"Wh..."

Show... much...

answer that one. Chloe took his face in her hands, met his eyes and said, "You kissed me in a dream."

"I dreamed the same thing," he whispered.

"I'd like you to do it again."

"You're…"

"A werewolf. And one who should be wanting answers."

She brought her mouth close to Morgan's while his hands, so warm and so talented, stroked down her spine slowly, leaving a trail of fire that scorched her flesh.

A wave of heat soared through Chloe, shooting sensations right through, bringing on an ache that wouldn't be appeased by a kiss, no matter how perfect it was. Tonight, she was both Chloe Tyler and someone else. Some*thing* else. And whatever that was added to her need for this man.

******

Don't miss the bonus short story included in this book!
Two stories for the price of one!

Wolf Bait *by Linda Thomas-Sundstrom*
was originally published by
Silhouette Nocturne Bites eBooks!

Books by Linda Thomas-Sundstrom

Silhouette Nocturne

Red Wolf #81
Wolf Trap #83

*Wolf Moons

LINDA THOMAS-SUNDSTROM,

author of contemporary and historical paranormal romance novels, writes for Silhouette Nocturne. She lives in the West, juggling teaching, writing, family and caring for a big stretch of land. She swears she has a resident muse who sings so loudly she virtually funds the Post-it company with sticky notes full of scribbles on every available inch of house and car space. Eventually, Linda hopes to get to all those ideas.

Check out all the books in the Wolf Moons series. It's all about humans morphing into other darker things—and finding love where it's least expected—in Miami under the full moon. Her first two novellas are included as bonus books in *Red Wolf* and *Wolf Trap*. And also now available from Nocturne Bites is her eBook short story *Moon Marked*.

Visit Linda at her Web site,
www.lindathomas-sundstrom.com,
and the Nocturne Authors' Web site,
www.nocturneauthors.com.

WOLF TRAP
LINDA THOMAS-SUNDSTROM

Silhouette Books

n⚫cturne™

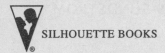

SILHOUETTE BOOKS

ISBN-13: 978-0-373-61830-9

Recycling programs
for this product may
not exist in your area.

WOLF TRAP

Copyright © 2010 by Linda Thomas-Sundstrom

The publisher acknowledges the copyright holder
of the individual work as follows:

eISBN-13: 978-1-4268-3056-3

WOLF BAIT

First Published in e-book form by Silhouette Nocturne Bites.

Copyright © 2009 by Linda Thomas-Sundstrom

www.silhouettenocturne.com

Printed in U.S.A.

Dear Reader,

WOLF MOONS... A criminal werewolf in Miami is biting innocent people! And eight people with wolfish tendencies of their own must join together to try to take this nasty guy down.

In doing so, four couples must face full moons, danger and each other, forming liaisons that will last a lifetime, whether or not they know this at the time of their meetings.

Secrets. Danger. Lust. Love. Welcome to the final books in the WOLF MOONS series.

Be sure to read the Nocturne Bite first— *Wolf Bait.*

Do check out my Web site, www.lindathomas-sundstrom.com, to keep track of what's upcoming. Let me know what you think of my wolves. Enter a contest or two. I'd love to hear from you.

Cheers—and happy reading!

Linda

To my family, those here and those gone,
who always believed I had a story to tell.

Chapter 1

"Just what am I supposed to be looking at?" Matt Wilson asked, massaging his temples with both hands as he walked. Fairview Hospital was one of his least favorite spots on earth, even if this was just a courtesy visit. Psychiatrics wasn't his job anymore, and he was certainly glad he'd veered from that into regular police detective work, in spite of the similarities.

Hell, the silence in this one corridor alone could drive a person nuts. Although the soundproofing was necessary for the sanity of the staff, who had to contend with these security wards on a daily basis, he was pretty sure that a complete lack of sound could eventually tweak their sanity, as well.

"New case," Jenna James, the supervising doctor of the hospital, said over her shoulder. A shoulder Matt knew intimately well and wished he could be alone with for a few minutes now on her office desk, as a precursor to having the rest of her. Dr. Jenna James was not only a damn good psychiatrist, but a great lover. So good, in fact, that Matt felt aroused just looking at her.

He knew exactly how long it had been since the last time he and Jenna were together. Three months. *Too long.* A necessary hiatus, but odds were good she'd be upset over the fact that he hadn't called her since then. She'd be angry. Furious.

Maybe he should confide in her about his current case, the one taking up all his time. Maybe he should have called her, anyway, just to let her know how strange his caseload had become lately, and that it had been demanding his time 24/7. He might explain to her that if he wasn't personally involved in this case, he'd have been with her in a heartbeat. Daily.

Sort of the truth, if withholding pertinent information wasn't considered lying.

He closed his eyes for a second. Hell, if he couldn't get himself together for sex, he was working too damned hard.

"I think you'll like this one." Jenna, her five-foot-six frame drop-dead gorgeous and alive with energy, swung her hips provocatively as she moved off in front of him, sexy even in her white lab coat. Her long, shapely legs caught his attention from beneath the hem of the coat, silky legs he'd had his hands all over twelve weeks ago. Legs that seemed to go on for an eternity, and which now ended in a pair of black suede pumps.

He almost smiled. If he had, it would have been the first light moment in a long time, and there was no doubt in his mind that this sexy psychiatrist knew exactly what effect she had on him. No doubt whatsoever. And he probably shouldn't be thinking about these things right now, or of what he might do with that body if given another opportunity.

No, most definitely he shouldn't be thinking about that. Finding time for this visit, agreeing to come to Fairview, had been hard enough. Besides wondering what Jenna might think of him, he had some pretty strange garbage to swim through these days, and problems that boggled his mind.

Jenna hadn't looked him in the eye once since he had arrived.

"We've kept this patient isolated, as much for her own good as anything else," Jenna said in her usual low-toned register that was a toss-up for the sexiest-part-of-her contest.

"Suicidal?" Only mildly interested, Matt tried to make a showing for Jenna's sake. Maybe she would take him up on a long lunch afterward? Engage in some afternoon get-reacquainted time? As much as he hated to admit it, what he really needed was someone to talk to. Someone with a similar background and an open mind.

Maybe Jenna would forgive him.

"She might be suicidal when she realizes what's going on. *If* she realizes it," Jenna said, fishing out a ring of keys, choosing a particularly draconian-looking one and inserting it into the lock of an iron-banded door.

Monster ward. That's what the staff called this area of the hospital. The worst mental cases were housed behind that door, now and then, making what lay back there the modern-day medical equivalent of a medieval dungeon.

The hair on the nape of Matt's neck prickled. He wanted to rub his forehead again, but refrained. With the word *monster,* in conjunction with the place they were about to see, one would have expected the door to creak. It didn't. A guard on the far side stood to attention when it opened soundlessly. This guard, more casually known around the hospital as an "attendant," had been sitting on a wooden, straight-backed chair. No padding. Nothing remotely comfortable. Not even a magazine to kill the time. The guy nodded to Jenna.

Matt reluctantly slid his gaze from Jenna to the long corridor beyond. Polished white floors, white walls, white ceiling. Sanitary-looking. Antiseptic. Fluorescent lights were inset, and high up. Cameras in white casings had been placed every few feet along the ceiling line, flashing tiny red beams indicating recording in process.

The doors in the walls were also white, making them difficult to see from this angle, although Matt knew there were twenty in all, and that so much whiteness could be deceiving when it came to what might lie behind the doors. His hands were already closing into fists.

He tossed the white-uniformed guard a brief nod of acknowledgment.

Back to Jenna. "Straitjacket?" Matt asked.

"Can't get one on her." Jenna replaced the key ring in her pocket. "Can't get close enough."

She walked off again, making it impossible for Matt to see her face. Checking out the sizable stature and build of the guard as they passed him, Matt said, "*He's* not big enough?"

"Two of him wouldn't be big enough."

"You said 'her.' Can't get one on *her*. Whoever is in here is a very big girl?"

"Well, not really a girl at all, maybe."

Not really a girl?

Futilely, Matt counted the doors they were passing. They were headed toward the far end of the hallway. Pesky hairs at his nape bristled again as Jenna stopped in front of the most ominous-looking door of all, the one set a little apart from the others, ruining the symmetry of ten on each side. Matt knew what this meant. Something conceivably worse than the other worse things.

Jenna turned to face him, her hands hanging helplessly at her sides. She carried no clipboard or file folder, nothing but a dangling pair of light blue cat's-eye-shaped glasses she used for reading and had probably forgotten to leave on her desk. The blue frames matched her eyes—eyes that were trained on him seriously, studiously, at last, as if waiting for him to play catch-up.

After contemplating the door, he said tentatively, "She's really a he?"

"No."

"You want me to keep guessing out loud, or shall we move into charades?"

"She's a she, all right," Jenna said. "Or was."

"Was?"

"She is something else altogether at the moment."

Okay. Now Jenna had his attention. "Split personality?"

"If so, this would set a precedent."

"Why?"

"There are…physical changes."

"What kind of changes?"

"Everything. Everything of what she once might have been is going, if not gone already."

Frowning, not quite sure if Jenna was yanking his chain for those weeks of silence, Matt ventured, "Dare I use the word 'insane'?"

Jenna shook her auburn-haired head. Her hair was tied back into a sleek knot at the nape of her neck, usual protocol in this hospital. Long hair was dangerous in the fingers of some of the patients. Jenna had glorious hair that could cascade past her shoulders in heaven-scented waves, waves he'd let slide through his fingers quite frequently, once upon a time. Burnished strands of loose curls that had brushed over his face.

He zeroed in on Jenna's expression, found it set and somber. Her lush mouth, full-lipped and, after hours, frequently painted red, was at the moment as pale as the rest of her, and didn't offer up so much as a hint of a smile.

"When I said 'something else altogether,' I meant just that. Literally," she said.

Considering her reply, Matt decided that if Jenna wasn't joking, she might be exaggerating. He had never seen this particular room, in this particular ward, occupied. Before bailing on the job as director of this facility, he'd worked at Fairview for three straight years and could count the patients housed in the monster ward on one hand, with two fingers. Though criminally insane patients were housed here occasionally before being transferred to a more permanent facility, even a brief stay was rare. No one under his watch had been hidden away here.

Lowering his voice, deciding to test Jenna one more time, he said, "We're talking…*alien?* Because I've seen *The X Files,* and—"

Jenna's facial expression cut him off. Frustration. Slight creasing of her brow. Reevaluating quickly, Matt frowned, said, "You're not joking."

"Never been more serious in my life. I called you because your specialty was once anomalies of the psyche, and I've never seen anything like this before. Your take on it would be truly appreciated before we bring in the big guns."

"You've called the FBI?"

Jenna nodded. "I was about to, and would have, if you didn't come."

"I come whenever you call. You know that."

Jenna looked him over, probably searching for evidence of a double entendre, and sighed. "Do you want to see her?"

"Yes. Absolutely." How could he not, after the vague and intriguing hints she'd dropped so far? Jenna had no doubt seen a lot since she'd taken over his position, and yet she'd seen nothing like this before?

Again, he took stock. Jenna's mouth, a mouth he had kissed, tasted, reveled in, taken full possession of in all sorts of wicked ways, was drawn up in a tight line. Her sky-blue eyes were huge, with traces of red weaving through the whites. She'd had little sleep lately herself. Because of this?

Reaching up to shoulder height, she used her long fingers to press open a panel, fingers that just weeks ago had been wrapped around his lustful body parts, fingers that had made him writhe in delight. Matt felt a buzz of recall as she hit a small black button in the door of the cell they were facing.

Yes, *cell* was the better term. These were no cushy prison holes, no normal spaces.

"New thing?" he said, ignoring the sudden, inexplicable roil in his stomach as he alluded to the glass revealed in the opening.

"One-way glass," Jenna explained. "We can see in, but whoever is inside can't see out. If you want her to see us, we press another button. If you want her to hear us, there's an intercom. I suggest, though, that we keep the noise to a minimum. I'd like you to observe her first, if that's okay?"

"Fine."

He stepped in front of the door, in front of the nonbreakable, nonpenetrable glass, and swallowed hard. Looking in, he blinked a few times in rapid succession, then actually felt his face drain of color. His hands went up and against the door with an audible thud.

Jenna James watched Matt's face closely, not bothering to peer over his shoulder at the thing in the room beyond. She had observed this room's activity until her heart just couldn't stand any more pain.

It had been a full twenty-four hours since the patient had been brought in by anonymous drop-off. Six hours since she'd called Matt, knowing he would come, and that what resided in this room was, in a way, bait. The dangling carrot necessary to see Matt again, face-to-face.

Now, she felt a pang of guilt. His face had lost expression.

He seemed to have stopped breathing. Was it because he hated this place, or because of what he was seeing inside that room?

Since Matt had left Fairview, she had never spoken to him of her work. Besides, when they'd been together, talking had always been kept to a minimum. More physical activities had precluded chitchat. Activities that usually included a king-size mattress. It was a fact that they were never able to keep their hands off each other, that their attraction was almost surreal in intensity. It was also a fact, she had realized lately, that anything other than small talk could have made for a charged situation, producing fear on both sides.

For me, the fear that Matt might close up tight and that I'd lose him in the end.

For him, fear of what? Commitment? Confiding? Being too close to the job he'd despised?

Losing him altogether was not an option she cared to contemplate. She had been in love with Matt Wilson since their first meeting, on her first day on the job at Fairview. She had instantly been drawn to everything about him: his rugged looks, dark, shaggy hair and perpetual five-o'clock shadow; his rangy, six-foot-two body; the way his green eyes, so light in his tanned face, seemed to see everything, take in everything.

The way those eyes of his had searched her up and down, as though they found nothing about her lacking.

For a long time, Matt had been absorbed in his work at Fairview. These days he was absorbed elsewhere, mainly with the Miami Police Department, where his medical accolades had been tossed in a drawer. She had been supportive of their time apart for a while, even made excuses for him. But lately her gut instinct told her that he was hiding something important from her, hence the distance, the quiet.

Matt had gone from an immeasurably hot pursuer to un-reachable, overnight. From lover to…nothing, without so much as a glimpse of the old Matt's soul, something so nec-essary in a true connection.

Was it clichéd to believe that talking would serve the major purpose of setting things to rights?

Had it been wrong of her to invite him here? She could hardly breathe around him.

Had it been wrong to keep what was in this cell?

Matt's hands kept him supported now. His knuckles, on either side of the glass, had gone white. She should say some-thing, but couldn't. Touch him? Every nerve in her body warned her not to.

Hating the awkwardness, Jenna waited a few moments more before looking into the cell.

Damn! Matt stared at the thing pinging around in there, and felt his own body react with a ripple of pure terror.

The thing inside of this padded cell was a woman, all right. Barely.

It was hard to get a good look. She was thrashing uncon-trollably. Hitting the walls. Ramming herself right and left, on her feet and then on her knees when she'd fall. She rolled, lunged, tore at herself with her hands—hands that weren't really hands anymore, that were more like an animal's paws that had been bound tight with surgical tape.

Her body was grotesquely out of proportion, as though she'd been stretched by some evil demon. She was naked, sort of. In actuality, her body appeared to be producing its own furry covering, though the process hadn't been com-pleted…yet. The thing in the cell was raw, and nearly com-pletely mad. She was half bare skin, half fur. Half human, half animal.

Matt felt a sound rise up from his belly, from somewhere so deep inside that it rolled upward as though moving through a mile-long tunnel. He stopped the sound in his throat, held it back with every ounce of willpower he possessed, knowing he had started to shake but unable to do anything about that if he was to keep the growl trapped inside. If he was to keep the secrets to himself.

Must hang on!

Jenna was beside him, and nothing if not observant. She'd note the shudders running through him, note how his insides were rippling and his pulse pounding. Jenna was outstanding at her job and in perceiving anomalies.

Which was why he hadn't called her after their last night together. Why he couldn't have called her. Not after what had happened to him. Not until he had gained some control, gotten some answers.

How could he have explained, exactly, lucidly, what had transpired three months ago, on the last night they'd made love in her apartment? What had happened to him on the way to his car?

How could he tell Jenna that this thing in the cell—the mad thing she had labeled a monster by putting it here—was merely a woman caught in transition? A woman who hadn't yet adapted to the new shape she was to become?

Possibly just an average female.

Until she had been bitten.

By a werewolf.

Whatever drugs Jenna's staff had given this poor creature had jump-started this transition, usually tripped in the dark of night, by a full moon, into high gear without the presence of those other governing factors. The confines of this eight-by-eight cell would be claustrophobic.

In essence, the woman in there was being tortured, kept

from attaining the new shape her mutated cells demanded she attain. Frozen in a horrifying sort of limbo, compulsively seeking her new self, her human side weaker than what was trying to take her over. She couldn't stop the process, become, ask for help, or go back.

I'm so sorry, Matt thought, fighting the urge to break down the damned door. *Jesus, I'm sorry.*

Next to him, Jenna's body was tight as she observed this so-called anomaly. She remained mute when the thing in the cell suddenly ceased its terrible gyrations. She kept quiet when the thing turned slowly, as if it could sense them staring.

Jenna said nothing when, even with the high-tech glass separating them, the thing in that cell looked at the door as if it knew he and Jenna were there.

But Jenna jumped back when the thing lunged, as it pressed its constantly morphing face, a face like some hideous version of a cartoon nightmare, to the spot where Matt was resting his forehead.

Jenna uttered something undecipherable as the thing in the cell stared back at them through terrified green eyes the same color as his own. As what had once been a young woman opened her mouth, exposing a set of newly formed, razor-sharp teeth, as if pleading with him to intervene.

Like calling to like.

Beast recognizing beast.

Through a two-foot-thick padded door.

Shit. Hell. No! Matt's blood began to sprint hotly through his veins. His fingers started to tingle—always the first sign in a mounting crescendo of dubious signals.

Darkness poured in suddenly from the periphery. From out of that darkness, and up from his gut, something unwelcome came tumbling. A unique presence. A horrifying one.

Needing to protest this dark entity's progress, assuming

this was being caused by his empathy for the poor, freaked-out woman in the cell, Matt let loose the howl he'd been holding—a howl that tore from his throat as a reciprocal cry.

Chapter 2

Jenna tumbled backward, slamming her spine hard against the opposite wall of the corridor, gasping with fear. She fought to breathe, then struggled with the uncertainty of whether the man over there could have been kidding. Whether this could have been some particularly nasty form of male humor.

The psychiatrist part of her voted for the joke. Her woman's intuition screamed that something truly odd and completely earnest had happened here—of which she wasn't a part and hadn't a clue.

Matt had howled. Like a wolf. Like a lunatic.

"Matt?" Shaky voice. She tried again. "Matt? What was that?"

The man who knew every inch of her body, inside and out, turned toward her, his face a mask of regret and, she thought, sorrow. Though he struggled to speak, he eventually said,

"You have to get her out of here. Right now. If you don't, she'll die in another couple of hours."

Jenna stared at him for a full minute more. "What are you talking about?"

"She will die if you don't get her outside, into the open."

Fighting the instinct to laugh, Jenna smiled nervously. "Right. Let her loose. In the open. And you would prescribe this because…?"

"I know what's wrong with her. I've seen this before."

"What are you talking about?" she repeated, at a higher decibel.

Matt pointed to the cameras near the ceiling and shook his head. He then pointed to her pocket, where she kept her keys.

"It's an automatic door," she said in exasperation.

"Which you can override with key number ten on that ring."

Was Matt starting to sweat? His face looked damp, and lined, though he was only thirty-two. His face seemed leaner than she remembered, more chiseled. His eyes, one of the features she had loved so much, seemed haunted as they gazed into hers.

And what? Matt was actually waiting for her to do as he'd absurdly suggested?

For a minute, she was at a complete loss.

Matthew Wilson had been at the top in his field, in investigating strange occurrences in the population. And he wanted her to unlock this door? Why? What could he possibly know?

Why had he made that ungodly noise?

"Shall we go to my office?" she suggested, still shaky as she waved at the cameras. Her office was one of the only places in the building free of constant surveillance. Matt would know this.

"You won't trust me, Jenna?"

The way he said her name brought a flush of heat to her

neck and a feeling of regret so tangible she could taste it. Matt had always whispered her name like that in the throes of passion, when they were about to climax. Her name had become synonymous with that dual moment of incredible sensation. And he would dare to use it here?

"I don't think I can, legally, Matt. Not without knowing the facts. You better than anyone should know this."

"Her life is in our hands," Matt countered.

"Then you'd better explain quickly."

He threw up his hands in a gesture of surrender and nodded his head. "First, let me in to see her."

His hands, she noted, were as shaky as her own.

"You are kidding?" she said.

"Never been more serious in my life. Let me into this cell."

"Matt…"

"I'll need a strong tranquilizer and a pair of scissors. It might save her from herself for a few minutes more while we talk."

A good hard bite to her lower lip brought not only a wince, but a piercing stab of uncertainty. She had always trusted Matt, at work and in the bedroom. No reason to mistrust him now, except, of course, for the months of infuriating silence. The almost complete disconnect.

He looked so…hurt? Why would he have an overabundant empathy for what was in that cell? Did he assume she wouldn't feel anything for what was going on in there? She hadn't slept or eaten since the woman had been dropped off on their doorstep. Until six hours ago, after calling Matt, she couldn't think about anything other than helping in any way she could.

Jenna tried to back up another step, forgetting about being tight up against the wall already. "How do you know it will help her?"

"Because," Matt said, "I know what she is. I'm willing to try to help her deal."

Another bite. Jenna tasted blood this time. "Why the scissors?"

"The tape is restricting her hands. Cutting off circulation. It's bad enough that she can't handle what's happening to her, but now she can't even feel herself. She needs to *feel*."

"She was cutting herself with her nails. Slicing her thighs open."

"What's it to be, then? Waste time by talking in your office first or let me in there now, when it might make the difference between the possibility of saving a life or just watching her die?"

"Possibility?"

Jenna watched the corners of Matt's mouth twitch as he concluded, "It might be too late already."

The phrase, and the way Matt had said it, chilled her. Jenna glanced down the corridor to where Jim, the attendant, sat in his chair, professionally looking the other way. She again scanned Matt's face, a face she'd repeatedly told herself was way too handsome for her own good, and confirmed to herself that she loved Matt Wilson with every fiber of her being. She trusted him, aside from their personal problems. She did.

But she had brought Matt here because she'd needed to see him again, not because she'd expected him to help. Now, she was torn. Despite her own desires, ultimately her responsibility was to try to help the woman in the cell. If Matt thought he could do that, he had to be given a shot.

"Jim!" she called out, watching the attendant jump to his feet. "Tranq number four, and a pair of scissors. Stat."

The attendant pressed a panel behind him in the wall, typed in his one-word code and moved his big hands over a shelf. In seconds, he was beside her, handing over a pre-loaded syringe and the scissors, handle side out.

In turn, Jenna handed the syringe to Matt, and motioned

for the attendant to open the door from his control panel by the chair. At least she would keep Jim from getting too close when this damn door opened.

Just in case.

Matt listened to the clunk of the door's lock releasing and sucked in a breath. God, he knew about this, all right. First-hand. But it didn't make what he was about to do any easier.

The important thing in this inhumanly painful transition the girl was going through was to get her through it. Changing from human to a human/wolf hybrid state for the first time had been so bad for him, he hadn't thought he'd make it. He wouldn't have wished that kind of distress on anyone. There wasn't anything comparable on the planet.

Still, he had lived through it, as well as the second *Change* a month later. He had persevered, in part because of his background in research and the need to find out what the hell this was and what caused it.

He had persevered also, in part, because of a pretty female cop named Delmonico who'd been first on the scene during the carjacking attempt that started this all off. A female cop who had taken one look at his badly chewed arm, a souvenir from the criminal they had chased off, and then handed him a card with a name and address printed on it. Just like that, along with the advice he'd never forget. *"I wouldn't bother with a hospital. The people on this card will help you."*

He had used that card out of curiosity, shown up at the address on it, and found help in the way of a family anyone in Miami would have recognized. *Landau.* The old man a well-respected judge, and his son the Dade County deputy district attorney.

But beyond those things, he owed his perseverance, along with his survival, to the woman who stood beside him now.

Jenna James—and the immensity of the love he felt for her. A love he had never put into words. Never once told her about. And now it might be too late.

The question that had plagued him, like this affliction had plagued him, remained. What better test would there be for love than confronting a partner with the worst sort of news? No, not a deadly illness. Something far worse. Something unbelievable. Unimaginable.

He was himself at times, yes, almost completely. But at other times he became and would continue to become a...

Werewolf.

Full moon as catalyst, just like in the movies. Body morphing into a beast's body, as this woman in the cell's body was trying to do. Infected cells knitting together to shove humanness out and allow an animal in. An animal that was tucked inside at all times, every day, every minute, waiting to get out, wanting to be free.

This initial phase of *becoming* had its own name. *Blackout.* The point where a human could no longer deal with the pain of being turned inside out and lost consciousness. A traumatic distancing of the body and mind from the body's first gleaning of its beast.

He had gone through it. Lived through it. So?

Jesus, Jenna. What will this do to us?

"Wait," Jenna said as he pushed on the door. "Maybe—"

He was already across the threshold. If it was too late for him, the least he could do was help out here.

The thing inside, frozen with her jaw partially unhinged and her eyes wild in a black fur-covered face, and with her muscles visibly rippling and expanding with a constant motion that Matt knew had to hurt like a son of a bitch, stood there, on her toes, edgy, looking back.

"It's all right," he soothed, his voice low and as gentle as he could make it, given how terrified he actually felt. "I'm here to help you."

The woman's beast was gaining on the human half, but pathetically slowly. A menacing growl issued from her throat that had the hair on his arms standing straight up, and his own inner beast squirming. But she did not attack.

"I can help," he told her, his fear now not whether this creature would believe him, but of having Jenna hear what he was going to say. In these circumstances.

Hell, he'd been afraid of this moment since the day after he'd left Jenna safe and sound and sleeping in her bed. And of what she might do. He'd been afraid of losing her, once she knew he was no longer completely human anymore. That for three nights a month, beneath a full moon, and though no one knew why, the beast inside him took over.

"Matt?"

His heart sank all the way to his ankles at Jenna's soft tone. Ignoring the spike in his pulse, he faced not the woman he loved more than life itself, but the other werewolf in this room.

"You know me," he said to the woman. "Because I'm like you."

Keeping his own beast tamped down where it belonged, Matt taunted the she-wolf in the only way he knew how. He opened his mouth, let out a chilling, bloodcurdling howl—a foreboding sound that would have echoed but for the thickness of the walls.

And as the she-wolf stepped forward, slow, tentative, irresistibly drawn to him, and as he felt her hot breath on his own chilled face, Matt muttered a very human "Sorry," and plunged the syringe into her hip.

The she-wolf's scream was feral.

Matt caught her in his arms as she fell.

Chapter 3

He was panting. The she-wolf's body temperature had to be through the roof, but she wasn't his main concern.

Jenna was.

Dragging the unconscious she-wolf to the corner, Matt laid her down. Warily, he turned, palm out, asking Jenna silently for the scissors, trying to keep his tremors under wraps.

Jena didn't move.

"I need to cut the tapes." His voice sounded strange, he knew. *Bad sign.* His inner beast was not only awake, but pushing adrenaline through his veins.

"That was quite a show," Jenna finally remarked, her own voice up an octave and not too smooth. Her skin had gone ashen. Nor was she steady on her feet.

She looked as if she could have used a bourbon, straight up. Hell, he could have chugged two or three. Maybe five.

"Yeah, well, I'm not a psychiatric specialist for nothing," he quipped. *"Was,"* he corrected right after.

Jenna still hadn't budged, at least not on purpose. She shifted on her feet, unconsciously rocking back and forth, her gaze riveted to him.

"Was this…was this all BS?" she said.

"Can we talk about it later? I'm not sure how long a tranq dosed for a small woman who isn't at the moment a small woman might last, and I need to get these bindings off her."

I'm not sure how long I can keep away from you.

"Do it," Jenna directed. "Get the tape off."

Whistling through his teeth, hoping to ease some of his gut-wrenching tension, Matt knelt by the she-wolf's side. Carefully, he cut the tapes binding her right hand, then moved quickly to her left.

"You howled." Jenna's voice was stronger.

"It was a distraction that worked." Finished with the tapes, Matt got to his feet. "The tranq isn't a cure for what ails her. As I said, she needs to be outside and needs help that this hospital can't give her."

I need help, too, God bless it.

I need you to understand what I've been through.

I need your acceptance, not your pity, and a clear path to the truth.

Just now, however, he needed a clear path out of there. Away from luscious, desirable Jenna. His beast was reacting to the downed female, and he didn't understand why. There were five floors of building over their heads. It was early evening. Not yet dark. There was no full moon in here. No horrifying kiss of silver on his skin.

None of those things should matter until later.

"Where could she get help?"

Jenna's question cut right through his thoughts and the

thick atmosphere inside the cell. The thing within him stirred. His stomach heaved.

Confession time. At least in part.

God help me.

"I know a family who will try to do something for her. They would be willing," he said.

The Landaus would help this woman, as they had helped him, because they were like him. Like her. Full of Lycan DNA. Seemed there were secrets all over Miami to be discerned by a careful observer. A fact that might be funny, except that it was all too real.

Honest to God, he wanted to shout to the woman looking at him now, there were such things as werewolves—although little comfort came from the knowledge that he wasn't the only one.

"What happened to you?" Jenna whispered, the full impact of her emotions packed into those four words. Emotions Matt could sense and smell with a beast's extraordinary new powers, and that shook him.

The room reeked of tension, unspoken questions, and Jenna's subtle perfume. A heady cocktail for a man, let alone a wolf. He felt an overwhelming desire to touch Jenna. Taste her. Be inside her. Maybe then he would be comforted, and in return comfort her. Maybe, like some damned fairy tale, Jenna could make him whole, provide a happy ending. A kiss to turn a beast into a prince?

He looked sadly up at the cameras.

"To hell with the cameras," Jenna snapped. "Talk to me."

The sudden variance in her voice dispersed the warm and wishful thoughts, snagging his already alert beast. Another growl trickled up through his solar plexus, followed by yet another.

But it wasn't time for the beast to reign. Not for a couple more hours. His beast should have been in its near-catatonic state.

Why, then, was the beast pressing at him?

Could strong emotions like fear and lust and love mess with already tweaked DNA sequences?

Was that why he was starting to shake again all over? Why his arm, the one that had been chewed by what he now knew was a damned rogue carjacking werewolf, ached to the point of his wanting to cut it off?

Could the—*no, oh please, no*—incurable Lycan virus be mutating further?

Some sort of reaction to this extreme environment?

A direct line to the beast's history, transferred and re-awakened?

Or maybe the early awakening had been caused by Jenna herself? By his close proximity to her? His feelings for her?

This may not be good.

In no way might this be good.

Jenna...

He was beside her in a flash, so quickly he hadn't noticed he had moved. Needing her. Craving intimacy.

Have to have you.

Her surprised eyes bored into his—big blue eyes in a face as white as porcelain. Eyes so deep as to be bottomless. She was taking shallow breaths and was visibly trembling.

What did she think was going on?

He almost wished she'd shout for help as he pressed himself close against her, against the wall. *Predator.*

Damn. He was searching her face with the beast's eyes, in addition to his own. Love was morphing into hunger, confusing the beast inside. He had to back off right now. He had to get out of Jenna's immediate vicinity.

Even as he thought that, he raised Jenna's hands over her head, pinning them to the pale padding, holding her captive.

He was so much stronger than she was.

He liked being the aggressor.

Jenna's hip bones cupped his pelvis. A perfect fit. Her breasts, soft, round and no doubt covered by a skimpy stretch of lace under the rest of her clothes, were tipped by rosy nipples drawn tight. He remembered the shape of those nipples between his teeth, on his tongue. Skin like shirred satin. Fragrant with bath oil.

He was hard in response to the memory and the present position. Hard as a rock, and aching. The beast might have been providing the impetus for a dangerous liaison, but the man was the recipient of all the feeling, the sensations.

You feel so damned good.

Matt brushed Jenna's lips with his own, closed his eyes as he rested his lips on hers, reveling in her clean, familiar scent, allowing his lungs to breathe in her essence.

Just one kiss.

We can handle this.

Encouraging her mouth to open, he kissed her tenderly first. Then he swiped his tongue sensually over Jenna's teeth, whispering his hunger into her…with the beast's voice.

She reacted as though she had been shot.

Her body went rigid, tight, distant. But he kept his mouth on hers, kissed her in the fierce manner she had always preferred. A devouring kiss now, long, wet and uninterrupted. An indicator of the fact that only reluctantly would he let her up for a breath. A golden promise of what might come next.

He felt himself slip. Felt the physical snap within his body that signaled danger. Oddly enough, though, as his own awareness began to fade, Jenna's body began to loosen. Never meek when it came to sex, there was a chance she was as intoxicated as he was by this incredibly savage meeting of their mouths, and in the risqué landscape of the cell. She pulled at his hands, moved her hips, flexed her arms.

Horrified by the hunger that was taking him over and by what he was doing, Matt tried to pull away, tried to separate from the part of himself that was guiding the hunger. The part that shouldn't have been noticeable, let alone acting on its wishes.

But Christ, the beast inside him wanted Jenna just as much as he did.

He tried to rally. Struggled to jam the snarling beast back where it belonged. Jenna's attempts to free herself were invigorating the beast further, inviting the beast to cling to the surface of his emotions.

"Matt…" Jenna's lips formulated his name with a quick, plush, blistering volcanic slickness.

Not now. No explanations.

Can't.

Have to get out.

Have to get away.

Releasing her hands, Matt, or whoever the hell he had become, didn't sprint in the opposite direction. Instead, he tore at the buttons of Jenna's lab coat as he continued to kiss her.

Surely she kissed him back? Drove her breasts and hips into him seductively? Wanted this?

If he could forget, lose himself in her…

Her coat came off with a tearing sound. He had no idea what she wore in the way of a shirt, except that it felt crisp to the touch. His need had built to a frenzy. His hands glided up under the fabric covering her, pursuing the purpose of the rattling, rock-hard, indescribable thing he had become. It was true that the roaring, morphable beast inside him couldn't show its hairy face or get a physical grip without the moon's light, but it sure as hell could force a daring rendezvous and create a long-overdue reunion.

Maybe, in some way, he should be glad about this?

Wasn't Jenna's willingness to take part in this situation confirmation enough that she loved him? That she'd forgive him?

Was he thinking clearly?

He had her on the ground, on her back, in a blink. His kisses moved over her cheek. She let out a staccato sigh.

Willing his hands to stop, but unable to control them, he ripped at her shirt, heard the buttons go, and feeling the warm, luminous skin of Jenna's stomach beneath his fingers, almost came right then and there.

And, miraculously, against all odds, Jenna's palms moved over him, kneading the tense muscles of his upper back, digging her fingernails in. She pulled him closer. He could feel her heartbeat next to his chest. He could see the pulse in her neck where it met the sharp angle of her prominent collarbones.

Her breath was fragrant on his face, rich.

His love swelled.

Her hands were on his lower back, working their way down his sides, onto his hips, traveling exotically toward the front, over his thighs, headed for an erection that virtually raged with need.

Jenna, I—

A sudden sting came, as though a thin-bladed knife had pierced the muscle between his shoulder blades. Followed by a similar painful stab to his left thigh.

His growl of distress hurled outward through his open mouth.

He roared again.

Hurts like a…

Like a…

Dammit.

Dammit to hell and back.

Jenna winced, rolled over, winded, and looked up. It took several more seconds to speak. "Thanks, Jim."

"No problem," Jim said, holding up the empty syringe he'd just plunged into Matt's back. "That's why they pay me the big bucks."

He offered Jenna a hand, which she took.

"The doc's not himself, I'm thinking," Jim added.

Understatement of the century!

"You'll okay the use of the tranq?" Jim asked.

"I certainly will."

Jim nodded once, made no mention of her state of disarray as she straightened her skirt. "You got him, too?"

Jenna glanced at the empty syringe she was palming, hoping with all her heart that a shared needle, in this circumstance between Matt and the other creature knocked out in the corner, wouldn't prove to be a horrific mistake.

"More for the surprise impact," she said, on her feet and still trembling uncontrollably. "There wasn't enough left in this syringe to drop a Chihuahua."

Pressing her loosened, disheveled hair back behind her shoulder, she signaled to Jim and then watched Matt being lifted by his arms.

Her gaze shifted from Matt to the motionless creature in the corner and back to Matt.

"What the hell," she muttered to herself out loud, "is going on?"

Chapter 4

The blackness behind Matt's eyes turned charcoal, then gray, lightening quickly, shade by shade, until the sensation became one of whiteness. The color of clouds.

For a while he felt at peace. Couldn't think of anything in particular, except that he didn't hurt, ache or feel pressured by anything at all. Which, in itself, seemed strange.

He wiggled his fingers, moved his head, unable for the life of him to remember where he was…until a familiar odor caused his heart and eyelids to flutter.

Drugs. Seeping out of his own pores.

And beyond that, the lingering aftertaste of narcotics, like he'd just sucked on tinfoil, mixed with one other chemical composition. *Lip gloss?*

Panic struck. His body jerked. Beating down the rising fear and inner commotion with a tremendous effort, Matt opened his eyes. Though he could have sworn he heard his synapses reconnecting, a whirl of vertigo all but hijacked the dryness of his tone. "Anyone here have an aspirin?"

"As a matter of fact, we do," Jenna replied, rattling a plastic bottle.

The small, next-to-insignificant noise thundered in Matt's ears, nearly overshadowed by the roar of the blood rushing back to his head. With the blood came more awareness.

"Oh, jeez," he muttered from between tight teeth, turning his head, having to look up to see Jenna sitting in a chair above him. A hard wooden chair that damn well looked exactly like the attendant's.

Chills dripped down his back. His forehead felt damp, though he didn't reach up to find out for sure, because he was flat out on his back, on a white surface. What had seemed like a cloud was, in fact, he now realized, a cell.

This hadn't been a nightmare, after all.

"One or two?" Jenna asked, concern evident in the question.

"Ten," he answered. "Unless salicylic acid is contraindicated for whatever the hell you hit me with."

"Least of your worries, don't you think?" Jenna rallied.

He waited that one out, coming up with no immediate response at all. Virtually tongue-tied.

"If you want aspirin, I'm afraid you'll have to chew them," Jenna added.

What she hadn't said was that a water glass in the hand of a nutcase might be as dangerous as a knife.

Just f-ing great!

Grimacing, Matt ignored the ensuing kick of pain that radiated up his neck and said, for lack of anything better coming to mind, "Well, that was mind-blowing. Was it good for you?" Stupid, lame-ass words to fill a space so terrifying, he wasn't sure if the space could actually be breached.

"Not particularly," Jenna gamely replied.

Matt's throat was so dry, he couldn't have gagged anything down, though he gazed longingly at the aspirin. "So," he ventured, "I suppose you'll want to talk about it?"

"Don't you?"

He had a flash of recall that was tainted with a reddish hue. The girl. Werewolf. The fact that he had to get her out of here. Equally as important, now he had to get himself out of here.

He moved his arms casually, and with relief. *No strait-jacket.*

"How long have I been knocked out?"

Tiny licks of anxiety nipped at his arms. As he shoved his body to a sitting position, he rode out a bout of light-headedness.

"Two hours," Jenna said. "Don't worry, you didn't drool."

"Where is she?" he asked.

A hesitation, then, "*She* is next door."

"We have to—"

"What are you?" Jenna interrupted calmly, though he heard the unevenness of panic underlying the point. "Who are you, and what have you done with Matt Wilson?"

Heart suspended for a beat, Matt said, "You really wouldn't believe the story behind that one."

"Today, I might believe anything, so at the risk of sounding clichéd, *try me*."

"Can we talk about this outside? Anywhere but here?" He added adamantly, gazing up at the lights, "What time is it?"

After considering him for several infuriatingly slow seconds, she said, "It's seven o'clock, and you haven't heard a word I've said."

Seven o'clock? He'd been out for two hours? He didn't even know a word bad enough to describe this predicament. He wasn't up on werewolf lore enough to know how he might react to the drugs. They hadn't worked too well for the girl.

His voice came out breathy. "Listen to me. We have to get her to my car. Before dark."

Something you can't see.

No time to explain.

"Are you ill?" she countered.

"Yes, but not in the way you might think. Nothing you can cure with a pill. Will you help us get out?"

"With no more explanation than that?" Jenna said, not exactly appreciating the finer art of avoidance.

"Only a hiatus, I promise. Get us out and I'll tell you everything. I owe you that and so much more."

Although Jenna drew back at the "everything," she said, "Just let her walk out of here? With you?"

"Actually, I'll have to carry her."

"And if I were to call the FBI?"

"I don't think they'll want to carry anybody."

Jenna's expression was stern. Matt knew that if he didn't get out of there, out of her sight, there might be no hope left to cling to.

"And if I've already called them?" Jenna said.

"Cancel."

"How?" she asked. "How would you cancel a call to the FBI?"

"False alarm. Woman high on drugs and beating on herself. Make something up."

"You mean ignore the fact that a woman is turning inside-out? That she's becoming a frigging animal in front of my eyes?" Jenna pointed a finger at him. "And that you said you're like her? That for a minute back there, I believed you were?"

Matt's heart rate spiked again. Reason was to a psychiatrist what food was to most other people. In her profession, Jenna James was part pit bull.

"You'll need to destroy the camera feed. All of it," he suggested.

"That might take care of the records, but what about the Hippocratic oath?"

"You can't do much for that poor woman here. Or me. Knowing this, are you willing to let someone else try? Are you so stubborn that you think you can help everyone, in every damn circumstance?"

"I don't know that I can't help. Not for sure. So, why should I believe you can?"

"Because you love me," he replied, getting at least that much out in the open. "And sometimes, love has to be blind."

Jenna smiled at that answer, without meaning to. Her expression was a burst of immediate sunlight in a grave and colorless situation. It was a smile that brought Matt a much-needed boost of confidence, in spite of the fact that it faded all too quickly.

"Not good enough," Jenna stated firmly.

But Jenna had slipped—from her technical voice to her real voice. The after-hours Jenna was here in this room, if only temporarily. The Jenna who had allowed him sexual leeway, in fact encouraged it. The Jenna who had given as much as she had taken, then sat on his bed, naked, legs tangled in the sheets, blissfully humming out-of-tune songs.

The knot of hope in Matt's chest doubled in size.

His inner whine had nothing whatsoever to do with the beast this time.

It was a given that he wanted to console her. It was also a given that he couldn't touch her again. Not here. Not tonight.

But oh, how he wanted to.

"Help me," he said, getting to his feet, almost pleading for her to believe him—except that he hadn't yet told her anything at all, actually.

There *was* that.

He shrugged it off. Of primary importance now was getting out of this hospital. In another half hour, outside at least, he wouldn't be able to utter a single syllable. He was good for only as long as the daylight lasted. In here, with the pressure, the anxiety, the closeness to Jenna and whatever had been in that damn syringe, he was a loose cannon. Sure of nothing.

Can't take a chance.

"Someone might question the missing tapes," she proposed, he guessed to get him talking again.

"Then it's a good thing Fairview is still in the Dark Ages, without updated recording systems," Matt shot back, steadier now that the vertigo had passed and he'd had at least a glimpse of that faded smile of hers.

"Where would we take her?"

"*I'm* taking her," Matt corrected. "You'll stay here."

Jenna got to her feet, shook her head. "She's my responsibility."

"Not anymore. This one is out of your reach. It happens."

"Are you saying I'm incompetent?"

"Not saying anything of the kind. Just that there are people better equipped to help her."

"And they can help you?"

He met her eyes, wanting to drown himself in their icy, baby-blue depths. "They are trying to help me, yes."

Her eyes maintained their defiant shine. "I can't meet these people? Know about them?"

"I've been sworn to secrecy."

"That's a bit vague, even for you, a bona fide detective."

"I know how it sounds. I just don't have time to talk now or beg. Night is coming. There's a full moon. If you thought what happened to us a while ago was strange and you press me for answers much longer, you'll be in for the ride of your life outside these walls. And not in a good way."

"Threats, Matt? Maybe you've gone off the deep end. Maybe you belong here, after all. For a while."

"Maybe I do," he agreed. "But I can't take you up on the offer just now. Not today."

Man, he wanted Jenna back. At least, she should be given a chance to understand. Without her, none of it mattered to him, anyway, or would ever matter to him again. Not the job, the research he had been doing since his own first *Change,* or the workings of the world outside, the one in which Jenna lived and breathed.

Thing was, he just couldn't tell her. He couldn't make himself say the words that would prove how life truly was at times stranger than fiction. Or that this was one of those times.

As he gazed at Jenna, willing her to help, to trust him, just this once…

As he saw himself running out of options and excuses…

As he inwardly vowed never to hurt her, leave her or hide anything from her again, ever, as long as he lived, if she would just give him this one chance…

She nodded her head.

Excitement rode the air like barely contained rage. Panic was in there, too, along with dread and the urge to hyperventilate.

Thank heaven, Jenna thought, Jim hadn't questioned her orders.

Matt had been out the door in a flash, motioning for the she-creature's cell to be unlocked. They had hit the woman up again with an injection, and she, as director here, had okayed all of this. Because it was the right thing to do? Jenna no longer knew. Maybe she'd done this for Matt as a last farewell. A parting favor. It was obvious he cared for the woman in that cell more than he cared for *her*. He would risk everything to help someone else.

End of story? Merely a really bad dream? Fact. Matt had become *more* than Matt in her presence. A blackness had slid behind his eyes when he'd pinned her to the wall, chasing out the green. She could hardly function thinking about it, vowed to get to the bottom of this, no matter what.

She watched Matt lift the woman, now nearly covered in hair that was clumped and matted with sweat, and whose breath came in great chest-rattling rasps, though she'd been given enough tranquilizer to knock out a horse.

It was downright freaky.

Matt cannot be like her.

Not my Matt.

A genetic mutation? A cluster of cells gone awry that had hidden behind Matt's flawless exterior until now? An illness carried in his lineage? Age-related, maybe? Drug-related?

Why hadn't I known?

Matt was all but running down the hallway, the creature's listless body held tightly in his arms. He anxiously waited while she unlocked the iron door.

His body was fending off a series of visible shudders that made her grimace each time she watched one hit. She heard him swear, suck in air, swear again.

His angular features were tight, but the same ones she had always craved. He looked the same. He just didn't *feel* the same. She'd noticed it the moment he'd entered the hospital, but had been too preoccupied with her inner thoughts and hopes.

If he was ill, seriously ill, she wanted to help.

Love him. In spite of everything.

In sickness and in health.

Just one more favor. She motioned for Jim to take the creature. Arms free of his burden, Matt reached out to her, silently, a whole lot of unspoken things in an action that did nothing to bring them closer together and only caused her heart to break.

Standing a good three feet away, he dropped his hands, tried to say something, but didn't. Couldn't, she supposed.

"Go," she said.

Just that.

Go.

Chapter 5

As soon as they had rounded the corner, Jenna was after them. Down the stairs she raced on foot. Around a sharp corner. Down more stairs as she observed the elevator's lights.

Into her office she ran, ignoring the stares of the staff, needing her purse, her car keys; stopping only long enough to type on her keyboard the prompts "Full moon. Hair growth. Howl."

Two more seconds to stare at the answer on the screen, one silent inward shout that should have shaken the rafters, and she was out the side door to the building, fleeing over the grass.

She fumbled with the lock to her car, banging her knees on the steering wheel as she dived inside. The sun was an orange blip on the horizon, then gone. In the oncoming darkness, she took a deep breath—one that would probably have to last her a while—and started the engine.

In her mind the word she'd seen on the monitor flashed blue, then red, then a blinding silver metallic, the color of the moon in tonight's sky. *Werewolf.* That was the word the computer had spit out. Again. As if she hadn't already hit that same key a hundred times since she'd first dared to look, always anticipating another answer.

Jamming the car into gear, she stepped on the gas, kicking up loose gravel. Time to face facts. There just wasn't going to be another explanation.

Now Matt was up ahead in a police-generic beige car, wearing a badge and maybe even carrying a gun these days— when he wasn't rescuing other…werewolves.

Her laugh sounded somewhat hysterical, she thought. If werewolves were possible, if a human could become a wolf, then the opposite surely could happen? A devolve process? A cure? *Somewhere? Somehow?*

Having never fainted in her life, Jenna tried really hard not to now.

Matt gripped the wheel tighter, to the point of ligament strain, and swore by moving his aching jaw.

Night had fallen. Behind the clouds, the moon was round and phosphorescent and calling to him. Using his first name.

Cold silver light bounced off the hood of the car as he screeched around a corner in a quiet old neighborhood where houses were double the size of his entire precinct. He felt the wetness of a lunar kiss on his left arm, soaking through his sweater and into his flesh, and yanked his arm off the dinged-up tan metal.

"Just a few more miles to go. We can make it."

There weren't many other cars on the old road. He'd passed two heading in the opposite direction. Another set of headlights remained in the distance behind him. If he had to pull over, get himself and the she-wolf out of the car, he could manage in relative safety. After that, though, if she were to waken, as startled as he was sure she would be, it might be bad news.

"Two more miles, max," he confirmed out loud.

The Landaus lived in a mansion on gated property. They wouldn't leave the estate with the moon like this, being what they were. The trick would be getting in if they didn't answer the intercom.

"Timing is everything." Matt checked out the backseat in the rearview mirror. No hairy face looked back. No strong, wolfish hands tried to choke him.

He gazed into the mirror at himself, opened his lips a crack, lips that were already drawing back to make way for a new structure of flesh and bone, and whispered, "Jenna," with the last human sound he would probably be able to formulate.

Jenna kept a decent distance behind Matt's car, until she saw it veer off the road suddenly, hurtling into darkness.

"No!"

She floored the gas and surged ahead, turning off the road onto a long, unlit driveway, aiming her headlights between the two tall stone pillars on either side. Once past the pillars, still able to glimpse red taillights, she switched off her high beams and attempted to run dark after him.

Concentration took everything she had, and then some. The driveway wound around several groves of tall trees, with head-high hedges filling in the gaps. She'd broken into a cold sweat. An ache twanged behind her eyes, doubling when Matt's lights disappeared.

Slowing, Jenna held fast to the wheel. *There!* A big gate. Ten feet high. Still open. Matt had gone through.

She put the pedal to the floor again, making it inside by

inches before the thing swung shut, absentmindedly brushing the hair out of her eyes.

More trees. Large swaths of lawn, looking as dark as lakes in the nighttime gloom. A giant house appeared, lit up by lights. Though Matt's car was small in the distance, she watched it nearly hit the front steps as it pulled up.

The front door of the house opened. Two people, possibly men, came out, tore open the car door, picked up the creature in Matt's backseat and carried her into the house.

Jenna rolled to a stop next to what looked like a deserted caretaker's cottage. Engine off, she watched in silence.

Where was Matt?

The people from the house didn't make a second showing. She hadn't seen Matt leave the car.

Her heart drummed irregularly in her chest, leaping when she heard a scratching sound. Had she parked too close to the bushes? She turned to look.

The sudden crack of her door opening brought a scream from her throat. A huge, fur-covered mass, rippling with muscle, sinew and electrified tension, stood there. Elongated face. Wolfish features. Eyes that reflected the blackness that was all around.

There was something recognizable in his stance.

Oh God, oh God.

"Matt?" she whispered, body heaving up one more irregular heartbeat before her inner world went as dark as the outer one.

She was being carried. Her shoulder bumped against something wide, something stretched taut and covered in softness. As the surroundings blurred into focus, Jenna saw that she was being carried through an open doorway right next to the car.

She didn't look at the face above hers, fearing what she might see. *Who* she might see.

Once through the doorway, she felt an immediate sway in the arms cradling her. A jerky motion nearly caused her to fall. The pitch-black space was filled with popping noises and a growl that lengthened into an audible groan.

Set on the floor, on her feet, she felt her heart career. Fluid rushed in her ears as more sounds filled the darkness, unfamiliar, freaky, reminiscent of the awful noise of bones breaking.

Numb, Jenna stayed where she'd been put on legs made of gelatin. If Matt had brought the creature to this estate, surely he considered it safe?

Matt. Help me.

A familiar scent floated to her, easily recognizable. Matt's apartment was filled with that same smell: just a hint of the aftershave he preferred, mixed with his exquisitely potent, all-male pheromones. He'd smelled like this in her hospital, not more than fifteen minutes ago. No mistaking that scent or how it had always turned her on. Now, though, Matt was giving off an additional scent: the unique odor of damp fur.

Feeling choked, her hands tight up against the stuccoed wall of wherever the heck she was, Jenna said, "Tell me."

"That I'm a damned monster, like the thing you had caged?" His voice was gruff and followed by a racking cough.

"Tell me," she repeated.

"Dammit, Jen, what are you doing here?" Matt countered.

"Following you. Are you okay?"

Hesitation. Then, "So far from okay as to be in another universe."

"Are you...*you?*"

"Yes." Another hesitation. "Most of the time. Tonight, only while I'm inside with a roof over my head."

"What is this place?"

"A haven for people like me."

"Why do you need a...haven?"

No reply.

Needing to deal, Jenna shook her head, wanted more. "I need to know what happened to you."

"You mean, what made me a monster?"

"Yes."

His voice cracked with the dryness of surprise. "So that you can analyze?"

"So that I can understand."

He took a step closer. Jenna resisted the urge to close the distance and pummel Matt with her fists, make him come clean, make him confess that this had all been one big joke, on her. They were on the Landau estate. She'd recognized Judge Landau's son as one of the two men at the car. She knew the Landaus; everybody in Miami did. But what would such a prominent family have to do with werewolves? Why would they take one in?

Her nerves starting to fry, she clamped her teeth together until her gums hurt and waited for an explanation.

Matt spoke at last.

"There's a criminal loose in the city with a special talent." He paused, began again. "Not killing his victims outright, but torturing them in another way, a more permanent way."

He had taken another step. His warm breath riffled through the hair at her temple. Automatic reflex; gone was the need to hit Matt. She now wanted to throw her arms around him, wrap her restless legs around him—and would have done that once, in this strange place, not long ago. This was the man she loved. Yet there was enough tension between them at the moment to blow the roof off the place.

"He bites his victims," Matt told her in a hushed, pained tone. "And those victims then become like him. No choice in the matter. No comprehension of what is happening to them. They don't always die from the savagery of his bites, Jenna, but if they survive the incident, many of them die soon afterward. Some of their bodies are found mutilated—by their own teeth."

"How could that be?" Jenna's rational mind made her protest. "Why would anyone kill themselves in such a gruesome manner?"

"Because what the asshole does is infect them. Infection through saliva. Very old virus. Ancient. Incurable. This infection, once internalized, changes DNA."

Horrified to stillness, Jenna sucked in air.

"The infection also changes the body's composition," Matt continued. "Triggered, as inconceivable as it sounds, by the light shed from a full moon. A frigging planetlike sphere. It's not like we could get away from that, is it?"

We. He'd said *we.* Her instincts hadn't been wrong, after all, no matter how much she'd denied it.

Again, in her mind, the word on the computer screen flashed with a sickly glow.

Werewolf.

Matt had been infected.

"The girl?" she asked, hands fisted.

"If you had searched the girl's body carefully, you would have found a set of teeth marks that might possibly have scarred over by now. A bite did this to her. A bite from either the same freak that bit the other bodies we found, or someone just like him. A bite is how she was infected. It's the only way a person can be infected if they weren't born with the genetic mutation."

He waited a beat, giving her time to assimilate that. Or try to. Jenna wondered if he could feel her terror.

"The girl in your care," he said slowly, "is now half-wolf."

Jenna held back a shout by the thinnest of threads.

And so are you, my love?

"I believe," Matt said, "that the girl has been mutating during the day because of the meds, and maybe even her strong reaction to the sterile environment of the hospital. Hell, maybe other things can bring about the *Change,* other than the moon and a shitload of mind-altering narcotics. What I don't know could fill a well."

Needing support, Jenna braced herself again, remained mute.

"Tonight, out here in the open, her body will go through the full transition—sort of like a rewiring of her central nervous system. The people who live here will help her with that and maybe even keep her alive."

"You have a bite?" Jenna whispered.

A hot forehead pressed against hers as he nodded. "Right arm. Twelve…twelve weeks ago. The night we were last together."

Startled by what this meant, Jenna felt her heart amp up its tempo. There were so many more questions, so much more to discuss. But just now, one thing took precedence over all of it. He hadn't left her. He hadn't found someone else. This man had been hiding. Hiding from her. Keeping this secret to himself. Protecting her.

Matt Wilson hadn't changed his mind, only his DNA.

As Jenna reached for her lover now, it was without a thought for how much longer her legs would hold her up.

Chapter 6

Soft feminine arms wrapped around him, enfolding him. She was in shock most likely, Matt concluded. Why else would she still be here?

Jenna's head was nestled against his bare chest, a bareness that was a necessity for transitioning into a creature twice his normal size.

Jenna pressed herself close. A lover's embrace.

A moment of sympathy before she'd recover her wits and run?

He looked down at the woman in his arms with enhanced vision, a new development that allowed him to see well in the dark. His heightened sense of smell had also developed to levels that were truly miraculous.

Jenna smelled like…heaven. But on his sensitive skin, where the pelt of the wolf waited for just the slightest sliver of moonlight, he felt wetness. Tears. Falling from Jenna's eyes.

He wanted to cry out against something so simple as a tear. Monster that he might any minute become, and as educated a doctor as he was, Jenna's tears nearly brought him to his knees. *Helpless. Useless.* For the moment a man, able to hold a woman. But what woman would want a monster in her life, in her bed?

The devil take him, he wondered seriously if there was a serum for mastering speechlessness.

Matt was holding her tightly enough to smother them both.

Or would have smothered them, if they'd both been normal people.

He had wrapped one of his hands in her hair. His free arm encircled her waist, so that she had to speak shallowly, in a whisper.

"It's all right? Will…be…all right, Matt?"

The deep rumble inside his muscular chest caused all the little hairs on her arms to stand to attention, and the spot between her thighs to quiver in anticipation. Moist anticipation.

A sudden flare of fire flickered deep inside.

The drama, intensity, danger and swirling emotions were heading them in a new direction. Uncharted territory. Not because of what Matt had told her, but because of what *she* hadn't told him.

Secrets.

She could feel this new thing growing between them, expanding, drawing them closer at last, snapping them tight. Beyond the sorrow and pain she felt for Matt and his plight, her body was reacting to his nearness with a lustful revving of her sexuality.

She hurt for him, yes. Wanted to cry for him, comfort him, yes. He would mourn the life he had always known. He would lament, swear, vow, want to hurt himself at times, because his beliefs would never be the same. If a man could become a werewolf, what else might be out there hidden from the masses? What other freaks might prowl the nighttime hours that a detective specializing in psychiatric anomalies might stumble upon?

Did people live in a world that wasn't at all what it seemed?

This was what Matt would be thinking.

And in thinking that, he would be right.

"I have to find him." Matt spoke those words vehemently. "I have to know if the same creep who bit me bit that poor girl, or if there are packs of criminals intent on infecting innocent people. A horrifying thought. I have to…"

Jenna tilted back her head so that she could see his face, let her fingers drift across his tortured mouth. His eyes were green again, though still haunted. He was all sharp angles.

She could see all this clearly. In the dark.

"Yes," she said simply. "You must do that. Find him. Stop him."

"What about you?" Matt said, seeming to read her without knowing why or how he could do so, or how she could be radiating the anticipation that continued to shake her from head to foot. "You aren't afraid, Jen?"

"I'm terrified."

"You smell like sex, Jenna. Not fear."

"It's you, isn't it?" she said. "Your body might change, but it's you inside, for the most part? You carried me in here. You cared. Whatever gripped you didn't fully take over."

She pressed on, needing to make a point that he might not fully understand unless she could spit it all out. "You have a job to do to save others. It's important. I support that. I want to help."

Matt's head shook side to side. "Not you. You need to stay safe. I don't know what I'd do if anything happened to you."

His mouth was on her cheek, her neck, his action urgent,

insistent. His fingers tugged at her hair, entwining ever deeper, the pressure holding her quite motionless. Breathless.

Yes, she would smell like sex. She wanted him, could barely contain herself. This was familiar ground, this sexually heightened moment. This was what usually happened between them, minus the new twist, the new hunger that lay waiting, camouflaged within the old. Not only within Matt, but also within herself.

Soon, gone would be the need for control. And the need for caution.

Soon, she'd be unable to hurt him.

Soon—and as much as she mourned and regretted the reasons why—she would, at last, be able to show herself to him.

Finally, they would have a full connection.

And dammit, should she feel guilty that God had, in this terrible way, answered her prayers?

She wasn't running. She wasn't screaming. Truly, Jenna didn't seem the least bit afraid. Not only did the woman in his arms smell like heaven, suddenly she smelled like dessert.

For which he was so very ravenous.

Have to possess her. Here. Now.

Yes, he wanted to.

And couldn't.

He didn't know his own strength yet. He didn't know what having sex with her might do, cause, with moonlight just outside the door.

Damn, though. Really want to.

He wanted to be inside her more than he ever remembered wanting anything. Wanted it more than he wanted to find the perv with the lethal teeth who had kicked all this off. Wanted it more than he wanted to breathe.

Jenna's body was calling to him, bending into him, her skin

as heated as his own, her lips parted. She gave off an electrical charge he could feel through her clothes. One that went straight to his libido and outward from there.

Must go.

Must leave her.

No. Can't leave her…here.

It crossed his mind to search for the door, invent a way to safely get her to her car without the moon doing its damage. Without her having to see what he would become. The Landau family were good at control, but they'd had years of practice, decades to prepare.

And Jenna…

Jenna's breathing was loud, ragged. Her lips opened farther.

An invitation.

For him.

It would have taken, he concluded, covering those glorious lips with his own and taking full possession of her feverishly hot, slick lips, something far stronger than a damn werewolf to have resisted Jenna James's lure.

Yes.

That's it, Jenna thought.

As their kiss deepened, the darkness around them crackled with sparks, as though live wires had come loose from the ceiling.

More, Matt.

Don't hold back.

Her clothes felt tight, restricting. It wasn't only Matt's body leaning into hers, nearly crushing hers to the wall, that had her clawing at herself, but her own skirt, shirt and the torn lab coat she'd donned to cover those missing buttons.

The sound of fabric tearing brought yet a new layer to the mounting tension. Cooler air met her hot skin. Her shirt had been ripped to shreds. Matt had torn the remnants of the coat and blouse from her quivering shoulders, growling as a man would growl in the heat of passion. And maybe more.

On to the zipper. The skirt slipped down over her thighs quickly, with a soft sigh. Nothing left to separate them now, save for the little lace barriers covering her straining breasts and pelvis.

After a day of hunting criminals, a day where everything was black and white, Matt had always loved the bright-colored lingerie that contrasted with her tanned, honey-toned skin.

In honor of seeing him again, she'd worn red.

Fire red.

Matt murmured his appreciation when he saw it, slipped his hand under the elastic band lying across her hipbones, his fingers angling downward—toward the source of her ache.

Jenna closed her eyes. She moved her legs to allow him room, muttered unrepeatable things as his fingers parted her own triangular pelt of auburn fur, gliding languorously over her feminine folds. As his breath, ragged, shuddering, whispered in her ear what he would do to her next.

Instantaneously, both bra and panties were nothing more than colorful wisps on the dark wood floor. Matt's smooth, naked skin slid over hers, each muscle rippling with need. His thighs were hard. What stood erect between his thighs was even harder.

Jenna's arms fluttered, hands still fisted. She sank a little, into his exploring right hand. He caught her by the shoulder with his left, held her to the wall. Matt had always been able to raise the ache within her to monstrous proportions and then appease it. Tonight would be a new test.

He brushed his lips over hers, but couldn't sustain the gentleness or keep himself back. It had been such a long while.

As she moved her hips against him, he dug in quickly, devouring her mouth with a force and a passion that unleashed a groan from her throat. On hearing her sound, he pressed his hard length against her, easily finding what she willed him to find.

He drove himself into her with a single thrust, absorbing her reaction with his mouth covering hers. Jenna closed around him, felt him shudder as she held him for one more trembling second, and then she opened the way. This is what she wanted, what she had missed. There was no life without this, without him.

Unable to stop shaking, she silently pleaded for more. As he thrust into her again, she closed her eyes, shoved her hips against his and whispered his name.

"Matt."

That one vocalization seemed to be, for Matt, the final straw. The rhythm, slap and tempo of their slick bodies meeting became fast, frenzied and almost angry. He was hurting, she knew. He was taking this out on her, sharing his hurt with her and apologizing to her, all at the same time. The result was glorious, terrible, shocking. Still, she found herself wanting him to throw her on the floor, break some furniture, tear the plaster loose from the walls, break her in two if he had to…as long as this lasted forever. As long as he would never leave her alone again.

Matt. Her werewolf lover.

And after this, she'd be able to confide her own dark secret.

He had her legs in his hot hands now, urging her to wrap them around his waist. It took only a few seconds more for him to reach the spot, hitting it dead-on. Spasms rocked her, forcing her spine to arch. Her entire body went rigid, suspended, as the climactic waves crashed, one after the other, each wave more powerful than the first. She felt Matt get carried away by her fever. He joined her with a shudder and a cry.

And then, suddenly, the dark room stopped spinning. The world again grew silent. Her body seemed lost in the stillness, even as a new hunger grew.

Matt's hands were the first things to move. He ran his fingers over her face, her neck, her shoulders, her upper arms.

Then he went rigid.

He drew back so quickly, Jenna nearly slid all the way to the floor. His hand had encircled her arm with a grip that would have been hurtful, Jenna knew, for anyone other than herself.

With a fluid side step and without thought for himself and what such a step might mean, Matt yanked her toward the door to the cottage and flung the door open wide.

A beam of chilled silver-white light hit them. Light so bright and sudden that Jenna almost cried out. Bathed in silver, body beginning to shudder, big-time, she looked into Matt's shocked, frozen face.

"What is this?" he demanded, his grip on her upper arm tightening further, his other hand fingering not her aching womanhood, but the scar just above her right elbow.

And of course, she didn't have the time or the need to answer.

Matt stared incredulously at Jenna, forgetting who and what he was. Where he was. As he ran his fingers over the scar on her arm, his beast slammed to the surface.

And so—dammit to hell and against anything he could ever have imagined—did *hers*.

Knuckles tingling, his hands exploded with a bursting of callused skin. Dagger-sharp claws flicked upward like individual unfolding switchblades. His arms pulsed, popped, as the bones and ligaments realigned.

He teetered when his chest expanded, ribs cracking with a spike of pain that made him want to shout every obscenity he knew. But his face had already lengthened, his skull reshaped with a sensation of red-hot pokers being seared into his brain.

Fur sprouted from his pores, all at once, in a singular push. His legs were the last thing to get with the program.

Once he could think again, internalize the pain and feel it ease somewhat, he drew to his full, new height, opened his mouth, and growled.

The growl echoed in the night. No. It wasn't an echo at all. It was Jenna. Jenna had growled back, softly, but adamantly. Standing her ground.

Jesus, what ground it was.

Jenna was…not Jenna anymore. What stood in her place was taller, fuller, anxious; every muscle defined and taut and covered with auburn fur.

Terrible. Poignant.

Magnificent.

And Jenna wasn't crying, thrashing, running or mad. Her eyes, in opposition to her body, were round, gray and as soft as her voice, reflecting back the silver of the moonlight.

The ease with which she stood there, the graceful lift of her chin, the softness of her eyes, could only mean one thing. Jenna had been a werewolf, a she-wolf, for some time.

And the world had become unhinged. Totally.

Until she growled again.

Because he understood her. He almost laughed, except that beasts didn't have the capacity.

He howled in reply, his hunger already merging with the beast's to form a need so deep as to be fathomless.

"It's okay," Jenna's beast sang. *"I understand. You needn't hide from me. I will explain everything, the girl, me."*

His hunger for her spiraled upward like a live thing, intensified by his animal side. He had always wanted her, and now he wanted her *more*. But he wanted her man to woman, fearing what damage their beastlike forms could do, yes, although that wasn't the entire reason. He wanted to look into her eyes and see Jenna there. He wanted her to be present, himself to be present, completely. If at least for a while.

When he glanced up, she was gone. His heart skidded in the beast's breast. A howl bubbled up. But a flash of movement brought him to the door of the cottage, where his feet straddled the threshold. Where he no longer cared how much another transition would hurt, or what might result.

He didn't have to hide from Jenna. He didn't have to hope she would understand. Jenna knew everything, felt everything, was everything. And she could help. Together, they would find some answers. It was possible that Jenna had some of those answers now. Important answers to important questions.

Such as: why hadn't he and Jenna known about each other's beasts? Had their love gotten in the way?

Jenna must have known about the girl. She would have helped the girl if he hadn't shown up. He knew her, knew this. The truth was that she had wanted him back badly enough to use any method to see him. Damn if he hadn't *made* her bait him. He had caused this. He was responsible. Although in truth, even fighting with himself, he couldn't have stayed away from her much longer. Every solitary minute without her had been filled with pain and sorrow. Looking now at the darkness inside of the cottage's doorway, knowing Jenna was in there waiting for him, the grand finale question, the mother of all questions he wanted answers to filled his mind.

How long would this cottage hold up, with two werewolves going at each other...repeatedly, and with all-out gusto?

Boldly, greedily, he stepped inside the cottage after Jenna. Out of the moonlight. Following the scent of her desire. Feeling himself rise to the occasion.

The other stuff could wait. Just now, he and Jenna had some unfinished business to conduct. Business that could conceivably take them well into the future, no holds barred.

He could see it, taste it. What a team they'd make, as man and woman and as werewolves, hunting anomalies—anomalies like themselves—together, day and night, full moon or otherwise. They'd know what to look for in others newly infected and where to take them for help. Maybe they would become the help.

They would find the creep who was loose in the city. The Biter. They would put him away for good, protect the public. Jenna would explain what had happened to her and about keeping her secret from him. He'd tell her everything about himself, things he'd never told anyone.

They might cry about this night, and maybe laugh about it eventually, if fate wasn't so terribly and continually cruel as to separate them ever again.

All there—inside the doorway that Jenna had gone through. His love waited for him. His life. The whiff of his lover's need trailed behind her like a mind-numbing cloud. Like a neon arrow leading the way toward a shared future.

Yes, he could let the rest go—for now. For a while. Though he was a beast, a monster and a detective, he could find a few stolen moments of bliss, and respite from the pain and turmoil his existence had become.

Happiness for him came in the form of a sexy, psychiatric she-wolf.

Well, okay, he said to the moon, looking up and baring his teeth. *Okay.*

And thank heavens, Matt told himself as he stepped out of the light, actually smiling for the first time in a long, long while…

We're already naked.

* * * * *

WOLF BAIT

Chapter 1

Night.

Soft velvet darkness on skin.

Frosted moonlight.

A sensual cocktail for the senses…

Parker Madison raised his face to the moon with a predatory gaze. He tossed back his curtain of black hair and felt the moon's light on his face—a touch that transferred to more personal places, reminiscent of the way a woman's fingers might stroke him to erection and keep him there, shuddering on the verge of orgasm.

The moon was such an indiscreet mistress.

Would he ever get used to that?

Maintaining his balance effortlessly, Parker crouched silently atop a high stone wall, shirtless, in jeans and boots, without the added benefits of the heavily muscled, morphed limbs he'd be able to access in twenty-four hours when the moon, in her full phase, would bestow more nocturnal magic.

He sensed the moon waiting even now—not quite full but paying close attention. Highlighting his naked shoulders. Moving him in ways only a lover should. Madame Moon's crimes against nature were intimate enough to make his groin ache, and tempting enough to draw him away from shelter with the promise of what?

Wildness? Inhumanness? Madness?

Well, it was useless for him to contemplate what her lure actually might be, since it was far too late to protest it. The fact was, he was starting to enjoy the physical changes the moon brought—the enhanced sight, hearing and sense of smell, the almost psychic rushes of perception that had already begun to help him in his job at the hospital. He possessed nearly endless cardiovascular output. In his alternate form, he exhibited the brute strength of four or five men.

Already, as each month passed since his initiation into the moon's cult, he needed more of an adrenaline rush just to feel alive, real, connected. He needed more of the dark, the wind and the moon's silvery breath just to deal.

He now looked forward to joining with his beast, letting it out a notch at a time to see where this new world would take him. Being a beast felt good.

"Damn good," Parker muttered softly.

A moon junkie was what he had become, longing to run, hunt, howl; counting the minutes until he could. Outcast. Loner. He'd become both of those things, too. But the inner arguments over giving up friends, free time and women had long since ceased, given over to the need for answers regarding his new existence. Answers as to what might have kick-started the beastly transformations in the first place.

He, Parker Madison, M.D., was no exception to the fact that physicians were nothing if not inquisitive. And if he continued to run real fast, real far, in the direction he was going with this moon business, there was a chance he might actually outdistance the nagging monologues arising from the rational side of his brain that questioned his liking these changes, and how quickly he had adapted in the past few months to being...*different*.

Hell, he had become about as different from the average thirty-one-year-old as was possible.

Shrugging off a twitch of apprehension between his shoulder blades, Parker adjusted his position on the wall. All those new senses bombarding him were in full evidence tonight as he stared at the house in the distance. The evening was hot and flooded with fragrance. Balmy Miami smells topped the list: crowded bodies in the distance, sun-soaked concrete, the subtle aromas of a hundred different types of food. Closer to him drifted green nature smells from the trees lining the wall and stretching off toward the city.

But those were tame things, the trees and the city scents. Surface things, masking the undercurrent flowing through the wall where he crouched, and upward into his body.

In truth, he didn't feel so tame anymore.

Neither did the house he'd been looking at for the past few minutes.

The feel of the place weighed heavily on his shoulders. The unusual scent that had drawn him to this wall, all the way from his city digs, saturated the area where he perched and the residence beyond it with the dense odor of Otherness. Creatures that were more than human had gathered here recently, in and around this place. More than one creature, if the strength of the scent meant anything.

How he knew this remained a mystery. No words sprang

to mind to match such a scent with a verbal translation. There was no real way to define the feeling of having found something similarly at odds with life as he'd always known it.

Otherness.

The house he watched wasn't a house at all, really, more like a genteel plantation mansion. Three stories of gleaming white wood and aged brick rose up from a wide expanse of lawn. Numerous tall pillars decorated its front. There were more windows than he cared to count. A long, unscreened veranda circled the base. The only thing missing from this pretty picture of Southern grace was a wicker table set with mint julep drinks, and men in ivory linen suits.

Calm Southern hospitality on the surface.

Then again, looks could be so deceiving.

There were no bright lights in this compound's acreage to compete with the moonlight. No guard dogs snarled or barked out their anger over Parker's presence. This in itself would have been curious in a city where crime statistics were notoriously high and rising, especially amid the luxury estates of the rich and famous lining this particular stretch of it.

He saw no electric fence. The gatehouse hadn't been manned for security. Yet the house set within these stone walls and meandering grounds was surrounded by a feral aura so virulent that any creature with the ability to breathe might have recognized it.

Which begged the question: were the others residing here like himself? Had his search for another genetic mutant ended?

Parker found those ideas both mind-altering and dreadful. More creatures like him meant he wouldn't be the anomaly he'd considered himself. Wouldn't be the only one afflicted with this strange shape-shifting ability. Finding others would mean no longer being the one-in-a-billion example of cells going awry, as he'd theorized.

If that house happened to be filled with other man-wolf hybrids, it would prove once and for all that human and wolf DNA really could fuse to form a new conglomerate, a new entity. Not a freak accident of nature or some damned Hollywood creation, but a fusion that happened on a regular basis. One with a title.

Werewolf.

Half wolf, half man. A man for twenty-eight days out of each month, and a hybrid for three. A man possessed by a more grisly part of himself. Sigmund Freud would have had a field day, though even an awkward description didn't do justice to the new thing that he, Parker, had become. Not by a long shot.

And he couldn't afford to forgo caution, no matter how many thoughts vied for his attention.

Studying the house intently, he found more questions bubbling up. Who lived there? What were they? Did the creatures inside await the next full moon, as he did? Would they shift shape, leave their fancy cars in the garage and run? Twenty-four more hours and he'd find out. In a little less than twenty-four hours the moon would be full, and werewolves, if there were any other than himself, would emerge to find him waiting.

Because believing in this beastly invasion of a man's body had been tough for a medical man like himself. Who knew better than a physician how impossible it should be for a body to split itself apart at the seams in order to accommodate the birth of a beastly form much larger than its host? Something long-faced, long-limbed and wolfish, partially covered in an inch-long pelt of fur—in his own case its color a deep black like the cascading dark waves of hair on his head.

But here he was. Proof.

Maybe these people know.

Maybe whoever lives here knows about the moon. That

circling silver presence so distant from the earth that directed his changes and dictated the way things were to be. The same moon that pulled at ocean tides and affected the blood pumping through human veins in such a way that caused surgeons like himself to refuse to operate on nights when the moon was full.

Screw his degree from Harvard Medical School. Textbooks couldn't help him. None of them could explain the reasons for the desires he harbored—the heady, almost sexual surge of power in his body that took place after dark; the insatiable hunger, not for food, but for the more primal urge to mate, bite, and lose himself over and over in a tight, hot place.

An animal's lustings. Dangerous cravings kept on a tight rein, with a choke hold, for eight long months now. Made worse every single time the moon showed her full face, and he became something he could not recognize.

Parker fended off a shudder, though he felt feverish so close to the moon's full phase. There would be no burning off excess energy tonight. He had to remain vigilant, keep still and concentrate. This could be it—the end of his search. It was possible that here, inside these walls, he would find out exactly what had happened…to make him this way.

He might find out if a further draining away of his humanity might be expected, if more changes were imminent, and whether or not he would lose himself altogether eventually. If the wildness would win.

Until he knew those things, maintaining his job at the hospital would be a precarious venture. Dangerous. Without a steadfast grip on himself and the assurance of being able to maintain full control, there would be no digging his way back into society. There would be no nuzzling anyone's long, graceful neck. No hot, tight places to explore.

"More's the pity," Parker whispered, truly missing the

latter. But then, he'd never felt so alive as he did this minute, with every fiber of his being tuned in and awaiting enlightenment. His body was producing a rush all on its own, and humming like a severed live wire....

Parker flinched midthought and brought his head up, his attention disturbed, his hearing mechanisms dialed in to a sudden vibration in the air.

He glanced over his shoulder, then straightened. Standing tall, he allowed the rare Miami breeze to ruffle his hair, caress his tanned, naked chest. In that breeze floated a fresh bit of sensory input.

Sound.

Too damned close for comfort.

She'd been fast once upon a time, Chloe Tyler remembered as she limped along in the dark. In school she had run track, trained daily and been an all-star. Now she couldn't get enough air into her lungs and her legs were dragging.

Her next breath shredded her throat, nearly paralyzing the rest of her. Fear rushed in. She felt *them* behind her. She hadn't gotten away. The filthy bastards were toying with her like a bug on a string.

Concentrate. Don't lose it, C. It hurts like hell, but you have to take in oxygen. You need to think if you're to make it.

Need to make it.

Not ready to die.

"Please don't...let...me die."

She knew where the hospital was, where to find help, and couldn't seem to get there. She passed trees, their silhouettes ominous in the dark, and felt what some distant chip of an idea suggested might be grass under her feet.

She wasn't thinking straight, didn't remember much. Blackness surrounded the pain slicing through her head. Big trees crowded in and over her, nightmarish, suffocating, stifling her attempts to breathe. No buildings, paved streets or lights were visible, though she should have hit the boulevard by now.

Had she gotten turned around?

No. Just too damned slow.

Her surroundings had taken on a grayish haze. Chloe fought off the rise of panic accompanying her sudden loss of sight. A wetness dripped in and around her eyes, thick, warm, smelling like rusted iron. Although she knew what this had to be, she refused to give it a name. She might not make it if she defined it.

She brushed at her eyes and tried again for a breath of air. The big moon overhead delivered a whiteness so bright it seared her skull, but at least, she decided, hobbling toward tree cover, she would see them coming for her this time. At least she knew they were there.

The thought of *them* paralyzed her further, so that she had to struggle to move. Not that it would do any good to move at this pace. She'd be caught soon enough. What could one small twenty-four-year-old do against five large men?

Not men. Gang. Very bad guys.

Looking outward, then up at the sky, Chloe choked back a sob and attempted to get her limbs in order, which no longer seemed like an option. She heard her pursuers clearly now as they noisily tromped through the bushes, without a care for life of any kind. The bastards who had hit her and left her on the ground—*yes, I remember that much*—were hot on her trail. The sickos who must not have expected her to rally or get away were closing in.

Her arms were shaking so badly she felt they were possessed. Ditto her legs. The moon seemed to sear pain into her bones, its light stinging her eyes. Tears mixed with the flow of blood dripping from her forehead, though she'd always prided herself on having nothing whatsoever to do with the words *weak* or *feeble*.

But the blood…

Oh God! Must…keep…breathing.

She managed one more step, but not another. *They* were coming to finish what they'd started.

These might be her last seconds on earth.

Gripping a tree with trembling fingers, gathering herself in spite of the urge to close her eyes and allow it all to slip away, Chloe parted her parched lips…and screamed.

It was the wrong thing to do. She found herself instantly surrounded. Five white T-shirts stood out against the darkness. Above the shirts, five angry faces scowled with dark intentions. Dammit, she'd just told them her location! She had called them to her! Hanging on now would be next to impossible. Remaining upright wasn't going to happen. Their very presence sapped the determination from her. Clenching her fists, Chloe sucked in one more breath and felt her legs go.

"Hey, baby girl," a voice whispered menacingly as her butt hit the dirt. "Where do you think you're going?"

Laughter followed, as if the comment had been funny. Chloe's stomach tightened, then did a rollover. An internal fuzziness closed in.

The heavily accented voice returned, closer to her ear.

"You would run away from me when I'm your daddy? Your soul mate? Your everything?"

More laughter arose from the animal's tattooed groupies. A grimy hand pressed against her throat and squeezed.

"I am going to make you special, little blonde. I don't have to, you understand. I could kill you right now and be on my way. I have important things to do. So, you see how much

I care? At much inconvenience to myself and my brothers I am here with you instead of doing what we set out to do. We hunted you down to tell you these things."

The night had grown darker, as if even the moon didn't wish to see what was going on. Chloe couldn't keep her eyes open much longer. She didn't have an ounce of fight left in her. Why? Had she been injured so badly already, or was she just scared out of her wits?

"Special," the voice repeated, in the tone of a nasty promise. "We will make you special." But a pause followed this hell spawn's evil insinuation, during which nothing awful happened, except the wind shifting direction to hit Chloe's face with a wave of summer heat.

Several seconds of silence ensued before a crunching sound sent her spiraling toward the pit of unspeakable pain.

Are those my bones breaking?

Hot breath dragged along her cheek. Just when she thought she wouldn't be able to stand any more, the sharpest pain of all hit. Indescribable torment. Choking back another scream, Chloe fought to regain her equilibrium in a sinking world. The pain was at debilitating levels—on her face, on her shoulder. No, her upper arm.

Everywhere…

Had she been knifed? Had the sick bastard threatening her stuck in a blade and twirled it around?

Thinking that, Chloe slid down in the rapidly gathering blackness, aware of a pitiful noise escaping her lips that she had meant as a threat, but was very probably the last sound she would ever make.

"No distractions. Not tonight!"

Parker protested vehemently under his breath against whatever that noise might have been. Finding out what went on in and around this estate was of paramount importance. Ultimately, his sanity depended on it.

A series of growls echoed grimly inside his chest before spilling from his throat, threatening sounds no human ought to have made.

Again he eyed the park behind him.

Yes. Sound. Not too far away.

His skin rippled in a reaction that had nothing whatsoever to do with the term *Homo sapiens.* A new flush of heat flowed through his limbs, all four of which were now buzzing with nerve fibers that pegged the sound in the distance as urgent.

Someone in trouble?

Parker inched sideways—for a breath, and to listen. Also to help deflect the blows of the beast pounding at him from the inside—a beast close enough to his night of freedom to tip the scales somewhat by urging the man into action.

What had riled his internal parasite?

Recognition hit Parker in the gut as soon as he asked himself that question. *Blood.* The metallic scent of blood wafted in the humid Miami breeze, discernible to both beast and surgeon. Had that sound come from someone injured?

Gazing out over the forested acreage bordering the wall, Parker heard nothing now except the dramatic beating of his heart. Not more than a minute later, the all-too-familiar noise of tearing flesh came, accompanied by a sting that hurt like a son of a bitch and nearly tipped him off balance.

Grimacing, swearing a blue streak, Parker glanced at his fingers, already sporting two-inch claws as sharp as switchblades, which had torn through him as if spring-loaded. Ten claws, long, curved, lethal.

Surprised, holding both hands up, Parker looked to the sky. "You're not full, so what the hell is this?"

Yes. What? Had the scent of blood caused the claws? Had

the eeriness of the sound in the distance inspired this unexpected little gift? Maybe the anxiousness of awaiting what lay behind this wall had done it?

Whatever the cause, the claws were a shock and damned unwieldy. He had the scars to prove it, scars that in turn proved the existence of his beast, beyond a doubt. And though the wounds he inflicted upon himself repaired themselves supernaturally quickly, the scar tissue they left behind remained his link to this new reality. All part of the *believing* thing.

A swipe to his right thigh now slashed through his jeans and into his flesh, bringing up another oath and a welling of blood that percolated to his skin's surface, causing a circular stain in the denim. Parker felt the blood trickle downward toward his knee as the laws of gravity dictated it should; not upward toward *her,* toward the moon. His blood didn't entirely belong to her. *Not yet.*

Relaxing slightly, he again sought the glimmer of overhead light that had become both his bane and his darkest secret. His darkest pleasure. What folly had she dropped on him now? What new game did the moon play?

Leaping from the wall, feeling the cool caress from above on his back, Parker landed squarely on his feet.

And then the sound came again.

Louder this time.

Grounded by the earth beneath his boots, Parker pigeonholed the sound. Didn't he hear this same kind every day in the E.R., coming from the lips of people in serious trouble? Unconscious people, and those close to losing it, keening for aid? A desperate plea for somebody to hear. A prayer for someone, anyone, to help.

His heartbeat amped up, fueled by a rush of pure adrenaline, just as it did each time he entered the hospital E.R.

Research here, at this mansion, would have to wait, because the Hippocratic oath was still strong in him—strong enough to rival the beast, the moon, the claws and whatever else went on between the black-and-white lines of life. He might be a freak, part wolf and predator, but he could not, would not, ignore his other calling. Not as long as he had one wit of his own left to him.

Then again, he concluded, whirling in place to confront both the sound and the distant scent of blood, "Dr. Werewolf" didn't have the ring to it he would have expected from all those years of training.

Chapter 2

Virtually skimming the ground, Parker ran until the scent of blood, arising like a solid barrier, stopped him.

The hair on the back of his neck prickled. His chest tightened. A huddled body lay on the grass, just yards from the wall. A human body.

Parker shook his head. *Too late? Maybe not.* The slightest movement of a hand on the ground, a mere reactionary flutter, encouraged him to step closer.

It was a woman, he saw, curled into a tight ball. A petite thing, young, slender, with a delicate bone structure, her blond hair fanning out around her as if she'd fallen where she lay.

Parker's beast gave a whine that he ignored. Moving in for a closer look, he heard the woman's breath rattle faintly in her throat. A slick red ooze covered her face, neck and shoulders. Long strands of hair that had probably once been silky stuck to the blood from a gaping wound on her forehead, so that none of her features were fully visible.

Quickly, Parker dropped to a crouch beside her.

She appeared to be in her early twenties. The skin on her bare arms was smooth and lightly tanned. Rounded breasts filled out a watery blue camisole. Her dark denim jeans looked expensive. She should have known better than to stray this far from civilization at any time, let alone after dark.

A surge of nerve burn flashed across Parker's skin as he reached out to touch her. Silently, he warned the moon to back off.

When the woman moaned, Parker's human heart went out to her. But the dark passenger he carried inside him felt something else, and reared back as if the spot might be contaminated.

Surely the cause for alarm didn't relate to this woman, so hurt and helpless, Parker reasoned. Someone else had to be there, out of sight. Maybe even more than one someone.

A flare of anger ripped through him, to go along with the claws. His beast's intuition battered at him as if the thing inside him truly was a separate entity, and as if the beast knew something the man didn't.

What's wrong with this picture, beast?

What do you see?

His hand remained suspended above the injured woman he hadn't yet touched, having been repelled by so much blood and at the same time drawn to it. This female, whoever she might be, was struggling to breathe, fighting to stay alive. Would he be able to help her? The claws, the intoxication of night on his skin, the scent of her blood and the nearness of his beast's time for freedom were filling Parker's body with vague warnings he wasn't able to grasp. *Too vague.*

He touched the woman's neck, careful to manage the claws. *Pulse weak.*

Carefully, he rolled her onto her back, then brushed the hair from her face with the side of his hand. "I have you," he said hoarsely, meaning it, yet feeling unpredictable. "I'll get help."

"No." It was a whisper, pushed by a shallow breath, after which her eyes opened, then quickly closed again, unable to sustain the effort.

Parker leaned in farther, silently assessing.

She'd been blessed with fine features: small nose, pointed chin, wide-set eyes, maybe blue, gray or green—they hadn't stayed open long enough for him to tell. Her lips were heart-shaped, a swollen reddish-blue, and surrounded by a blood-less, ghostly pale face. A face disfigured by deep lacerations that ran from her hairline to her chin, leaving one cheek a bloody pulp.

Parker's muscles seized in protest. He blew out wordless sound. This female had been badly beaten and slashed. He'd seen a lot of terrible things in the E.R., but this?

In spite of the severity of the damage and the possible clog of blood in her throat, the woman tried to speak. What Parker heard was, "Trick."

"No trick," he countered in a tone as gentle as he was able to make it, given his feelings of disgust for what had hap-pened to her, and his own recent events. "You're hurt. I'm a doctor. We'll—"

He didn't get the last sentence out. With a neck-snapping turn of his head that would have severed the spine of any typical human without a beast's connections, he scanned the dark. Jumping to his feet, Parker recognized this particular wave of cooler air as a warning of imminent danger close at hand.

A voice carried to him over the grass. "Look, my brothers. The woman has brought us a new toy to play with."

Parker counted one, two…no, five figures emerging out of the shadows to form a loose circle around himself and the injured woman. The newcomers were too close not to be taken seriously and too far away to wring their necks for taking necessary time away from the girl. He'd been too concerned about her injuries to have seen this coming.

The night was just chock-full of surprises.

"Or maybe," the same heavily accented voice chided, "what we have found is a pervert in his own right, since he appears to be missing some clothes."

"Clothes be damned. Did you do this to her?" Parker demanded, knowing the truth well enough. These jokers' scents permeated the woman by his feet. They smelled of overcooked fat and wore the baggy uniforms of a typical street gang. Miami gangbangers. Security in numbers. And these filthy scumbags had savaged the blonde.

Parker's body gave a heave of disapproval. Blood gushed through his open thigh wound as if his beast were attempting to slide through the hole.

Tensely, Parker stood his ground as three of the gang members inched toward him in the way hungry coyotes crowded in on a meal. That image made him sick to his stomach, and he knew why. His wolfishness was growing more substantial, lured to the surface by anger and uncertainty. His beast wanted to burst out ahead of his scheduled release time to take over the driver's seat. His darker side wanted to confront the danger these lowlifes presented.

Maybe on another night he could have shouldered a surprise like the pop of unexpected claws and the lively interest of his inner beast, but not this one. It wasn't time for a transformation and he wasn't the only person involved here. Even so, he felt a distancing from himself, as though his humanness danced on a last remaining thread of control.

"It speaks," the spokesman for the group quipped. "And isn't that just too bad. Now we will have to hear his screams for mercy."

Heck, maybe he should sic the beast on these guys, Parker thought. It would serve them right to have the tables turned. But it just wasn't time for that. And no matter how he looked at this, and whatever form he might long to take, five-against-one odds were going to be bad.

"Buzz off," he warned, flexing his clawed fingers. "First and final warning."

It was a fine threat, but a wave of light-headedness washed over him with very bad timing. His head needed to be clear if he wanted to live. Plus it was completely insane to believe that his beast could emerge unbidden. The claws had been a mistake, a slip. Say he could open up to the beast, let it take over early, and together they managed to kick some gangland butt. What then?

Parker's anger tripled as he breathed in the faintest trace of perfume drifting to him above the odor of blood, coming from the woman on the ground. Perfume and blood. Blond hair and a slashed face. Sure, he might be some kind of monster, but the jerks facing him were much worse.

He knew what these guys would be thinking, could almost hear them laughing. *How much trouble would one unarmed, half-dressed guy be?*

"Plenty," Parker answered, without the benefit of the question being asked aloud. "And willing."

The three thugs closest to him paused to glance toward their brother. Parker looked at him also. *Big guy. Dark-skinned. No shaved head, bucking trend.* Waiting a few seconds more, even though his ligaments and tendons were starting to strain with tension, Parker brushed his claws back and forth over his jeans with a swishing sound.

"We don't like your tone," the big guy spat.

"*We* don't much like yours, either," Parker said. *Me and my internal friend.*

"Are you hiding a knife under your armpit?" the leader droned sarcastically. "A gun in your pants? Because that's what it will take to keep us from dragging your ass off to our boss. He prefers his entertainment alive, you see, even barely."

A moan, faint but noticeable, came from the woman on the ground. Time was wasting. Her life had to be draining away. While he…was feeling so strange.

Pulsating biceps sent an icy shiver of apprehension up his spine, a familiar sensation Parker couldn't ignore. He heard the pop of one vertebra realigning. Then another.

Oh yes, he knew this feeling, all right. He knew what it meant. He was going to morph, full moon or no full moon, willing or not. The claws had been a precursor, a warning, for which the scent of blood and the state of this poor woman's face had sealed the deal. His beast was about to blossom and there would be no holding it back.

Angling his neck, Parker heard a crack. *Better than knuckles.* The sound caused an instantaneous fire in his belly that rapidly spread upward into his shoulders, then flowed down his arms like molten lava, to leave a trail of sparks all along his overstretched nerve fibers. His claws raked his palms as he fisted his fingers. His jaw tensed.

"Maybe we can continue this chat later?" he suggested, afterburn dropping his voice an octave. "The woman needs help."

And the beast needs twenty-four more hours to chill.

This is not a good precedent.

"So, you would like us to call you a cab, maybe?" A wave of the big guy's hand caused his four brothers to step forward in unison, like puppets.

"Tires might ruin the grass," Parker said, disgust riding his skin in the form of yet more heat. "But transportation would be nice, all the same. Will you have one of your merry men call for it, or actually do something yourself?"

The next sound the woman made seemed to ruffle through Parker. Right through him, as if her raspy plea somehow slipped beneath his skin to meet his beast face-to-face, stirring up trouble of another sort. That longing for a hot, tight place.

Parker felt his heart stutter, stall, then immediately start back up. He had suddenly grown rock-hard below this belt. Something about this woman appealed to his beast.

Glancing down, he said to her, "I'll get help. I promise."

"We just don't think you can keep that promise, perv," the thug said with a laugh. "Because who is going to help *you?* You have no idea who we are and what we can do."

In spite of the threat of violence tainting the air, Parker got another whiff of citrus emanating from the ground, a fragrance almost as ethereal as the woman wearing it. He didn't have time to think beyond that. A second scumbag barreled forward, as if urged to action by a silent cue. A third followed. Surrounded, knowing he would have to fight, Parker chanced another look. At *her*.

Inexplicably drawn there.

Struggling with the pain threatening to take her down, Chloe stared at the man standing above her, supposing that her mind had to be going. The man looked like an avenging angel.

His face had become visible to her now in the drip of eerie, dappled light from above, a face composed of taut, tanned skin over sharp angles. Dark hair hung past his ears, frosted by a silver liquid shine. His eyes, light, extremely bright, bored into her, stirring long-dormant feelings she was unable to tap into, rekindling something that had been about to slip away.

It felt to her as though he, whoever he was, had called up through his gaze the single spark of life left in her, that little flicker about to be extinguished by so much hurt and chaos. Sensations soared through her, one after another, weaving in and out of her pain. She felt damp grass under her body, saw the twisted shape of the trees beside her, smelled the foglike humidity of the night.

Emotions flowed as if a tap had been left open. Anger, fear, love, hate, longing, lust were all there and exposed. Yet the lure of this man's eyes lifted her up from the blackest depths, as if he had gripped her soul and was tugging hard. His blue eyes were both fire and ice, beautiful and disconcerting, taunting and sympathetic, strange and yet familiar.

Did she know this guy? Where had she seen those eyes before? At the university, where she worked? At the hospital lab she utilized for her research? In some hallway? Outside a grocery store? Did it even matter? The ground seemed to be slipping out from under her. She felt about to float off.

"Sorry," she tried to say, knowing that what came out sounded more like a grunt than a word. Still, the guy responded as if he had understood.

"I'll get help," he said. "I promise."

She believed him. God knew she did. In order to do that, though, this man would place himself in jeopardy. He already had. She had been dessert for this gang, and now he was new bait for them to continue their rampage of evil. She didn't have any money, carried no purse. She didn't wear jewelry. What had attracted them to her so near that freaking wall she'd been watching? Why had this happened?

The air swelled with their wily, eerie presence. The beautiful guy who stood over her had no idea what he was getting himself into.

Must get to my feet.

Unfortunately, neither her arms nor her legs responded to her will to move. Whatever these freaks had done to her this time had been the final straw. The horror of it came crashing down.

Not gone yet.

Not a quitter!

Chloe plunged her fingernails into the dirt so forcefully, she felt the strike ricochet through her. With a small, inward shriek, she felt her fingers sink in. Gripping the earth, she pulled with all her might, and succeeded in moving her body only half an inch. But that was half an inch toward the light, not the dark. Toward the light in this man's eyes.

"Run!" Again, it was nowhere near a word. She cleared her throat, gurgled up blood that trickled down her chin and tried again. "Run!" So much energy needed to say one damned word and travel one inch. "Save…yourself…."

A quick touch caused her to recoil. The man with the luminous eyes, close again, had gently laid the back of his hand on her face. In this moment of imminent danger, he had taken the time to reassure her. Reacting to the kindness, Chloe's heart gave one good strong pulse.

"Hang on," the black-haired avenger said to her. "I have to take care of something, but I swear I'll be back."

The young woman's eyes were open, and trained on him. Green eyes, Parker noted, and dazed because of what had happened to her. His insides clenched again as his eyes met hers. His beast rumbled. Recently unused body parts stirred. But it was too late. Whatever message she had beamed to him with those bloody, beautiful eyes slammed the beast the rest of the way into him, and into action.

Head. Neck. Shoulders. Chest. Ligaments began to stretch at their insertions with the sound of wet meat being slapped on a plate. Pain soared through Parker as his hips realigned and his thighs bulged. Both knees crackled. His stomach gave a lurch. Acute distress accompanied this transformation, because this wasn't supposed to happen, had never happened, not without the full moon's prompting. Not without her very special attention.

His face stretched, bringing a sting reminiscent of being knifed behind the eyes, but it was only a portion of the discomfort he usually encountered with a physical shift. Faster than the time it took for him to blink a second time, his bones had settled into their new shape. A stranger-than-usual kind of strange shape. Only a partial semblance of the normal routine. Parker could see past his nose. He was panting, but not much fur sprang from his pores, other than on his chest and forearms.

The birth of a beast, and yet not.

Head raised, and holding tightly to his mental faculties, Parker straightened up to his full new height, a few inches taller than his usual six-two. He could see in his peripheral vision that he had indeed only attained part of the beast's shape. Half of the beast emerged—as if somebody had hit the pause button too early. It was an astonishing feat.

His jeans were now tight, but not tight enough to constrict further development. His arms looked somewhat like his arms, only better. His skin felt thicker. His body was hard all over.

Longer now in this incarnation, his hair swept across his bare, muscled shoulders. He tasted blood. His mouth, though not fully developed, contained a full set of razor-sharp teeth that made the claws seem like child's play.

Rolling back his enhanced musculature, baring those

canines, Parker studied the freaks surrounding him, absorbing his personal discomfort with a ferocious howl that, if translated, would have meant:

Be bested by a bunch of stereotypical street thugs?
The hell you say!

Chapter 3

So. He'd done it. Shifted early—if only in part. *No time to think about the ramifications of that.* The five guys were close enough now that Parker could see details—such as the long stripes of scar tissue on their forearms that looked like white, ridged tattoos.

He stepped forward to narrow his attention on the three in front of him. Their reaction to his appearance had been expected, and had provided him with some lag time, but the idiots were soon on him anyway, like crazed infants in need of a lesson from a monster. Like insects on honey. Were they completely nuts? So high on drugs they failed to notice what had just happened?

They beat at him with their fists, kicked at him, tried hard to wrestle him to the ground. They were strong suckers. He knocked one of them over with a right-fisted punch to the face, and felt his claws swipe the guy's flesh as he went down.

Parker twisted sharply to gain access to the second and the third, noting how the two others remained apart, maybe waiting for signs of fatigue in the fighter the way a pack of hyenas might, and content to watch their brethren fight. He would have yelled "Cowards!" if his teeth hadn't been in the way.

One of the bastards jumped onto his back and hung there. Parker spun again, tucking his arms into his sides, shaking that guy off with a mighty twist, ready to deal with the one remaining imbecile.

He was distracted midblow. Not by a sound this time, more by an internal alarm that had nothing of the smell of cops or more creeps arriving on the scene. This new perception was fierce, nagging, unusual.

The atmosphere in the park changed. A new scent reached him, similar to the one near the mansion's stone wall.

Otherness, coming on.

Likeness nearby.

The heft of the pressure drift that reached Parker was altogether new. A stunning slap to the senses.

Someone else had arrived. Someone special.

Maintaining distance between himself and the guy swinging at him by keeping his hands on the idiot's throat, Parker sent his awareness outward. His focus snapped to a spot by the distant trees, deep in shadow. And there he was. *It* was.

Barely visible, his form blending into the night as if a part of it, this onlooker's presence seemed like a shout never uttered, a silent bell being struck with such force that the unheard vibrations soared through the ether, changing the air's consistency. Except that this newcomer could definitely be heard when he wanted to be. A howl of challenge broke through the scene, causing Parker's attackers to freeze where they were.

The two guys left standing looked at each other, turned and

took off. The two on the ground hauled themselves to their feet and followed. Parker let go of the idiot he'd been holding and watched him hightail it in a southerly direction. Parker let him. He'd witnessed too much destruction in the emergency room to want to inflict his wrath if he didn't have to. He wasn't all beast, in fact.

What parts of his beast there were leaned toward this new presence. Chills raised goose bumps on his back. Everything seemed to center on the newcomer, for which a name tickled the edge of Parker's tongue. *Evil?*

Standing stock-still, staring hard, Parker felt his heart race at impossible speed. All of his muscles spasmed at once. A man stood by the trees. Part man, that was. And part something else.

Werewolf.

Transfixed with disbelief, Parker continued to gape. The thing over there looked like nothing he had ever seen, except tonight in himself. The pale half wolf, also naked from the waist up, pointed at Parker, then at himself. *Same?*

Then he cocked his head and howled with an ominous, forlorn sound that echoed in the night and filled Parker's mind with flashing pictures of mountains, valleys and forests, with an almost subliminal speed. In those landscapes dark things ran on two legs in a tight pack. Many dark things.

The images dissolved when the albino-pale wolf took off after the fleeing gang, leaving Parker rocking on his heels, having just glimpsed, however startling it was, his future.

Not the only one.

Half-crazed, bewildered, lured by that wolf's presence, Parker started after the thing so like himself, then stumbled to a stop, hauled back by remembering the woman.

The girl. The oath.

His promise.

He teetered, torn between a man's logic and a beast's

desires. Here lay the proof of the existence of another person like him, the very thing for which he had been hopeful and at the same time dreading. Another werewolf roamed this earth, this city, perhaps in possession of answers to the questions that had plagued Parker for months.

Parker stood rooted in indecision. *The animal? The gang? The girl?* Should he chase the thugs clear out of Miami, helping the people who lived here? Should he go after the beast who had come to his aid? Wouldn't it be selfish to allow the other wolf to fight his fight?

Was it crucial for him to fulfill the promise he'd made to the woman to see her to safety and help? The badly injured young beauty who had tried to warn him of the danger? How could she know what this meant for him? How could anybody know? He had seen a werewolf!

His head whirled with questions as one of the toughest decisions he'd ever had to make nailed him in place. Find out about his own life or save the young woman's? Whatever direction he chose meant maybe losing the other option.

Parker ached to follow the wolf. Everything pulled him that way, except *her*. Her and those large, green, pleading eyes she had turned on him.

Casting one more glance into the distance, uttering one more guttural growl, and filled with a longing so intense to be with his own kind that he swayed back and forth on both feet, Parker dug his teeth into the side of his mouth and turned.

A promise was a promise.

With his body all revved up with the tension of a lightning storm, and barely able to breathe, he headed back between the trees, wanting to bang his head against one of them. He'd had his shot at answers and had lost. Why?

God Almighty, why?

Not just for a pretty pair of eyes. He knew that, of course.

Parker had let that wolf go because the man in him had won this round, and it was imperative the man remain in control.

No. That's not it. There's more.

There was another human being to be considered here. A woman owed help for many reasons, but in part because, after all was said and done, she had caused the healer in him, the best side of him, to shine.

Still more, his mind nagged.

He delved further beneath the surface of his feelings.

He was going back because…yes, dammit, because her eyes were an intelligent green. And because they had briefly connected with his in some new and inexplicable way.

He would find her, help her.

Parker closed his eyes and willed his body to stillness. Inhaling deeply, he found her trail easily enough. The woman had dragged herself from the spot where he'd left her. Droplets of her blood, smelling like crushed aluminum, blackened the ground. The unique scent of citrus-dipped flower petals mingled with the fragrance of mangled grass, disturbed earth, injury and fear.

Parker cast one more look in the direction the other were-wolf had run. Then he eyed the blood by his boots, gritted his canines and forced a growl through tight teeth.

A promise is a promise.

Ducking beneath the tree cover, Parker willed his beast into submission, into the background, with a concerted effort. There would be no helping anyone like this.

Changing back from beast to man always took longer than the other way around. All those added muscles had to contract, then be stuffed into a much more lithe frame. The process took twice as much effort as the expansion did, and hurt beyond belief.

Disorientation usually followed, accompanied by the feel-

ing of having been run over by a truck. But he'd gotten better
at managing his discomfort each and every month since he'd
been cursed. Since the first bone-breaking full moon eight
months ago, when he'd thought his life was over.

Half the beast, half the hurt, maybe, this time?

The discomfort started as his ligaments reeled themselves in. His shoulders retracted, molding themselves back
into his normal human configuration. His bones tapped out
a protest. Each muscle complained. All the while, Parker
held his breath.

The change was bad at the best of times. With this newest
ability, this half shift, his beast parts were protesting submission with an internal tug-of-war. It took a final series of
whiplash gyrations for his body to more or less finish its transition. Last thing to go, his teeth.

What was left in the crazy hybrid's place was a shivering
thirty-one-year-old human male, his skin glistening with
sweat that had already begun to cool, his mind flipping over
the proverbial question: *What the hell just happened?*

Breath ragged, legs antsy, Parker gave the moon a wary
once-over through the branches and started off after the
injured blonde as though he were a bloodhound on the scent.

It didn't take him long to find her. She hadn't gotten far,
crawling on her belly, weighted down by fear and distress.

Parker was certain he had done the right thing the moment
he saw her. "It's okay," he said, halting her progress by placing
himself in her path. "I'm here."

She made a pathetic attempt to shout, and Parker understood this need. Too much had happened to her in too short
a time. Bad things. She wouldn't know who to trust, if
anybody.

Rubbing a gentle finger across her swollen lips to wipe the

pooling blood away, Parker quietly reassured her. "The bad guys are gone. The hospital is close by, and I'm taking you there right now."

He scooped her into his arms and lifted her off the ground. She was as light as a feather, as if the weight of her life had already started to scatter.

He placed her injured head against his bare chest to steady it, and staggered sideways a step. The girl was so hot she was electric, raging fire in a feminine form. Her temperature was soaring.

Sucking in a breath, Parker rode out several more shocks accompanying this first meeting of their bodies—shocks that slid down through him, chest to groin, sparking to life the hunger he had so diligently tamped down.

Mate. Bite. Hot, tight place…

He riveted his attention to his slight bundle, shaking his head, shaking all over. *Sick bastard. She's ill, and you think you want her? Will any female do after all this time alone?*

The answer to those questions drove Parker forward, in the direction of the city lights. He held the wounded female almost close enough to suffocate her, fearing to look at her again. He had to ignore the beastly needs that tipped the scales of a normal thirty-one-year-old's insatiable libido. It was imperative he maintain the upper hand on the beast he'd just shoved back inside, the part of himself at that very moment testing his resolve.

There was no full moon. The change had been an accident, that's all. Repeating a mistake wouldn't make it right. But damned if that mistake didn't carry over into an almost desperate need to have this woman—to know her, taste her, explore every inch of her with his hands and mouth. Trace the sharpness of her collarbones, bury his head in the curve of her neck. See what promises lay beneath her jeans.

He would kiss her pain away if he could. Inhale that taunting combination of citrus and petals up close. The urge to turn around and take her to his apartment was so powerful he could hardly keep to a straight line.

The plain fact was that he had to take his mind off her somehow, to keep from doing any of those things. The very idea of him thinking them came as a shock. In order to make it to that damned hospital, he'd have to pretend those green eyes of hers hadn't bewitched him in some way.

How did someone pretend that?

"Talk."

He would talk to her all the way to the street. Keep up a dialogue.

"Okay." He used a soft tone reserved for badly injured patients who needed comfort and reassurance, one he had to work at to keep level.

"Well," he said, as if they were to have a real conversation. "I'm a doctor at Metro Hospital. My parents were both doctors, so I guess you might say that healing people is in my blood."

Along with what else?

Parker cleared his throat and started again. "Although my folks didn't live to see me graduate, I owe the career to them. My doctoring honors them both. At least that's the way I look at it."

The smell of this woman's blood, mingled with those citrus petals, drifted up with each step he took. The sensual slide of her jean-encased legs against his bare arms kept his hunger hovering like an animal on the sidelines. As a man who had sworn off dating and relationships of any kind, and who had maintained a celibate life month after month, it was no big stretch to realize why he wanted this woman so badly.

Talk!

"I don't know about the werewolf part. I don't understand

how the wolf thing came about. That's why I'm out here tonight, looking for answers."

It was all right to confess his secrets here. There was a ninety-eight percent chance she wouldn't remember anything he said. She would be beyond experiencing pain now, and residing in the grayer spaces—the places where each breath mattered and time was of the essence, but where the soul could, for an indeterminate amount of time, escape the trauma. Her body was limp, her arms and legs lifeless.

"I did my residency at Harvard and became a surgeon, a life's dream. But no one at Harvard or anywhere else warned me about what else I was to become. No one told me anything about that."

He inadvertently brushed the top of her head with his chin, felt a growl stick in his chest and made a stern note not to repeat the gesture.

"Thing is, I've started to like the changes," he continued. "At the same time, I have to wonder how much longer I'll be able to keep the old me together. Tonight was a surprise. If I can shift early, as I just did, provoked by excitement, threat, or even the scent of the blood of a helpless woman like you—then how can I live any sort of a public life where I'll be around those things on a regular basis? What will keep me in check if things get worse?"

The woman in his arms could not, of course, answer that question. Who could? Yet telling her the things he'd kept inside for months, getting them off his chest, suddenly seemed like a bonus for behaving himself.

Parker chanced a downward glance at the fine, fair hair that was tangled, blood-matted and still soft as cornsilk as it brushed his arm. The bloodless face resting so close to his thundering heart, so seriously wounded, looked nearly transparent and un-earthly beautiful by moonlight. He couldn't take his eyes off her.

"Don't worry," he whispered earnestly. "You won't die on my watch. That's another promise."

But was that promise for her or for himself? Yes, she felt so very good in his arms.

He could see the glitter of lights between the trees. Civilization. Moments ago he had shunned all of that, hadn't wanted it. "Now," he said to the woman in his arms, "I'm not so sure. It's where you belong, little one."

Just perhaps, Parker concluded inwardly, this little package he carried was in essence a lifeline of sorts. Something to keep him grounded on a night when he'd contemplated wildness. Something to keep him Parker, the man.

Remember that guy?

Maybe, he reasoned further as he walked, finding this woman would turn out to be the saving of his soul, instead of the other way around. A reminder for him of what really counted. With his beast battering his insides enough to break a rib or two, he was, in fact, feeling more like a man than he had in months.

He might have lost this opportunity to find another wolf, a thing he had desperately wanted, but just possibly he'd found something else instead: some of his sanity and a sense of direction. A piece of those things, anyway.

Maybe.

After so much darkness, the lights of the boulevard were blinding. After the softness of the grass, the hot pavement felt sticky beneath Parker's boots. The noises of people rushing here and there seemed absurdly removed from what was happening to him.

The city park was large. Parker skirted it, crossed from one side of the boulevard to the other, keeping to the darker places. The hospital, his hospital, was only a block away. The woman in his arms dangled by a precarious ribbon of consciousness.

Blood had soaked through her blue sleeveless top, not from a single wound, but runoff from several. Her sleek hair had fallen over part of her face, making her appear half girl, half—

"No, I'm the anomaly here. No sense wishing that on anyone else."

Heading for the hospital's circular driveway, Parker knew he'd be hard-pressed to explain to the E.R. staff how he'd come upon her and why he was half-dressed. He would probably be arrested before reaching the door for this awkward picture they presented, but get to that door he would. Whatever else was to become of him, he'd at least get this woman to safety, as he had promised. For whatever part she had played in returning him to himself, even temporarily, he was thankful.

Lights. Cars. Deafening noises. Those things were dreadful notations at the edge of Chloe's consciousness. Her eyes wouldn't open, she couldn't take in enough air, and still her brain kept up a chaotic chatter. She felt trapped within a paralyzed body, tripping toward an unknown chasm, and all she had to hold on to was the security she felt in this man's arms. Lulled to a slightly calmer place by his whispers, Chloe felt as if she mattered, as if this man truly cared what happened to her.

She shouted inside when he adjusted her position, though no sound emerged from her damaged vocal cords. She regretted the abrupt change in his tone as his discourse became that of a person talking authoritatively on a cell phone. Giving orders. "Meet me at the door," she thought he said, as another wave of lightness spiraled her further away from herself and into the ether.

"Now!" he directed.

There came a whooshing sound. A blast of cold air hit her,

instantly chilling her bones. She shook as if death were trying to squeeze all of the life out of her but was having a difficult time.

They, whoever they were, had cold hands, and tried to separate her from the comforting heat of the man holding her. She protested uselessly.

She was laid on her back on a hard surface and covered up, hurting in unimaginable ways, in unimaginable places. What she desired most was for the warmth to return, for *him* to return. Her rescuer. Her savior. The glorious man with moonlight-tinted black hair and that serious, haunting face. She wanted to feel the rumble in his chest that his words produced. She wanted him to urge her on.

Who would protect her now from death's clutches? Who would care whether she lived or died? There was no one in Miami, and no one left anywhere else since the car crash that had taken the rest of her family.

Please don't leave me!

"Stay!" she tried hopelessly to say to the man who might have been as mad as a hatter, but had done something special for her tonight. The man who believed he was a werewolf.

Not a single word actually made it past her constricted throat. But the deed was what counted, not his crazy belief, Chloe told herself, before a new wave of blackness descended.

Chapter 4

"Shit, what happened to you?" Jim Woodsen, the E.R. doc on call, asked as the girl was wheeled away.

Parker stared down the crowded hallway, his heart refusing to slow. He wanted to go after her, certain he felt her reaching out to him.

"Where did you find that woman?" Woodsen persisted. "What happened to *you?* Man, it looks as if you've been in a war, Madison."

Parker gave his coworker a sideways glance. "Attacked. In the park."

"No kidding? Come with me." Woodsen pointed to a bed.

"No way."

"Let me dress those wounds."

Wounds? Only then did Parker take a closer look at himself. Sure enough, he had some deep scratches and a few other bumps that Woodsen shouldn't have seen, since they'd be gone by the time Parker returned to work the next morning. Another werewolf perk, miraculous regenerative powers. If Woodsen treated him, Parker would have to try to remember to reapply bandages in the same exact spots—which wouldn't be easy with his mind spinning so fast in all directions. He hoped he hadn't slipped up too badly.

"Maybe a tetanus shot." Woodsen was already calling for one.

"I don't need a shot," Parker argued. "They're surface scrapes, nothing more. I'd like to know what they find out about the girl."

"Right. Like they'd let you anywhere near her in the shape you're in."

"What shape is that?"

"Dirty," Woodsen replied. "You'll need a shower and some fresh clothes if you're going to hang around. And," he added, "since when do you have time to work out? Who knew you were so buff, my friend? Do the rest of us overworked MDs a favor and don't let the nurses see your abs. I want to ask Nikki out. Shit, Madison, have you always looked like that?"

Already Parker was feeling the strangeness that kept him distanced from everyone else. He'd forgotten about his new musculature, and here he sat, without a shirt to cover himself, after being careful for so long.

Another potential mistake.

He had to get out of here, pronto. He didn't want to make small talk with Woodsen, get a stitch or a Band-Aid. He wanted to follow the blonde, see how she fared, make sure she got the attention she needed.

He wanted to be with her. He felt responsible. At the same time, everyone in this hospital knew what to do, so his promise had been fulfilled. He had gotten her the help she needed. End of story.

Not quite. Emotions were running rampant and astray. He

should go back out there now, into the dark, and find that other thing so like himself, the thing keeping him separated from all these people. That had been his goal.

Being in the hospital, in this current mental state, was dangerous. Since he'd said they'd been attacked, Woodsen would have already given the signal to call the police. The cops would show up within ten minutes if the rest of the city was relatively quiet.

Not much time to beat the foot traffic out of here.

Damn. If he had just accomplished a partial shift and was still on edge, what was to stop a morph from happening in here, under fluorescent lights brighter than the moon? Under police scrutiny? In front of everybody?

"Okay," Woodsen said, yanking the curtain back, "I've got to go. Accident coming in." He handed a syringe to Parker. "Shall I send in a nurse?"

"Don't bother." Parker prepped the needle. With his colleague not turned completely, he jabbed the syringe into his own upper arm and remembered to wince.

"See you in the morning," Woodsen called over his shoulder.

"Yeah," Parker mumbled, already on his feet.

He got no farther than the lobby, where the receptionist pointed a long finger at him, and two of Miami's finest blocked his exit. A third man with "law enforcer" written all over him approached with his hand extended in greeting. What was this, a frigging tea party?

"Are you Dr. Madison?" this guy, a detective most likely, asked.

Parker took the offered hand, pretty sure he couldn't get away with lying about his identity in his own E.R., though he would have liked to. "Yes," he replied. "I'm Madison."

"Detective Wilson."

The detective was a tall guy and stood eye to eye with Parker. He was leanly muscular, with brown hair worn on the shaggy side. Maybe he worked Vice? He was dressed in faded jeans, his blue shirt open at the neck, and he'd pinned his badge to his belt. Doctors were so used to making quick assessments, Parker didn't bother to mask his scrutiny. Detective Wilson, however, didn't seem in the least bit bothered by his overt once-over.

And why had they sent a detective, right off the bat? This wasn't usual procedure. There'd been no homicide.

Or had there?

No. The girl was alive.

"You were attacked in the park?" the detective asked, his voice falling somewhere in the lower portion of the sound register. "Mind if I ask you a few questions about that?"

"I'm in a hurry." Parker waved a hand to allude to his state of undress.

"It'll only take a minute," Wilson said.

Somehow Parker knew that wasn't going to be the whole truth. He'd been through this many times in discussing patients brought into the E.R., and he didn't want any part of it. He needed air. He needed to get outside, into the night. He needed to do some running to ease off his incredible high. He wasn't feeling at all civilized.

"The woman with you," Detective Wilson said. "We'd like to know what happened to her."

Parker felt an odd stirring in his chest with the mention of the blonde. The detective would have called her "the victim" if she had died.

His sense of relief was a surprise. Had he developed feelings for the girl that he didn't want disturbed? Deep-down raw emotion that he wasn't at all sure about? The fact that she might make it seemed of the utmost importance all of a sudden.

In these familiar surroundings, standing at the edge of the lobby, Parker found the dichotomy of wanting to be in two places at once tearing at his soul. Find out how the girl fared, versus getting outside to seek the pale wolf. Parker wasn't able do the one—look in on the girl—appearing as he did at the moment, but he could do the other. He could go back out there, do some prowling, then shower and return for her.

Return for the girl...

As if she belonged to him. As if she'd want anything to do with him after this. He'd be a reminder of a very bad night. He would probably never see her again, except through a plate-glass window in the surgery ICU.

Not true. I will see her again.

Glancing down the hallway in the direction the staff had taken her, Parker found that his legs were starting to move nervously in that direction. Funny. He showed concern about his patients on a regular basis, but the pull to go to this girl was so strong that he remained idiotically mute.

Detective Wilson signaled to the receptionist. "Dr. Madison?" the detective said. "Are you all right? Should you be getting some help here, also?"

Parker responded automatically, "I'm fine."

The receptionist sidled up to him anyway, waiting for directions. He knew her, of course. Older woman, kind to everyone. He wasn't sure of her name.

"I'm fine," Parker repeated, directing his reply to the woman, who nodded and went on her way.

"Can we sit down somewhere, then?" Wilson asked.

Obviously, this guy wasn't going to let up. Parker led the way to a cubicle behind the reception desk, wanting to stay the hell away from Woodsen and the rest of the night crew behind the door. But he couldn't sit. Energy skittered throughout his body. Somehow he'd managed to swallow a lightning bolt. Again he looked to the door, to where he'd last seen the girl he'd held so possessively.

What was it about her?

"I don't know her name," Parker said finally, as Wilson leaned against a desktop with a small notebook in one hand and a pen poised in the other. "She's a small blonde. Five-three or -four. In her twenties. She'd been beaten up by some guys on the far side of the park. Most of the damage was to her head, her face in particular. She had numerous other wounds and contusions—shoulders, neck, probable broken wrist. She was dressed in jeans and a blue top, and missing her shoes."

Parker stopped his own discourse to stare yet again at the door to the hallway…swear to God, as if he were possessed. What was it? Why should he feel so interested? Did he need to feel human so badly?

Detective Wilson cleared his throat in the way that polite people did to call a wandering mind back into the present. Parker found this another anomaly—a polite detective.

"Did she have any identification on her?" Wilson asked.

"None that I saw, but I wasn't looking for it."

"Purse? Wallet beside her?"

Parker shook his head. "She had a pulse."

"Did you see her attackers?"

"I encountered what might have been her attackers. I can't be sure. They were close to her when I heard her call for help."

He couldn't say that their scent was all over her. What would the good detective think?

Wilson nodded. "And you just happened to be out there, close by?"

"I was running."

Wilson raised an eyebrow, probably having noticed that he had on boots, not running shoes. As far as Parker could tell, the detective hadn't written down one single word in the notebook.

"I sometimes go off by myself after a long shift," Parker explained, figuring he most certainly would be the only one in the room to catch the double meaning and sheer irony of that. "I like to be alone, so I sometimes lose track of time and distance. The fresh air gets me cleaned out. You know, from in here."

"Fresh air is supposed to be great for de-stressing," Wilson agreed. "I sometimes run myself." He let a beat of time go by. "You encountered the guys after this woman, and then what?"

"I tried to fight them off her."

"How many were there?"

"Four or five." Okay, admittedly he should not have mentioned those numbers to the detective, whose eyes had just narrowed. Parker needed to tack more details on to that explanation to make it sound more credible.

"They were getting to me, ganging up, when another guy intervened on my behalf. Then it became two of us against the rest, and the guy who came to my aid was big. The creeps out there didn't seem to prefer those odds or his size. They ran away."

"Did you know this other guy?"

"No. He disappeared right after they did. I picked up the girl, needing to get her some help."

"That was a pretty brave thing you did—going up against four or five guys in such an isolated area, in the dark."

"Yes, well, I didn't realize there were more than a couple of them when I barged in."

"Any description of the guy who helped out?"

Suppose he just said the word on the tip of his tongue? Parker thought. The *W* word. How would Wilson view this case then?

"To be honest, I didn't see his face. All I had time to notice was that he was tall and well built."

Wilson absently scratched his chin with his pen. "Do you know how she is? The woman you helped?"

"I've been chased out of my own E.R. for looking the way I do. I'll get cleaned up, then check back in."

Wilson nodded again. "Appears as though you took some decent punches."

Parker glanced at his bandaged chest and arms. "The damned tetanus shot hurt worse than anything they threw at me."

He wasn't surprised to see that his skin was riddled with black-and-purple bruises already starting to form yellow centers. In this instance, he was healing in minutes rather than hours, a phenomenon that must have been due to that partial shift in shape. Maybe his beast was still precariously close to the surface, even now.

Getting away from here had become crucial, the sooner, the better. This detective probably knew about the color palette of a bruise, since he encountered problems every day in his job. Parker hoped the man wasn't paying close attention.

"Well," Wilson said, "it turned out to be a good thing you were out there tonight, Doctor. That other guy, as well. Is there anything else you can tell me?"

"Yeah. There should be signs posted all around the darker parts of town, warning people to keep out."

"I agree." The detective nodded. "Then again, you'd assume people would know this automatically, wouldn't you? Especially young women?"

"Yes," Parker replied thoughtfully. "One would assume that." Why had she been out there? Maybe just running in the wrong direction to get away from the guys chasing her? In jeans and bare feet? The thought brought on a chill, seemed incomplete.

"So," Wilson said, picking up on the same idea. "I wonder why she'd be out there alone, at night."

"You'll have to ask her that," Parker replied. "Hopefully you'll be able to if you return tomorrow."

"She won't be able to talk before that?"

"I doubt it. After treatment she'll be drugged up good."

"There will be a necessity for the usual tests," Wilson said.

Parker cringed. Of course the police would have to know if those gang guys had abused her other than with their fists. However, since she'd had on her jeans, all zipped up, Parker was pretty sure that sexual abuse would prove to be unfounded. Nevertheless, he didn't want anyone touching her in that way, for information's sake or not. He didn't want her any more violated than she already had been, and stopped himself from throwing open the door and marching to surgery, off duty, bare-chested and dirty as he was.

That girl had been lucky, even if some folks wouldn't think of it that way. Her fate could have been much worse.

"Has there been a lot of this sort of thing going on?" Parker asked, just to have something to say to the detective eyeing him. "We've been seeing more than a fair amount of victims of violence in the E.R. lately."

"The heat brings the violence to a head," Wilson said. "Traffic in and out of the department quadruples when the thermometer reaches ninety."

Spoken like an experienced law enforcer, Parker noted. No devil in the details. And Wilson, he knew, was holding back.

"Okay. Thanks for the time, Doctor." He closed the notebook with a flip of his wrist.

"No problem," Parker said.

"We'll need to see her clothes."

"Of course. Someone here can get them for you."

"Oh," Wilson said, turning toward the lobby. "Can we bother you to show us the exact spot where you found her? There might be some clue as to who she is. We'd need to notify her relatives if she can't speak to us about it. You up for that?"

Was this detective kidding? No way was he up for that. Going back out there with a couple of cops and a detective? Unable to run? Unable to try to find remnants of the other wolf? It was a big freaking inconvenience, but there was nothing to be done about it. Detective Wilson awaited a reply. The woman—*his* woman—had been wheeled to the operating room, and he was stuck between a rock and a hard place.

"Sure." Parker gritted his teeth in between breaths. "I'll take you there if someone can loan me a shirt."

"Got a spare in my car, for emergencies," the detective said. "Shall we go now?"

"Now is fine, but if you'll give me that shirt I might be able to check on her progress before we head out."

"Deal," Wilson agreed, contemplating Parker a few seconds more before heading for the lobby door with his blank-paged, spiral-bound notebook stuffed into his back pocket.

God, she looked pale, and so small on that table that Parker wanted to go in there and pick her up again. He wanted to put her back together himself, though it seemed the team was doing a good enough job. They always did. Still, those damned tubes seemed invasive in a body so frail. He didn't want to leave, but he had to. Wilson was waiting for him.

Parker tapped on the glass. Only one attending nurse glanced his way, and nodded. Nurse Nikki Reese, the newest addition to the nighttime E.R. team—the nurse Woodsen coveted from afar. Parker was grateful to her for that nod, which let him know that the patient on the table would make it, and had stabilized. Only then did Parker breathe.

But he didn't leave. Didn't move. Why was that, exactly? She was just another woman who had made an error in judgment and paid for it. He felt protective because he had found her. Because he had shunned his own deepest internal desires in order to help her. Helping her meant a lot. He was invested in her outcome.

Her hand hung over the side of the table, white, long-fingered, elegant. Parker remembered the way it had fluttered in the night—the signal that she was alive. He almost expected it to flutter now.

He remembered the way she had felt in his arms, as if her body had made a permanent impression there. He already missed the easiness of speaking with her. Okay, not with her, *to* her, since she must have been all but unconscious at the time. So perhaps that's all he needed—an unconscious sounding board for the strange turn his life had taken. The freedom to say things out loud that had been pent up, like steam. There was no real reason to feel so connected to the girl. Theirs had been a chance encounter, nothing more. Good Samaritan. Good deed. His job.

The thing was, he did feel connected. And way too possessive.

Nurse Reese looked at him again with a lingering glance that said "Time to go." The girl would be all right. He'd done his bit and the team had done theirs. She would be here tomorrow, recuperating. If the need remained, he would see her then. As he'd told the detective, he would check back. If he felt like it.

It took five more minutes to tear himself away, and then only by sheer force of concentrated thoughts about placing one foot in front of the other. Police were in the lobby. Wilson's pen was waiting to sketch out the details that might further help this woman, whoever she was. Her relatives certainly would want to know about her condition.

They were all on the same side, wanting what was best for the female in there on the table. A young woman who would not, could not, sit up and see him there. A woman who wouldn't know he'd been at the window. At the moment, she didn't know much of anything.

So why did he feel as if she knew of his presence and willed him to remain? Why did his heart continue to pound as he looked at that small white hand on the table?

Why? Because against all warnings to the contrary, he was imagining those warm fingers moving up through the hair on his chest with an agonizing slowness. He was imagining how those hands would feel on his shoulders, his waist, his bare thighs.

Man! The woman he lusted for was in the operating room being patched up, and he was out here losing his mind. He didn't know her, not even her name. There was nothing to do here now except help the cops.

Frustrated, Parker turned from the window, finished buttoning his borrowed blue shirt and made a pact with himself to think more clearly in the morning.

He'd have to be more focused tomorrow, since the moon would be full when darkness fell the next night. He might not be able to help anyone after that. Not even himself.

Chapter 5

The humid air brought it all back: the feelings, the unusual shift in shape that had occurred, the fight with the scumbags, the surprise of finding the new wolf. Add to that seeing the creature go after those gang guys, plus the virulent scent of wolf surrounding the walled compound… Thinking of those things, Parker had to try hard to remain civil to the men in uniform who were accompanying him on this sojourn.

But information went two ways.

"Detective," he began as they walked between the rows of trees stretching from the road to the distant wall where he'd been perched not long ago. "Do you know who owns the house bordering this land? The big Southern one behind the walls?"

"Judge Landau and his family have a place there. It could be the one you're describing," Wilson replied.

This information stunned Parker. Landau? The name was familiar to everyone in Miami, even to a more recent transplant like himself. James Landau was not only a well-respected judge, but a member of every committee and non-profit organization in the state. He was a philanthropist with old money, and lots of it. His wife incarnated Miami charm at its best, so the newscasts and tabloids suggested. His son was the deputy district attorney. The Landaus had it all—looks, money, prestige, power.

Parker grimaced. If the Landaus' estate was behind those stone walls, then the family had a dirty little secret that TV, magazines and the newspaper media hadn't mentioned. Realization of that secret settled over Parker like a big black net. Either the Landaus themselves weren't altogether human, or they fraternized with nonhumans on their property.

The realization of those possibilities stirred confusion in him. Whatever way it went down from here, the Landaus were now people of interest in his book. They might be public figures who weren't afraid to show themselves often—at art-gallery openings and the opera—yet odd things were taking place at home, behind those gates. Near which an innocent young woman had been accosted.

"Do you know them?" Parker asked Wilson, keeping his rising anxiety in check. "The Landaus?"

"I met the judge recently," the detective replied. "He helped me out of a jam."

If Parker asked any more questions about that family, Wilson might become suspicious of him having been so near their home. A judge of Landau's standing had to have weirdos after him at least half the time. Maybe those bastards who had harmed the girl had been on their way to Landau's place, and her untimely presence had been too tempting to ignore.

Way too much supposition and no proof made the ideas seem silly in afterthought. Parker Madison was a physician, not Sherlock Holmes. And Detective Wilson seemed competent enough. Parker had to keep a low profile, due to his own secrets. It would be best to keep from connecting the dots, even when his intuition screamed foul play.

Settle down. Get this over with.

The night had grown darker, with the moon partially obscured by vaporous clouds. Miami had a weather system all of its own when humidity rolled in; the trees virtually dripped with moisture. People sweated a lot, and got cranky if their air conditioners went on the blink.

Parker's sweat was dampening the good detective's babyblue shirt, and it served him right for making Parker return here. At the moment, though, he wanted to do anything but mosey. Given the option, he'd sprint right back to that stone wall and see what went on inside a judge's mansion. He had to be alone to do that. The sooner he got this investigation over with, the better.

"This is it," he announced, halting. Scenting dried blood as easily as if it were fresh, Parker scanned the area. The hair at the nape of his neck didn't rise. The earlier chills stayed away. He tried not to picture the woman here, curled up and in pain. His beast offered no further shove of acknowledgment.

"The idiots ran off that way," he said, pointing. "Most of them headed east."

Four cops were already searching the scene with powerful flashlights, several beams sweeping back and forth like miniature searchlights. Detective Wilson bent his knees and crouched low to the ground, touching a patch of grass darkened by the girl's blood. He plucked a handful and raised those blades to his nose.

"No purse. No ID. No shoes. It's an enigma, Doctor," Wilson said. "What a terrible way to learn a lesson about the precariousness of venturing too far from the crowd."

"Can you tell anything by that?" He gestured to the bloody grass.

"Not really, other than it's here because of a recent injury, and still somewhat damp. You knelt here beside her?" Wilson pointed to boot prints that wouldn't have been visible to most people, even in daylight. He then rubbed his fingers together to clean them. "And you were out here for the air," he said.

"Yes."

"Do you come here often for air and exercise, Doctor?"

"Frequently, yes."

"Why here?"

"For the exact same reasons nobody else should. It's quiet, peaceful and far enough from crowds."

Wilson looked up at him. "Peaceful?"

"Until now."

"Well, I hear you on that." The detective straightened, took out a handkerchief and cleaned his fingers more thoroughly. "Thanks for showing us the spot. You can leave if you want to. We'll have a team go over the area. They'll light it up and have a look around."

Parker nodded, waited.

"You'll go home?" Wilson asked.

"Do I have to check in with you, Detective?"

"No. Just wondering. You look tired, and there're all those bruises to take care of."

"I'm afraid I know exactly what to do about the bruises," Parker said.

"I'm sure you do." Wilson smiled wearily. "If we have further questions, we can reach you at the hospital?"

"I'll be there tomorrow, first thing," Parker told him, turning on his heels. No use remaining out here with the place lit up like Disney World. What self-respecting werewolf would hang around that?

"I'll have your shirt cleaned and returned to you," he added, wondering if these cops might follow him, and knowing he couldn't chance a return to the Landau compound in case they did. That damned wall would just have to wait. The only option left to him would be to return the next night, as planned, in order to find out why such a respected public figure's grounds reeked of something that might be wolf. Parker's quest had become so very interesting, so very quickly.

Tomorrow night, he'd slice through the dark with the moon to guide him. He would be able to perceive those little nuances he might have missed before.

"'Night," Parker said, walking away from the flashlights and the disruption in search of darkness. He stopped twice to glance over his shoulder, but no one followed.

"Very well, then. They won't see this."

He upped his pace from a walk to a jog, then punched the jog up faster. In minutes he was far from the scene and relishing the breeze on his face, a relief for overheated skin.

Nothing about this night had been usual. He already knew it was impossible to escape the questions sticking to him like shadows. Questions such as could he do it again? Shift shape early? And what made him so into that girl?

More stuff to make his current complex life even more complicated. More things to file away in the annals of the strange.

Yanked off his pace by another realization, Parker slowed. He hadn't been the only werewolf who had changed without the lure of the full moon. There was another. He'd seen it. Had felt the other's presence as if it were a piece of himself that had been bitten off and spat out elsewhere. *Similar, but not the same.*

All this had happened too close to Judge Landau's stone wall to be coincidence. The place smelled like wolf, and Parker had seen one. Had the pale wolf come from the Landau property, taunted by the scent of the girl's blood, just as Parker had been?

Uninvited chills returned and he spun around abruptly. Waves of gooseflesh surged up the back of his neck. His skin pulsed with static electricity and his heart gave one audible thump after another.

"Strange night," Parker muttered, fearing it was already too late to hold himself back. He checked out his hands by raising them to his face. His knuckles were visibly throbbing, as if the claws wanted a comeback in spite of his decision to restrain the beast.

What was he reacting to now?

Intrigued, Parker searched the dark, found nothing. No werewolf, nor any sight or scent of another person. Still, more chills came.

Certain that he must have missed something, Parker scanned the area more closely. He found what he'd been looking for on the ground, not far from his feet. A shoe. One black ankle boot, smelling not of hot pavement or dirt, but like citrus and flower petals. Like *her*. The woman he'd held in his arms. The woman with those big green eyes.

This time when his claws burst through his flesh, rising long and stiff in the humid air, it seemed to Parker a lot like a sexual metaphor. Yet another promise.

Staring at his knuckles as if they were harbingers of doom, Parker took off—not for home, but in the direction of the hospital.

Chapter 6

Chloe worked to open her eyes, wondering all the while if she should. She sensed nothing but darkness beyond her closed lids. Her body no longer felt like hers. It was as though she had become someone much weightier.

She knew she was on her back, but couldn't feel her limbs. Panic surfaced at the realization, the way it did when her arms fell asleep under her pillow at night. She hated numbness of any kind. She hated it now. She'd only recently gotten over the emptiness, the numbness, that followed her parents' death. She had just begun to feel, and wanted to experience everything, the good and the bad, all the emotions, all the pain. At least pain proved that she was alive.

She felt a strangling sensation when she groped for a breath. Coughing, choking, struggling to move, she managed to open her eyes at last, and she stared about wildly, helplessly, trying to remember where she was. She heard breathing. Hers? No, these were deep breaths, while she continued to gasp for air. Someone else was here, out of sight.

Who's there?

Nothing but more breathing.

Who's there?

Warmth touched her face, and Chloe shuddered. Her heart overcame its sluggishness and started to race, surpassing panic levels for a whole new realm of reaction. Out of the darkness came an escalating beeping noise, electronic sound getting louder as she listened. Then sudden silence.

Chloe tried hard to focus her eyes. She noticed a glow to one side, a panel of lights that jump-started her memories. She tried to call out, coughed again, gagged. She felt so very cold.

The pinpoint of warmth returned, on her forehead, as if she had willed it back. Yes, she felt that! On her face!

Help me!

An unexpected reply came out of the darkness.

"You're in a hospital," a smooth masculine voice explained. "You've been in and out of surgery to repair some wounds. You're going to be okay."

The voice brought an immediate feeling of calm, as if it, too, were woven of warmth. Both it and the presence behind it filled the room like another subtle layer of atmosphere. Even without being able to make out the man's outline, Chloe felt strangely comforted, and knew who this had to be.

Him. Her brave rescuer hadn't gone away. She had willed him to stay and he had.

"I'm going to remove a tube from your throat," he told her, his tone a husky collaboration of richness and raw nerve. "It will be uncomfortable."

Chloe wished she could see him, see his face.

"When I do," he continued, "try not to talk. I'll spray something inside of your mouth to help soothe the irritation."

Yes. Please hurry. I feel trapped.

"Promise me you won't speak," he said.

I promise.

"Are you ready?"

Yes!

A long, hard length of something began to slide outward, out of her, feeling like a petrified snake that she'd half swallowed. The need to gag returned, and fast on its heels, more panic.

"It's all right," the voice told her. "Almost there now. Relax your throat. Try."

Chloe did as he asked, and felt the end of the tube rub her dry, cracked lips. She coughed again and wanted to retch. Then the man's fingers opened her mouth and she smelled antiseptic spray. A sudden coolness quickly coated the irritation. *Better.* The urge to gag died away. Moisture spilled from her eyes at the potency of the spray, and the man beside her wiped the wetness away with a gentle action incongruent for so large a presence.

"Sleep," he directed. "Sleep now."

Can't. She had promised not to talk. This was unfair. She wanted to know who this man was. She needed to thank him for helping her and for remaining by her side.

"I'll be here." His tone slid over her, almost exotic in richness, but the thought of so much darkness brought the panic back, and along with it memories of the men chasing her, the sound of bones snapping. Was that why she didn't feel her limbs? Had her arms been broken? Her legs?

"Sleep," the voice repeated.

Afraid to sleep. Don't want to close my eyes.

"I'll keep watch," he whispered to her. "I'll be here. No one can get to you. You're safe."

She felt his breath on her forehead. He was close enough to touch, and he had made good on his prior promise.

She was so very tired.

Don't want to sleep.

"Close your eyes, little one."

The endearment he used caused some of her panic to ebb. *Little one.* She liked that from him, though, growing up, she had made an art form out of rebelling against all comments about her size. It wasn't as if she were a true shrimp at five-foot-four, in heels. She was just small-boned.

And her mind was wandering. Bad sign. Chloe blinked several times, thought, *Let me see you!*

She felt the bed move as he either pressed his weight against it or sat down beside her. Heat radiated from this man with the wattage of a sunlamp, while she continued to shiver.

Warm me, please.

"You have a fever." Her rescuer's voice had dropped to a lower tone, yet he stayed, as if he had heard her plea. Chloe's shivers calmed. The darkness got blacker as his wide body blocked out some of the peripheral glow.

"Sleep," he whispered. "Heal."

Trusting this man, whoever he was, Chloe felt more of her anxiety drain away. She'd take him at his word. She would be all right, and he would stay. She didn't have to fear anything while he kept watch. He had saved her before. The numbness would be kept a bay with him there to protect her. Someone cared, even if temporarily. That meant a lot.

Enveloped in the stranger's warm aura, at peace having him beside her, Chloe allowed herself to drift off.

Parker sat motionless, wondering how he could remain still with the baser parts of himself kicking and tumbling with desire to touch her again. Big reminder—his feelings of possession and protection weren't logical. They were just another crazy new event for him and the beast he harbored.

He would not allow himself to get too close, but he wanted to cradle her in his arms, keep her shivers away if he could. Telling this sleeping beauty he would stay, with his body in such turmoil, was a promise he was finding difficult to keep. On the contrary, his mind was warning him to get away, with all the subtlety of flashing lights. He was unstable. The beast, having taken over once already, out of turn, crawled beneath his skin, searching for signs of weakness.

"Just one touch."

Parker rested a hand on the blanket, on top of the girl's right hip, and waited to see what might happen. The beast pressed at him, but did not escape.

The girl's bones felt fragile beneath his palm. Her belly was smooth, concave. She didn't have much flesh on her. Once upon a time, his mother would have had fun fattening her up.

Her head lay on the pillow, not all that far away, making it impossible to breathe without taking in the uniqueness of her scent—a fragrance not yet overshadowed by trauma. Being this close to her was a dangerous thing, he knew. Possibly also self-destructive. Whether or not there existed such things as animal magnetism and lust at first sight for human beings, this current conglomerate of man and beast made sure those feelings registered. The emotions enveloping Parker were so much more intense than a simple man-woman attraction.

He had dialed right in to the extremes of this emotional high. The closer the moon got to its full phase, the more trouble he had coping, especially here in the hospital, where so many people were in turmoil and needed saving. He hated the feel of fabric of any kind on his skin. His overly active appetite kept him on edge with curious, unrepentant cravings. Sensations, one after another, bombarded him from the inside out, his constant companions. All of them centered here, now, on the woman in this bed.

He didn't know who she was. And she didn't know him. She had no idea what he would change into the very next night, how much he had already changed, and that his life was complicated enough without adding a female into the mix. A female who tripped his arousal switches.

He didn't want to throw his quest aside. He needed more than ever to find out what had happened to him earlier that year. Parker had given up nearly everything other than his job to find out why a man might be a man one day, and the next find every bone and muscle in his body rearranged.

And this woman was fragile enough for the beast to break in two.

Her head was shaking slightly from side to side now, as if she was trapped in a nightmare. Each move made her groan softly, those sounds reaching Parker below the belt, as if an invisible hand, her hand, had cupped him there.

"Stop!" he whispered, to her as much as to himself. "Enough!" She was now a patient in this hospital and deserved better treatment than libidinous thoughts from one of the physicians on staff. Parker knew how to calm her, knew what had worked before, but speaking to her now might make things worse. For him.

When she groaned again, the sound tore at his heart just as surely as if she had reached into his chest to take hold. He swallowed hard, unlocked his jaw and closed his eyes briefly. He would talk to her. That had worked before. In order to erase his covetous thoughts, he would talk about whatever came to mind.

"The night the changes began," he said, listening to her struggle for breath in her sleep, "I was sure I was dying of some lethal disease. I was sequestered at home for days, alone, sick, believing death would inevitably arrive. The pain of my body changing was excruciating, debilitating, draining."

Parker stared at his hand on the blanket, surprised that it had returned there without his awareness. He half expected claws to pop. They didn't.

"All that money, I thought at the time," he said. "All of my parents' hard-earned cash spent for my education, and I was going to die without ever realizing the dream."

But he hadn't died. On the contrary, he had given life to something new inside him.

"I've gone through the scenarios many times since the night the changes began, and I'm tired of rehashing old possibilities. Maybe I had been exposed to a toxic chemical in med school, I thought. I might have a genetic disorder, some sort of bent DNA sequence starting to show itself. If that were the case, however, shouldn't my parents have counseled me before they died? Advance warning of such a potential problem would have been nice. Not exactly helpful, maybe, since I might have morphed anyway, but at least I might have understood what happened."

No, he hadn't died. His parents had. He'd gone through a living hell on earth and had been spared. He had torn his apartment apart and shredded every stick of furniture he owned, but had eventually wakened from the nightmare to find his own reflection in the mirror. Looking like death, feeling like death, but breathing.

"To this day, I'm not sure how I survived that first ordeal. I put a name to the symptoms only after watching television. An old Hollywood movie had used the term *werewolf*. What other title described my condition? The transformation, the mindless ripping to shreds of my belongings and the remolding of my body. I used the Internet for a diagnosis, searching not medical records, but the horror genre, and going from there. More specifics came to light, terribly, unbelievably. All there. All pertaining to me. Full moon. Lunar draw on my outsides and insides. The shape of the hybrid creature I became."

Parker blinked slowly, and continued. "In all my research, the one specific I missed was that I hadn't been bitten by a wolf or werewolf, as the stories and legends went. I had never been close to a wolf at all. No camping, hiking, zoos or nights under the stars were possible for dedicated med students attempting to get through our courses. So, how did a man become a werewolf?"

And where had the impulse come from that made him want to bite the woman beside him now? To take the smooth white skin at the base of her throat between his teeth and slowly, agonizingly, clamp down?

Parker drew back, creating more distance, pressing his lips together. His hands shook.

Reluctantly, he went on, confused, knowing he had to.

"My parents hadn't seen this side of their son, thankfully. Although they didn't live to see me graduate, they knew I'd eventually become a doctor. They had started me on this path. It had always been my dream and theirs that I follow in my father's and mother's footsteps, only in this country, rather than in some foreign place. There was plenty to do here to take care of people."

He had to hand it to his parents, though. They gave back. Doctors Without Borders and treating the sick in every way possible had been their passion. The last time his folks had seen their motherland had been when he'd been accepted at Harvard. They had arrived from the Brazilian rain forests looking half wild themselves, and had thrown him a party.

He hadn't seen them since, and never would again. They were gone, both of them lost to a landslide in some remote woods, leaving no trace of their bodies and no goodbye note. Parker missed them every damn day. He missed the closeness, the memories, the talks. He missed belonging.

And now he had become a monster.

But not so very far gone, maybe. This girl, this woman, had been beaten and left to die right in his path. Whether by chance, accident or serendipity, single-handedly and half-unconscious, she had somehow drawn him from his objective. She had sidelined his vow to keep his distance from others. By being here, and in her present state, she had reacquainted him with his humanity, the part missing since the death of his folks and what had happened to him since. A big accomplishment for such a small female.

Parker blew out a sigh as he studied her, lying helpless in the bed beside him. He had informed the night nurses on staff that he would take care of this patient tonight, personally. In the morning, the E.R. docs who'd done the repairs would check on her. The cops would arrive, like clockwork. Detective Wilson would flip open his notebook and ask the woman lying here what the hell she had been doing out there in the dark—questions that would bring her anguish back.

"There's no way to keep you from that," Parker whispered, his eyes flicking hungrily over her face. "There's no name on your chart. There are no numbers for us to call to notify someone of the events that have taken place."

There had been no cell phone hidden in her pocket. "Who doesn't carry a cell in this day and age?" he asked her.

What had taken her out there, only to put her in harm's way? And so near to that stone wall, where he'd been waiting? The simplest thing would be to ask her, as soon as she was able to speak. Would those questions hurt her?

A second sigh moved through Parker as he surveyed her

bandages. Her closed eyes showed through the turban of gauze, and also a small patch of her forehead, and one cheek. The undamaged one. Parker feathered his index finger over the swollen contour of the bandages swaddling her features, and fended off another spark of arousal.

Better not touch her at all.

"Better not be here when you wake, little mummy."

She wasn't a monster, he reminded himself, just bandaged to look like one. She probably had a very normal life, a boyfriend, fiancé or significant other. Parker detested the thought of her being "taken." And despite the inner warnings, he wasn't able to keep his hands off her.

Very carefully, he pressed a stray strand of hair behind her ear. A silky golden tendril. She would carry the scars of this night with her for a long time, physically and mentally, he knew. If she had great insurance, plastic surgery would take several passes at her, after which she might be recognizable to herself and others who had known her before…he met her.

A shudder of empathy moved through him for her future as someone marked by a certain kind of otherness. The better parts of him, the good and honorable parts, told him to run, get out now before it was too late and he became seriously attached. Before he might injure her further with the knowledge of what he had become. Other parts of him, the darker, unexplained parts, maintained their appetite for her with a heated, palpable passion.

She was a delicious morsel for a man-beast. An unexpected feast. She'd feel nice under him. Her green eyes would stare deeply into his when he made love to her. She would be a quiet lover. She hadn't shouted or thrashed in the midst of her horrible crisis. Small, yes, and at the same time tough enough to take him inside her. This woman would accept all he would give her, and give some part of herself in return. The part of her that adhered to life so vehemently told him this. The part of her that had rebelled against her pain.

Heaven only knew he wanted to take her now. Wanted to miraculously heal her, then make love to her. The desire was so strong, Parker brought his face close to hers—this woman who had ensnared him, captured a part of him, and would now have every right to mistrust men.

He swept his gaze over every bit of her face that showed. Her long lashes lay golden against the ghostly pallor of her skin. Her lips, pink, lush, swollen, were slightly parted.

He ached to taste those lips.

Leaning even nearer, Parker paused with his mouth suspended above hers, a mere breath away, millimeters, imagining what a kiss would be like. One turn of his head or hers, one good shiver, and he would have that taste. Weren't there kids' stories about princes waking princesses with a kiss? What if fairy tales were based on truth?

One kiss. Parker closed his eyes to savor the sweetness of being so close. But rationality reminded him, on the verge of a traitorous act, that there was a syndrome for patients who fell for their doctors. This woman might feel beholden if she found him here when she woke. She might transfer her thankfulness for survival to him, in the form of adoration. Extreme emotions would come into play, none of them viable or lasting. He had seen this before with his colleagues.

So, what about the reverse? Could his interest in her be due to having paid such a hefty price for helping her out? Couldn't he be groping for a reason to justify the loss of his objectives?

Had something deeper happened that he didn't yet understand, in the simple act of his eyes meeting hers? It had been in that instant, out there, that he'd imagined he felt something snap between them, a connection.

He thought back to that, and what she'd said. The word she

had used, the only word she had been able to mutter, was *trick*. He remembered that clearly now, and the effort it had cost her. *Trick*. What did it mean?

The answer that came to him was as dark as the night outside the window, and twice as unsettling. What if this woman had been some sort of bait, meant to lure somebody else to the scene? Beat up a woman to catch a male they could rob, maybe? Plausible, and also quite gruesome.

Unless maybe they wanted to snare something other than a man? Something *more* than a man?

Nonsense. This girl had likely just been in the wrong place at the wrong time. Maybe she hadn't said "trick" at all.

Parker lifted her hand from the covers. He stroked her open palm with his fingertips, experiencing both a thrill and another warning he chose to ignore. It was all right to hold himself in check. Good practice. There would be time tomorrow to prepare himself for what he might again encounter out there—how many hours away now? Maybe he would find that pale wolf, a gift from the moon for helping this girl.

Hovering over the woman like the guardian angel he most certainly was not, Parker blew a faint breath across her mouth, wanting to say to hell with it all, wanting to go backward in time and just live. Maybe he should have buried himself out there in the middle of nowhere with his mother and father, and this newest temptation was payback for desiring a more comfortable life.

Comfortable? Had he thought that? What a joke. His head hurt. His hands hurt. His teeth hurt. His heart ached. The beast within lay curled up, waiting to spring. The moon ruled his outer shape, and there was nothing comfortable or comforting about that!

"It's lucky I found you," he told her. Lightly, with his body continuing to shake as if negating what he was about to do, Parker brushed her lips with his own. It was the merest touch, yet his insides roared and turned over. His awareness began to distance itself from the room around him, all senses focused on this meeting of their lips.

The sharpness of the antibiotics they were feeding her lingered around her mouth to mix with her sweetness—a heady cocktail for a physician turned wolf. His beast unfurled, wanting in on the action, wanting to take part. Both halves of him were in full accord now, with the beast struggling for the lead.

What would that part of him do to a female? Parker didn't want to think about that, lost in the illicit sweetness of the moment.

Holy hell!

His heart rate suddenly spiked and his eyes flew open. He heaved himself backward, away from her.

Whatever the hell she was.

Eyes wide, fearing to breathe, he searched her bandaged face, not quite sure what he expected to see, but knowing, through that kiss that wasn't a kiss, that the woman in this bed wasn't completely human…either.

Chapter 7

Her thrashing started after midnight, causing alarms to go off. Great explosions rocked her. She moved jerkily, back inside her nightmare.

Parker left his place at the window, where he had been studying the stars in a night that called to him fiercely. He leaned over her, careful not to touch her this time, wary of being too close, no longer trusting himself.

"It's all right," he soothed, not so sure about that, after all, or even what she might be.

She didn't waken. Nor did she seem to hear him. Her gyrations increased. Her broken left wrist, in its splint, came loose from its binding. The machines were going nuts and, instructions or not, would bring the night nurses running.

Parker beat them to the door, barked for a sedative and strode back to the bed. "Who are you?" he whispered.

The sedative arrived and was inserted into her IV by a

nurse, who checked the monitors and then stepped back. "What is it, Dr. Madison?"

"Hell if I know," Parker said, waiting for the drug to kick in, wondering if it would, since it took a while for the woman in the bed to calm down. For her weight, which he guessed to be about a hundred and five pounds, the sedative should have immediately knocked her on her butt, right before sending her off to Never-Never land. Instead, the meltdown took its own sweet time—two minutes, maybe three, though the medicine had gone directly into her vein.

Not quite human.

Eventually, she gave up the struggle, caving to the call of twilight. Parker waited through a few more erratic heartbeats of his own before remembering the nurse.

"She's all right now," he said. Though it was pretty damn clear that he wasn't.

"She's sweating," the nurse noted.

Recognizing the voice, Parker turned to find Nikki Reese from the E.R. "She's been alternating hot and cold," he said. "It's probably her fever breaking. Aren't you working late?"

"I'm taking Lucille's shift. She had an engagement. Literally. Big shiny ring and everything." Nikki came back to the bed. "Have you got her name?"

"She's scarcely opened her eyes."

"You brought her in?"

"Yes," Parker said.

"She has broken bones. The wrist, and a bunch of ribs."

"I saw the chart."

"Did you notice anything funny about it?"

Parker tilted his head. "Funny?"

"She has some pretty significant wounds, including that hit to the head," Nikki Reese said. "On top of it all, though, she has a series of punctures, as if, having gone through every-thing else, she was attacked by a pack of dogs."

Parker felt a wave of sickness knot his stomach. "Punc-tures? Where?"

"Upper arms and shoulder."

He peeled back the blanket and pushed up the loose sleeve of her gown, appalled. No extra light was needed for him to see the damage. He hadn't even thought to look the rest of her over, he had been so focused on her breathing, on her face, on her lips, and on the latest discovery. Plus the beast would have liked seeing what lay beneath the covers a little too much to dare anything of the sort.

Parker had assumed her injuries were all related to the beating she had taken, but any doctor worth his salt should have found the strange marks on her shoulder and the upper arm. His odd feelings of connection might have ended up hurting her chances of getting out of this.

"That one's the worst," Nikki said, probably noticing his scrutiny. "Whatever did this tore out a chunk of muscle and flesh. It was already infected, and must have hurt like—"

"Hell," Parker finished, carefully lifting the adhesive bind-ing the bandages to her skin. Upon seeing what lay beneath them, he bit back an oath. This wound was indeed serious. Although the injured area had been stitched closed expertly, it was puckered, red and weeping. Ringing it were indenta-tions that presented in the shape of a set of teeth.

Parker felt himself blanch.

"A really big dog must have done that," Nikki said. "Some nasty beast. Rottweiler. German shepherd. Doberman. It would have taken a huge effort to shake such an animal off. Poor thing, beaten and bitten out there. What's the world coming to?"

Parker fought for a calm that eluded him. The mysterious

wound nagged at his mind. A dog bite would have wrapped around her arm. This wound was circular, like…

Feeling as if the room didn't have enough air to sustain him, Parker ran a palm over his own upper arm, able to detect the scar on his left biceps, which had the same general outline as hers. But he'd always had his scar. She'd just received her wound. There were no parallels to be drawn. His mind was attempting to establish connections where there were none.

Bitten. The word stood out like a bright neon sign.

Under Nikki Reese's watchful gaze, Parker traced the outline on the girl's arm, a wound that showed no atypical or miraculous signs of healing. So, he had to be wrong. Maybe she was human, and just very, very ill. Maybe what he had felt in her closeness was in fact the effects of a dog bite. His own scar was a leftover from an early allergic reaction to a tetanus shot, or so he'd been told. A kind of reaction that a werewolf with miraculous healing powers no longer needed to fear.

Looking at the woman in the bed, though, he suddenly wondered who needed a sedative more, her or himself.

"No bite."

"Excuse me, Doctor?"

"Nothing," Parker replied. "Nothing. Thanks for pointing this out, Reese."

Nikki nodded and walked to the door. Pausing, she said, "What's kind of strange is that this is the second wound like that I've seen lately."

Parker turned to face her.

"Last month we treated a guy with a chunk missing from, of all places, his throat. We stitched him up in the E.R. He wouldn't stay, ran off when we got busy, but he had to be hurting. His wound was as serious as this one."

"How much like this one?" Parker managed to ask.

"Same kind of hole ringed with indentations that looked like teeth marks. The guy had lost a fair amount of blood, but wasn't the chatty type. We pegged him as the recipient of some new kind of gang violence. Maybe we have a rogue pack on the loose?"

Pack. The word stuck a chord. But Reese had meant a dog pack, nothing more.

"Don't you think?" Nikki pressed, when he failed to respond.

"It would seem so," Parker agreed, with a continued sense of foreboding.

"Well, I'll be here for another hour. Let me know if there's anything else you need," Nikki told him.

"Any chance you might have some whiskey?"

She eyed him, then retorted jokingly, "Alcohol of any kind on the premises is against the rules of this hospital. Though the pharmacist is downstairs, and I believe you have a prescription pad."

Parker smiled. His first smile in months, and an automatic response. He would have liked tall, well-built, quick-to-make-a-wisecrack Nikki Reese at one time. He should have been interested now. But of course, Woodsen had claimed dibs as soon as she'd arrived. Then there remained Parker's own loner ways, which he'd just all but broken because of the woman in this bed.

Beyond those things lay the puzzle of his new life. And the two similar bite wounds.

Nikki Reese waited by the door. It was obvious to Parker that she had something further to say.

"I'll stay with your patient if you'd like to get some coffee," she told him, leaving Parker with the sense that she had changed course in midstream. Her attractive oval face, however, showed nothing of that.

"I promised to be here," he said.

"Would you like me to bring some coffee to you?"

"Thanks, but no thanks."

"Sorry about the whiskey."

"Me, too."

Reese smiled again. "Yell if you change your mind."

"Don't you think yelling might be against those rules?"

"I suppose it is, so I'll be right outside. You can whisper instead."

Parker turned back to the bed as the door closed, intent on the woman in it now that he again had her all to himself. She seemed to be resting more easily, although every once in a while she arched her back, caught in the throes of that bad dream he sincerely hoped was nothing like his.

"Welcome to my world," he whispered, reapplying the bandage on her arm, feeling even more unsettled inside. What had caused this wound? That gang might well have had dogs with them that he hadn't seen. Pit bulls were said to be the beast of choice for gangs in Miami. Animals trained to fight could inflict the most damage.

Bandage secure, Parker again fingered the scar on his upper arm through the detective's blue shirt and frowned. He would have smelled dogs in the area, if there had been any. Beyond the jerks he'd fought, there had only been one other presence in that park. *One other.*

A rush of cold, like an ill wind, raced up Parker's neck, as if the pale, half-morphed creature who had helped to scare the fighters off had just breathed on his back.

Shit, he mouthed, then repeated the oath again. Had that wolf found this woman first and taken a bite out of her? A goddamn, good-size bite? For real? If so, what did that make her?

Biting, the legends said, caused a person to become a werewolf. Through a bite, infected saliva and blood were transferred, containing the Lycan virus, an ancient pathogen causing the recipient to then become a werewolf with the arrival of the next full moon, as well as each and every full moon thereafter.

Parker had already discarded that theory as fiction, since there had been no bite for him. Nevertheless, an icy cold spread across his chest as he stared at his patient in an attempt to see right through her skin to what might or might not be forming there. To what she now might harbor in her veins.

Lycan virus? Absurd.

All of a sudden he wasn't too sure.

Suppose, he reasoned, that werewolves—if there were more of them than the one he'd seen, and that's what they really were—didn't all maintain a spark of human intelligence? Suppose werewolves weren't good guys? Maybe like humans, there were good and bad Weres. With the sort of power and strength he'd gained since his first transition, a strength still in its infancy, one bad werewolf would be terrible news for Miami. More than one wolf gone over to the dark side, and the entire city could be in jeopardy.

Biter? Hell, *he* had wanted to bite her. Maybe that was the way werewolves showed their affection—with a good nip or two to the neck.

Parker searched his Jane Doe's swaddled face. She was medicated now, but when her senses returned would she imagine he had done this to her? Had she seen him out there in his half-morphed form? Was there a chance she might have heard his awful confession?

If she had been given an infusion of wolf saliva, would she walk out the door in a day or two, miraculously healed?

Was the brave little soul in this bed about to become like Parker?

No. No, she couldn't be a wolf, he told himself. He had imagined it all. Still, there were so many reasons for him to run. Not only for fear of being accused of this heinous crime, but for the elusive unknown that now seemed only an inch away.

Mired in bleak thoughts, Parker knew how important it was, now more than ever, that he find what roamed the Landaus' property and sniffed around its walls. Somewhere out there a pale wolf wandered, one that had been at the scene of the brutal crimes against this woman. In order to find that wolf, Parker would have to leave her.

How could he remain? How could he guarantee her safety or anyone else's if that dark side he had been giving in to, piece by piece, might eventually cause him to harm others? Where would this mutation take him as time passed? Hadn't he been contemplating that very idea?

Returning to the window, Parker looked out at the city with a deep, almost gut-wrenching eagerness to be out there in it. He wanted to be free from the constraints of walls and sickness and having to deal with being a beast in a doctor's clothing, tethered to the word *human* by the most slender of definitions.

And, Parker concluded, unable to forget the sight of the holes in this poor patient's flesh, a girl who might soon become so much more than she appeared if his intuition proved to be correct... For the moment, though he wanted to run, he could not. He was, in fact, hobbled by something as delicate as a silken strand of an anonymous woman's golden hair.

A woman who perhaps held another key to the secrets he harbored.

A knock came at about the same time the sun began to rise. From his position near the window, Parker turned.

"I was told I might find you here." Detective Wilson stood in the open doorway holding two plastic cups in his hands.

"You brought coffee?"

"The coffee is courtesy of the nurse in the hallway. Perez, I think her name is," Wilson said.

"Bless her." He went to meet the detective, feeling like hell warmed over, desperately needing that coffee.

"You've been here all night?" Wilson asked.

"Yes. How about you?"

"Out in that infernal park for most of it. I did manage to get home for a quick shower. Man cannot live by caffeine alone."

For a detective, and as surprised as Parker was to admit it, Wilson seemed okay. First the loan of the shirt, and now the coffee. He didn't seem as pushy as most of his kind often were. Yet things were not always what they seemed.

"How is she?" Wilson handed one cup over.

"She had a rough night, had to be sedated."

"She didn't open her eyes, offer any clue as to her identity?"

"No, and no." *Mostly the truth.* "I'd like to keep her sedated for a while longer, then bring her out of it slowly."

See what she is.

Wilson blew on his coffee, then took a sip.

"Did you find anything out there?" Parker asked, sipping his from his. The coffee was lukewarm. Wilson had wasted a breath.

"Lots of footprints, her blood, not much else," Wilson replied.

It didn't take extraordinary brains to know that the good detective withheld information. "And?" Parker prompted.

"We found a trail of blood on the ground. Drips leading from a certain point in that area. Which means that some of her injuries had happened in another location, before you found her."

"I see." There was more. Parker waited.

"We picked up her trail pretty close to that stone wall you asked me about."

Fairly sure he kept his face expressionless, though another chill made it down to groin depth, he said over the rim of his cup, "The wall around the Landau place?"

"That very one."

The questions Parker didn't ask brought on another round of anxiety. *Am I going to be a suspect? Is this how it will go down?*

"We found other prints there, besides yours, and in another place farther east, mixed with hers," Wilson explained. "And we found her shoe. Only one shoe."

A black boot.

"So, you think she'd been chased by that gang?" Parker asked.

"Seems likely," Wilson affirmed. "Can you tell me anything more about her condition?"

"She has some serious injuries. A broken wrist and cracked ribs. The wound in her head has been stitched. Her face was sliced open three or four times by something sharp. My first guess would be a knife."

My second guess would be claws, Parker silently added, liking the idea of another wolf out there less and less.

"She has a chunk missing from her upper arm," he went on. "Even I can't explain that one. One of the E.R. nurses thought it resembled a dog bite."

He had to tell Wilson most of it, didn't he? The detective could see her chart anytime he wanted to. This kind of information wasn't protected from the cops.

"Has she been tested for rabies?" Wilson asked.

"I'm sure some blood work would have been done when they found that particular wound. You said she had been pretty close to that wall, Detective? Do the Landaus have guard dogs roaming the property line?"

"No." Stated adamantly, as if Wilson knew this for certain.

"It's usual for a property that size to be guarded, isn't it?" Parker pressed.

Wilson shrugged. "I suppose so. In most cases dogs would be a decent deterrent to trespassers."

Parker picked up on that. "Do you think this woman might have been about to become a trespasser?"

"We won't know until we talk to her."

"But you found evidence she had been near the wall."

"Yes. Alongside evidence that you had been there."

Parker blinked. Wilson moved closer to the bed, adding, "We found the same boot prints near that wall that were near the girl. The ones belonging to you."

"I didn't do this," Parker said.

From across the bed, Wilson met his eyes. "So, why don't you tell me what you were doing up on that wall?"

"I didn't mention anything about being *on* it."

"The deeper prints where you jumped down were fairly easy to see, Doctor."

"I'm afraid I can't tell you that," Parker said. "Why, I mean. I wanted to see the place. Just curious, I guess."

Wilson checked out the unconscious girl again. "What I find curious is that you didn't see the girl, since you both were there at about the same time."

"She wasn't near me, Detective. I heard her call out, and went to see what was wrong."

"You hadn't been drinking, or…"

"Or what? Have a split personality, one of which is a psychopath with a penchant for mauling young women, so that the other side of me can put them back together right afterward?"

Having said that, Parker experienced a familiar stab of uncertainty. In fact, he did have what was in essence a split—not in personality, but in physicality.

"It would, of course, be pretty silly of you to bring her in here to get her patched up, and then hang around," Wilson agreed, his attention on one of the machines. "However, stranger things have happened in an attempt to throw us off a scent."

Scent. Parker's tension increased with Wilson's choice of that word. "You found evidence of the gang?"

"Yes. Five of them, just like you said, tearing up the ground all over the place. Heavy bastards, by the prints. They also were near the wall, and then beside the tree where you found this girl."

What shouldn't have been relief, but was anyway, flooded through Parker. Maybe Wilson didn't consider him a suspect. Maybe he wouldn't be under careful scrutiny—because that would put a damper on his nighttime plans.

"Are you going to bring her out of this state anytime soon?" the detective asked.

"She's had several convulsions."

"Will she have them again?"

"I don't know. I'm not sure what caused them in the first place." *Yet.*

"You'll find out?"

"I will. If you'd like to force the issue, I'll wake her now."

"You'd do that?" Wilson said.

"If it was for her benefit."

The detective smiled, but it was in no way a happy expression. "Can you show me the wound on her arm?" he asked.

"That, I can do." Parker set his coffee cup down on the table by the bed. Carefully, almost loath to touch her again in case some part of him might slip from his control in front of the detective, he removed the gauze from her upper arm, exposing the wound.

Detective Wilson made an indecipherable sound that Parker took for disgust. "Is it infected?" Wilson asked.

"Yes, but it's been cleaned out, and she's on antibiotics."

"Are those the teeth marks around it?"

"That's what they look like."

"Are you sure they belong to a dog?"

"No." Parker had let that bit of truth escape, and attempted to cover it by diligently reapplying the gauze.

Wilson was not to be deterred. "Do you think they're human teeth marks?"

"I would certainly hate to entertain the idea," he replied. "I've seen *The Silence of the Lambs*."

"I'd like to take impressions," Wilson said. "I'll get someone in here to do that, if it's okay."

"Fine. Did you find any evidence of—"

"No. Turns out she wasn't harmed in any way other than the obvious, as far as her clothes and the other tests went."

Parker's heart actually pounded with relief. "Well, it's time for me to get cleaned up and get to work. Is there anything else you need me for?"

"You'll bring her out of this today?"

"When she's stable."

"Then I'll be back."

"Would you like me to call you?"

"No need. I'll be around, Doctor," Wilson said—rather ominously, Parker thought, considering his own need for privacy.

Chapter 8

Parker was beyond exhausted. Flat-out dead tired, and in the grip of the kind of fatigue that frequently accompanies stress, prolonged turmoil and sleeplessness. A state all too familiar to E.R. surgeons, as well to a night-loving werewolf.

"Not much time for a reprieve," he muttered, tossing his keys on a table by his apartment's front door.

The long shower he took felt like heaven and seemed to wash away his sins. Parker let the hot water scald his skin to a ruddy red for what felt like an hour, despite the rising temperature outside.

Afterward, with a towel wrapped around his waist and beads of moisture clinging to his torso, he flicked on the ceiling fan to air dry. He shook his wet hair back from his face, lathered and shaved, wiped the vapor off the mirror, and only then dared to study himself. Thankfully, the person in that mirror looked just like him.

"Always a comfort, eh?"

He paused to run a hand over his scarred upper arm, and used the mirror for a better look. It sure looked like a ring of teeth marks, and freakishly similar in shape to his patient's wound. Odd as that similarity was, however, the question that dominated Parker's thoughts was who or what had caused hers.

The particles of morning light streaming through the bathroom window seemed to make details about the pale wolf he'd seen in the park more elusive. Daylight always brought with it a fresh take on darker things, for a while—after which the questions would begin their unending loop all over again, starting with *Had she really been bitten?*

Parker had ordered enough sedative to keep a woman twice her size dreaming. No way did he want her to waken when he wasn't there. And this break, quick as it would be, had been necessary. He'd looked like hell.

Donning clean clothes had never felt better. Parker skipped the pile of new jeans in favor of a faded, worn pair. His skin had grown increasingly sensitive in the months since his first transition. He could handle the worn jeans, but preferred the soft scrubs he would wear at work. The jeans were a last holdout in his leisure time; he had never been much of a tan slacks, button-down shirt kind of guy.

He remembered to replace his bandages with fresh ones, covering scrapes and bruises, most of which had already disappeared. He hoped actual injuries wouldn't be a necessary part of this investigation for Wilson and the other officers on the case. The lack of even a single scratch on his body, if he were to be a suspect, would be impossible to explain.

He covered the bandages with a fresh-from-the-dry-cleaner's white, long-sleeved shirt, and tugged the collar into place.

Being in his own apartment, if only for an hour, felt good,

normal. Parker forced himself to eat a stale bagel, for fuel, and gulped down one more cup of strong, hot coffee. Eyeing his soft leather couch with regret, and giving the newspaper-strewn living room a last glance, he closed the door on his small haven. He'd be lucky if he got back there today. Really lucky.

"Time to face the firing squad."

Time also to figure out how to ditch the cops if they tailed him after work, so he could get on with the current progression of things. Tonight, he would go back to the Landau estate. He'd go there as so much more than himself. And if he met another wolf or two, all the better.

He kept the top down on his red Jeep, liking the hot air. At nine o'clock the sun was already hot enough to fry an egg on his hood, and maybe a pancake or two.

Nostalgia trip. His parents had made pancakes often. Pancakes had been his father's favorite food. Parker had always liked them, too, loaded with blueberries, and couldn't remember the last time he'd eaten a hearty meal. Food didn't top his priority list these days, although the lack of it hadn't affected the size or shape of the muscles he'd inherited along with the curse.

And now that he'd taken that short journey down Memory Lane, Parker found himself wondering what his folks might have eaten on the morning they'd died. He hoped it had been pancakes, in outback Brazil. He also wondered what they would feed *her* today, his Jane Doe, when she woke. Lime Jell-O? Orange juice through a flexible straw? Would she be able to stomach anything? Did she like her coffee black? Did she like pancakes?

Would she have miraculously healed by the time he got back?

An impossible thought, yet wasn't there a chance of such a thing happening if she now had wolf in her blood? And if she did make a swift recovery, how would that be explained?

Driving took concentration in Miami, where traffic got worse in the summer. For that reason, and for convenience, Parker lived close to the hospital, even though downtime was a joke.

Ten minutes after leaving his apartment, he pulled into the hospital garage, welcoming now the coolness of its shade. There were fifty stairs up to the lobby, then he walked undisturbed through the corridors to the physicians' locker room. He climbed out of his jeans, hung them on a peg. Ready to pull on his scrubs, he heard a sound alerting him that he wasn't alone. A purposefully cleared throat. For all intents and purposes naked, save for his dark blue underwear and bandages, Parker turned toward the noise.

"Sorry," an unusually throaty female voice apologized. "They said I'd find you here, but they didn't warn me you'd be naked if I did."

A female police officer faced him. Parker grinned in surprise and his inventory switch turned on. Attractive female of the cop persuasion. Maybe some Italian tossed in. Classic features. Creamy bronzed skin. Dark hair pulled back severely from her face. No hat. Large eyes. Full mouth wrapped around very white teeth. Not quite tall enough to reach his chin, the woman was curvy beneath her crisp uniform. His attention didn't stray any further. After all, he was in a hurry. And she had a gun.

"Name's Delmonico," she said. "Detective Wilson sent me to check in with you. I'll wait outside while you get dressed."

"Yes," Parker said. "This isn't Chippendale's, though it might look that way at the moment."

Officer Delmonico did not blush or smile. She did, however, pass very close to him on her way out, hesitating briefly when she caught sight of the bandage covering his upper arm.

"Knife?" she asked.

"Tetanus shot," he replied.

The officer raised an eyebrow at that but continued toward the door. Parker stared after her, disturbed in a way he was unable to name. Having a cop visit this early wasn't a good omen. And he hadn't realized that police officers were allowed to wear perfume. Then again, he supposed he'd never thought about it before. He hadn't encountered many female cops.

This officer definitely smelled like gardenias, and also a trace of another indiscernible fragrance buried beneath the florals. Damp hair? Probably she was as fresh from a shower as he was. Of more importance was the fact that Officer Delmonico's presence shouted loudly and clearly that not only were the police going to watch over the woman upstairs, they were going to keep him on their radar, as well.

Great. Who the hell else would Detective Wilson send calling? Whoever they might be, Parker sincerely hoped they weren't so well trained in stealth that he wouldn't notice them following him after dark. Tagalong cops would pose a real problem in terms of his agenda, and be a big thorn in his side. If there were wolves at the Landau estate, they certainly wouldn't want Miami law enforcement to know.

He pulled on his scrubs slowly, his thoughts again on the pale wolf, and the possibility of that wolf having faked him out. Of that wolf having beaten the malicious gang members to the girl.

Parker closed his locker and headed toward the door to the hallway, but stopped with his hand on the knob. "Okay," he told himself. "Enough with the conspiracy theories. Wilson did not purposefully send the female into this locker room to check out my bandages. Surely detectives have better things to do than pimp out their female counterparts."

All well and good as a pep talk; nevertheless, the officer's presence made Parker uneasy. With an overexuberant tug, he flung open the door and almost ran into Officer Delmonico, waiting right outside. She hadn't been peeping through a keyhole or anything, he noted with satisfaction. She stood with one shoulder against the far wall and her arms crossed.

"I can only talk if you follow," he said to her.

"Are you going to check on the girl?" she asked.

"Yes."

"Then I'll follow."

The elevator took them to the surgery recovery floor. The female officer who marched after him down the hallway garnered plenty of attention. A pretty cop was an anomaly, as was her adherence to silence. Officer Delmonico didn't speak or try to slow him down. For that, Parker felt grateful.

Halting at the end of the corridor, his nerves starting to jump, he faced his police shadow. "I need to go in there alone first," he said. "When I come out, I'll answer any questions you have for me. Is that all right?"

Officer Delmonico nodded and again leaned a shoulder against the wall. She was probably used to waiting.

Feeling the female cop's eyes on him, Parker headed for room where his true interest lay.

Chloe had been shaking so badly, she'd brought the nurses in seven times after the man she called her savior had gone. She had pretended to be asleep.

With his company, the level of pain had been relatively manageable. But now it seemed as if it had been lying in wait until she was alone. First returning as a trickle of aware-ness, as a dull but persistent ache, that ache then began its wicked attack. Slowly, steadily it progressed, and from the inside out.

Her head felt as if it had been hammered, then split open like an overripe melon. It seemed as though her organs had caught fire, having first been dowsed with flammable liquid to ensure they burned for a very long time. Next, her skin had caught the heat of those internal flames and seemed to bubble, though no blister became visible.

Immediately after that awful burning sensation came chills, a galloping external fire department with the objective of putting out those invisible flames. The chills were severe in intensity, and the shaking they caused doubled the pain and allowed the internal fire to spread.

Fire on the inside, cold on the outside. A damned reverse chicken barbecue. Throughout this worrisome event, a fresh onslaught of pain, shockingly electric and way too persistent, took over. Her head really was going to explode. Her eyes burned and watered. Stifling a shout, Chloe glanced to the drip line attached to her arm, then to the monitor by the bed, then to the curtains at the window between her and the hallway. The nurses would probably be on her in another minute, checking her vitals for the eighteenth time.

Have to get out of here!

Not only had the room become stifling, she couldn't afford this kind of treatment on a genetic researcher's meager salary. The man she so stupidly longed for in a completely unvirginal way, though a doctor in this place, was quite probably insane. Either that, or the meds had allowed her some pretty strange dreams.

He said he'd come back.

The thought flitted across her mental screen. The man, her savior, would return. The guy who thought he was a werewolf. The guy who went out after dark looking for other werewolves. A werewolf doctor.

Well, whatever the hell he thought he was, he wasn't here

now. And he wouldn't have let her go anywhere if he were. Things were clearer this morning. He would have helped her because he felt responsible for her. Nothing personal about saving her and then tending to her afterward, just the Hippocratic oath he'd taken to do those very things. She was probably just one in a long line of patients.

Did he confess his own nightmares to everyone he rescued?

There was no need to hang around or make him feel any more responsible. She'd send him a thank-you card and a box of chocolates. She'd even pay her bill someday, if she got ten raises in a row.

Chloe's mind flipped through the reasons for feeling so bad. Being a geneticist, she knew that some of the pain might be a reaction to the meds. She'd also be groggy from surgery, whatever they'd done to repair her. In the past few hours they had injected a lot of pain-killing liquid into her drip line.

But she was wide-awake now, and wondering how bad the damage had been. Her chart wasn't hanging on the end of the bed or on the bedside table. No help to be had there. She had been struck by a hard object out there in the night, by the feel of the thudding above her eyebrows. Her dark angel had confirmed this. She didn't remember all of the details, and that was frustrating. Concussion? Minor brain malfunction?

Had it been only last night?

Nearly her entire head was covered in gauze, she discovered by feeling around with the fingers of her right hand. Her left arm, from the elbow down, was hindered by a splint. Navy blue, with a white racing stripe.

Maybe the blow truly had addled her brain, and the bandages worked to keep her head together. Her torso was bound by a girdle of tape that smelled like a men's locker room prior to a football game. Diagnosis: her ribs had to have been bruised, maybe fractured. Probably that's why she couldn't breathe.

All of that, and a totally illogical directive rose up so strongly that she gasped.

Run! an inner voice told her.

Don't make him feel responsible for you.

Feelings of being trapped, tubed and isolated added to her claustrophobia. The bed was small. The room had snowy-white walls and lots of steel.

Run.

With the quickness and precision of a veteran scientist, and with a stern reminder that she could do this, that it was possible to rise above the debilitating pain threatening to take her down, Chloe switched off the valve near the clamp of her drip linc, then hit the off button on the machine beside her.

She had about two minutes before the nurses would notice the sudden lack of wavy green lines, she figured. She'd heard them moving around outside and guessed they'd be busy changing schedules. Not so good for other patients with beep-loss, perhaps, but good for her.

How fast could she get up and out of here?

Fighting off wave after wave of light-headedness as she sat up, Chloe slid her legs over the side of the bed. She would go to the hospital lab and find a computer. She had work to do. Her medical chart would be there, and she knew how to access it, had accessed files in those same computers hundreds of times, since she'd been hired by the university to help track statistics on unusual viruses passing across Florida's state line.

Her research had been sidetracked by those bastards in the park, important research needing follow-through.

"You can do it. You will do it."

The tile floor felt chilly under her bare feet. There were no tubes sticking out of her to catch body fluids, she found with relief. Chloe tore off the tape holding the needle in her arm and

groaned, ignoring the drops of blood pooling at the IV's inser-
tion site. Tossing the needle onto the bed, she got to her feet.
Next to come off were the heart-rate monitor attachments.

"Two minutes and counting."

All well and good in theory, of course, but her legs didn't
want to move. She made them. Both knees refused to bend, so
she shuffled, feeling as if she'd been dipped in lead.

Leaning in any direction from her waist was impossible;
she'd been taped too snugly. Dragging the blanket with her
to the tiny bathroom, Chloe latched onto the sink to support
herself, and took a look in the mirror.

Whoa! She flew backward, startled. Was that thing in the
mirror herself? The thing that looked like death warmed over?
Worse even than that?

She tried to swallow around the lump in her throat. Her
heart thudded rapidly against her taped torso. But she had
always been tough, she reminded herself. An only child
growing up in the desert had to be. Cacti and rattlesnakes
made for major alertness training. There was nothing to be
done about the way she looked at the moment.

In need of clothes, she scanned the space, found a robe on
a hook. She put it on with difficulty, panting from the effort
of covering the ungainly blue hospital gown that would leave
her rear end visible to the world were she to exit sans robe.
And, lucky for her, her jeans were also there, wadded up on
a shelf. She'd slip them on in some other bathroom down the
hall. Time was wasting.

Barefoot, holding the sides of the robe to her body and
knowing she didn't have time to remove the turban of
bandages in order to be more inconspicuous, Chloe Tyler,
mummified, unable to draw one significant breath, lifted her
head as regally as a queen's and walked right out into the
hallway as if she owned the place.

* * *

Parker came up short after entering the room. He stared at the two nurses who were staring at the empty bed with expressions of mingled surprise and horror, and managed to find his voice.

"Where is she?"

Nurse Perez, as her name tag read, looked to him with startled brown eyes and didn't say a word.

"Gone," the other nurse said. Nikki Reese, either still there or returned after a couple of hours of sleep.

Frustrated, Parker surveyed the scene. "How can she be gone?"

"No visitors have been in or out," Nikki replied. "No time for that. So I can only assume she walked out."

Parker's shoulders knotted. Had she…had she healed enough to do that?

"She was too ill to walk out," he snapped.

"It appears not," Nikki countered, pointing to the clamp on the drip line and to the heart-rate monitor attachments discarded on the bed. "It also appears that she knows something about medical equipment."

"When?" Parker demanded.

"Not more than a couple of minutes ago."

"How did she get by the desk?"

"She couldn't get by the desk, in theory."

"Were you on duty, Reese?"

"I just got here. We were chasing down charts. She might have exited at that time. We watch and listen for the monitors, but we don't expect anyone on a recovery floor to be able to untangle themselves and run away. Or even want to."

"Unheard-of," Nurse Perez seconded.

"Well, let's look for her, shall we? She couldn't have gotten far." The word *bite* appeared before Parker's eyes in large blinking letters that left him breathless. "Put an APB over the speakers for a mummy walking the hallways."

"On it," Nikki said.

"Those broken ribs should have been hurting like a son of a—" He broke off, noticing Officer Delmonico beside him. Facing her, he threw up his hands. "I'm sorry, Officer. We seem to have lost your victim."

Delmonico didn't rant, rave or throw accusations. Instead, she went into a corner and spoke softly into the radio attached to a curly cord at her shoulder, most likely to Detective Wilson. When she had finished, she said calmly to Parker, "Maybe you have time for that talk now, while the others search for her? If it's possible, over a cup of coffee?"

Every singe emotion known to man, plus a few beyond those, were pummeling at Parker. He couldn't rant or rave, either. Not here. What good would it do, anyway? The staff would find the girl. As Nurse Reese had pointed out, she couldn't have gotten far. A first transition from human to wolf didn't work as easily as that, if his own experience was anything to go by. She would soon, if not already, be in serious trouble. If they did find her, she wouldn't be long here at Metro. Treating a wolf would be far too dangerous and disconcerting for everybody. Most likely, they'd put her in a zoo.

Certainly, she would be easy to spot in the crowd, a standout, wearing all that gauze. But why had she gone? Should he feel better, more optimistic that there didn't appear to be that same sense of connection on her part? That she might just up and walk away? If he'd been mistaken about her condition, how could she have disappeared?

No. Optimism wasn't an option. He felt sicker than ever. And if they didn't find her, he'd be free to follow his own path toward enlightenment, toward his own kind.

Parker took another long look at the empty bed, and wanted to shout.

"Coffee? Sure," he said to Delmonico, hating the thought of sitting nose to nose with a cop when he needed to find the girl, but not wanting to call further attention to either her or himself. "I have some time before reporting in."

Delmonico smiled, as though losing a patient, aka crime victim, was routine. Noting the brightness of her slightly crooked, contagious smile, Parker gestured for the officer to precede him to the hallway.

Only when she'd turned her back did he allow the terrible internal turmoil he was experiencing to have its way with his expression.

Chapter 9

Chloe made it to a public restroom one floor down and locked herself into a stall. There wasn't any way she could get into her jeans with a splint on her good arm, a girdle of tape on her torso and her head throwing fresh rounds of dizziness at her every time she tried for a decent breath. She'd need to continue to the lab dressed as she was, and hope hospital personnel would ignore her.

First, though, she would have to get rid of the bandages, an awkward task without a pair of scissors to start the ball rolling. Plus, her hands were trembling so badly, she might puncture some other body part if she wielded a sharp object.

"I *can* do this," she repeated with conviction. "I will."

Slipping her fingers underneath the bandage closest to her ear, she tugged, got nowhere, felt faint, and had to sit down on the toilet, awkwardly. The bandage stuck to her cheek. From the slight gap she'd made came the smell of clotted blood and antiseptic dressing, odors that sent her equilibrium spinning.

God, Chloe. You are tougher than this.

Somehow, she made it back to her feet, hardly able to draw any breath at all now, due to the pain in her chest. She must have been bruised pretty good to hurt this much. So, okay. She'd have to be more careful, rearrange her immediate goals. The bandages would have to stay put until she got to the lab. There were scissors there.

Easing forward, Chloe opened the stall door, looked out, saw no one. Clutching her jeans as if they were a talisman to get her through this crap unnoticed, she set out.

"Are you all right, Doctor?" Officer Delmonico asked from her place across the table from Parker.

"Yes, why?" he replied.

"Did you hear my question?"

"Sorry." He shook his head. "I was thinking about the escapee."

"Is there anything special about her?" the officer asked.

"Special? In what way?"

"I believe I asked you that question."

Parker wrapped his hands around his coffee cup to give his hands something to do. "No. Not special, in terms of being different from any other patient who falls into my path after taking a beating." *Sarcasm, and lies.*

"Can you tell me what her injuries were?"

"You don't already know?"

"Broken wrist, cracked ribs, hole in her head," Officer Delmonico recited. "What else?"

"Isn't that enough?"

"She didn't speak?"

"She had a tube down her throat for a while. She drifted

in and out of consciousness." Parker searched Delmonico's face. "Do you work with Wilson?"

She nodded. "On occasion."

"What's that perfume you're wearing?" He was pressing the limits of personal information here, but dammit, he felt feisty, antsy, anxious. He had work to do. He had to find the girl, then get out. He had to prepare himself for the night ahead, was already feeling the effects of the moon's imminent rise. Nothing in the last two days had been ordinary, that's for sure. Tonight was certain to be more of the same. The hospital felt confining. The officer across from him added to his uneasiness.

"It's lotion," she replied easily enough, but it was clear by the set of her jaw that she didn't want to play games. Neither did he, really, but talking about the woman who had gotten away wasn't in his realm of capability at the moment. He had guarded, mixed feelings about her disappearance. He still felt possessive, as if he'd just lost a piece of himself.

"Detective Wilson is in Homicide?" Parker asked, getting back to the reason he was facing an officer of the law.

"Yes," she said. "And he is particularly interested in the area where you found the girl. There have been problems in and around the parks lately, though not as far out as that. Gang-related problems. Muggings, beatings, the violence escalating into a couple of recent deaths that were quite gruesome. One of those victims was an undercover detective, and the reason Wilson got involved."

"So you're worried this gang's territory might have expanded?" Parker asked.

"We thought we had cleaned up the mess. We found a warehouse on the east side where an illegal fight club had festered. Really bad guys. Lethal drugs. Weapons cache. Some of the members of that club killed themselves before we could round them up—a sort of mass suicide generated, we believe, by the properties of the drugs they'd ingested. Others were killed trying their damnedest to kill us. In the chaos, we missed the main guy. A truly ugly fellow got away. Our concern is that he's back in business, back in the game."

"Does this guy have a name?"

"Chavez."

"Distinctive appearance? For the record?"

"Black hair, dark skin, unusual eyes—at times. He has other disguises and can look completely different, which makes catching him harder. He hasn't been seen since that raid. Before that, we had him locked up for a while for that detective's murder, but he was released on bond. He is now wanted by everybody, but can lie low since he has a seemingly unending supply of idiots willing to do his bidding."

Parker nodded. "You think that the five guys who turned up out there could be working for him? They fit typical gang descriptions, but didn't really offer up any discernible leadership qualities, even though one of them acted like a king. I wouldn't have pegged that one for a ringleader, though. He seemed more along the lines of a wannabe to me. Dangerous, yes, don't get me wrong. He quite probably used my patient for a punching bag, and then ripped open her face, in a 'five strapping jerks to one tiny female' ratio, which certainly places him in the upper echelon of creeps."

Delmonico set her cup down. "So, you and another guy chased them away?"

Parker eyed her warily. *Better be careful now.*

"It seems that we did," he said.

"Did you have a gun with you?" she pressed.

"I don't own a weapon, Officer."

"Then the guy who helped you must have had one?"

"He didn't brandish one if he did."

"Was he a big man? Large enough that the two of you

chased five gangbangers off, earning only minor scratches and a tetanus shot?"

"Are you questioning my ability to fight?" Parker teased, guardedly.

"Oh, I'm sure you're intimidating enough, Doctor, in a physical scrabble. I'm just wondering why the other guy didn't stick around. You say you didn't know him?"

"Maybe you should read Wilson's notebook, but the answer is no. He came out of the bushes. I'd never seen him before. I'm sure I would have noticed if I had."

"Why?"

"He was unusual."

"How so?"

"He had pale hair, platinum or silver. I couldn't tell which in the dark. He wore it long, to his shoulders, and seemed to me like a guy who knew how to defend himself."

And also bite an innocent woman, despite the way things had looked at the time?

Delmonico's eyes were on her coffee cup. Quiet for minute or two, she then said, "Did he actually join you in this fight?"

Careful. "Actually, I think the sight of him, appearing out of nowhere and with all that white hair, scared the pants off those buggers. All he had to do was shout at them, give them one good look at his muscle, and they ran like hell."

"He had a lot of muscle?"

"Enough to do the trick."

There was that word again, *trick*. Was it going to stick to his brain like a Band-Aid? Was there a possibility the girl had known ahead of time about this wolf's imminent appearance?

Delmonico tapped her empty cup on the table, the way other people absentmindedly clicked pens. "Thank you, Doctor. That's all the questions I have, for now," she said.

Relieved, Parker got to his feet, not sure he had fed her anything new, but ready to hit the road.

"Oh," she said, getting up. "Sorry. One more thing, if you don't mind?"

"Shoot."

"It's sort of a strange question, but I'd appreciate it if you took me seriously."

"I'll answer if I can."

Her gaze met his and held. Parker saw a certain fierceness in her eyes, no doubt often easily overlooked in such a pretty face.

"When you fought these guys, did any of them try to bite you?" she asked.

Parker waited out two shallow breaths before answering, "No." Then adding, "Is that some new kind of secret weapon? Teeth?"

Delmonico kept right on eyeing him. He didn't look away.

"We believe our girl had been bitten, though," he explained. "That chunk out of her upper arm had marks around it that Wilson wanted to take an imprint of."

Aside from the intensity of her eye contact, Delmonico's face remained passive. Still, Parker detected a hint of rigidity in her shoulders that suggested he had given her bad news. Obviously, Detective Wilson hadn't yet passed that particular piece of information along to his affiliates.

"Well," Delmonico concluded, tossing her cup in the wastebasket—a perfect shot. "I hope you find your missing patient, Doctor. Sooner rather than later. I hope she's okay."

Delmonico walked off, just like that, leaving Parker stumped as to whether the newest chilly breeze cooling the tender skin at the base of his throat was caused by a recently upgraded cafeteria air-conditioning unit, or by the possibility that the team of Wilson and Delmonico knew something he didn't know...about those bites.

* * *

Chloe concentrated on the computer screen with rapt attention, sure there must have been some mistake. If she had cracked ribs, she wouldn't be sitting upright at all. She had cut those bandages off her torso first thing after reaching the lab, then had gone for the ones on her head.

With the tape and white gauze turban removed, she looked even worse. Really bad. She'd nearly cried when she saw herself, pinched with pain and as white as a sheet. Three creases down one side of her face had been stitched together with blue nylon, near an eye swollen nearly shut. Beneath yet another bandage, she'd found a dent in her forehead, its edges zipped together with the same blue stitches.

Her hair was matted with traces of dried blood; this was, after all, a hospital, not a beauty salon. As she'd stared at herself in the tiny lab mirror, she'd felt sicker than ever, and in desperate need of a shower and toothpaste.

The only other researcher making use of the hospital mainframe, a skinny young guy in a plaid shirt, hadn't looked up when she came in. Riddled with chills, she had swiped his sweatshirt from the back of his chair, but couldn't get it around her shoulders due to the unwieldy wrist splint. She sat huddled in a chair. Holding her elbow elevated, she used the tips of her fingers to type, a little like a lobster with big claws might. In this slow-motion pecking at the keyboard, though, she traipsed on familiar ground, which provided a mental boost.

Finding her chart was easy. Most things were computerized these days, and notes on patients were inputted regularly. She had been the only unknown female, aka "Jane Doe," ushered into surgery with cracked ribs, a broken wrist, surgery to sew up her head and the placement of a temporary ventilator due to possible serious side effects of the head wound.

"Tell me something I didn't know," Chloe murmured, continuing to type, refusing to address the seriousness of those notes. The doctors must have been off their game, tired and overly quick to diagnose. Her ribs were black, sure. Beneath that tape she had found just about every inch of her chest black-and-blue. Her ribs did hurt when she breathed, yet here she was, walking around. Sort of.

She really did feel like hell, though. Nausea had set in, more than likely from the effort and exertion needed to get here. Her right cheek pulsed terribly, as if something underneath the muscle wanted to get out.

"Important things to do here," she whispered, ditching the chart, hacking into the human resources files, typing in the M.D. listed on her chart. *Parker Madison.*

A sexy name, whether her guy or not. Surely the hospital wouldn't allow a *werewolf* to tend to the sick.

The screen blinked, then lit up. She'd found a page highlighting everything about Parker Madison except for his biceps measurements. Or a photo. A quick scan of that page turned up no evidence of psychological slipups or an overactive imagination. On the contrary, Parker Madison had quite a résumé.

Chloe read on. Top of his class at Harvard, residency there, good reputation here in the last year as an E.R. surgeon. There was a note about his parents having been surgeons of some repute. *Been.* Meaning that Parker Madison's parents were deceased. Hadn't her avenging angel mentioned that his parents were dead? She and Parker had that in common, then.

Chloe typed in more key words, found nothing about any charts of his own. No list of allergies, broken fingers, immunizations. No blood tests on record. Again, no mention about psychiatric sessions or counseling. If this was her guy, maybe he didn't use his own hospital for treatment.

If this was the man who had helped her—and it was possible she'd been experiencing a few of those head trauma repercussions the chart suggested she might have at the time—it was also possible, she supposed, that she had imagined the *werewolf* part. A shock-induced brain addling, maybe, where instead of seeing stars, there were dark-haired avengers? Post-traumatic hallucinations for the over-twenty-and-still-single crowd?

Maybe this wasn't the right man at all.

Retracing her way to her "Jane Doe" chart, Chloe checked the name of the attending doctor again. Parker Madison. No one else had touched her chart after he'd taken over the watch.

Intrigued, she combed through more of the HR files, and leaned forward intently when a photo eventually popped up. She didn't realize how long she'd held her breath until her lungs offered up a searing protest. With the expansion of her rib cage came a blinding pain that tipped her sideways in her seat and conjured up several choice curse words.

It was him. Parker Madison. He was her rescuer, all right. And he was a sight to behold.

Even in the crummy ID badge photo, this guy stood out like a face from God's heavenly realm. Chloe's heart gave an unexpected lurch as she peered closer at the screen.

Parker Madison's overtly alpha, just-the-right-amount-of-everything angelic beauty was, in fact, startling. The man was inhumanly beautiful. Seeing him brought back a dis-comforting lightness inside her head, along with the sensa-tion that he was there now, behind her, watching. Chloe glanced over her shoulder, swore at the pain that movement caused.

A lumbering set of recurring memories she'd been trying to repress accompanied the curse word: the night, running, being chased, the sound of her pursuers, the progression into terror, the unique sound of breaking bones. The awful tearing of her upper arm.

After that came a clear picture of this man finding her. And of the way his voice had shuddered through her. The power of his eyes looking into hers. His whispered reassurances. His strange confessions. His larger-than-life presence.

This man. The one that long-dormant places deep inside her had recognized all along, though she'd refused to admit it. Her body called out for him now as if he had touched each and every one of her private, hidden places personally, instead of merely directing her to sleep.

Had there been a kiss?

Her hands were shaking so much now it took her a few seconds to magnify the image on the screen. She studied Parker Madison's face, needing to internalize every detail. As if she could ever forget any part of him. There were some things a person just never forgot—such as experiencing death's breath on your face, and then having your life saved.

Parker Madison couldn't have been described as a hunk. He was as far from the muscled construction worker stereotype as was imaginable. He wore his black hair long, chin length, as she remembered. In the night each strand of that hair had flashed with a luminous sheen—moon-kissed waves, the opposite of the quintessential Miami sun-kissed blond. Or in her case, the Arizona-born-and-bred blonde.

There were so many other differences between them. The man on the screen was big, while she was small. Dark, while she was light. Hurtfully handsome, whereas former boyfriends had described her as "cute." This guy was special, a doctor, the real deal, while she was a southwest transplant who didn't care much for balmy climates or pretentious occupations, and who would have never considered lusting after a man like him in her past, since he'd be in a league all by himself. Like a real angel.

All six-foot-whatever of him.

So, the reason behind this ID invasion? All this reference checking? Did she want to find out where to send a thank-you note? Did she have damsel-in-distress syndrome—a condition that caused throbbing sensations in intimate places not related to the throbbing pain associated with her recent misfortunes? Insanely *lustful* sensations, leading to an undercurrent of desire?

She wasn't a fool, only a scientist. The chasm separating herself and this doctor loomed as wide as the frigging Grand Canyon. The only other thing besides deceased parents that she and Parker Madison had in common was their desire to help people. His job was to heal them here in this hospital and hers was to help find and mark the viruses that brought patients here, so that there could one day be a cure.

She loved what she did for a living. He probably did, too. And although she had never allowed herself to be easily intimidated, the sheer wealth of Parker Madison's incredibly sexy looks, with or without the physician part, rendered him off-limits.

"Hey. Are you okay?" the guy at the next desk asked, checking her out for the first time as he got to his feet.

"Yes, why?" Chloe retorted wryly, daring him to comment on her appearance by fixing him with a steady gaze, and not even trying to cover up the fact that her entire body had started to quake, vibrating her chair to the point of rattling its wheels on the linoleum floor.

"Uh, well, you were moaning," the tech told her.

"Was I?" *Was I?*

"Plus you look a little bit like the bride of Frankenstein, so I'm wondering if you need help."

"Nope. Fine. Thanks, anyway." Chloe closed her eyes, deciding maybe she should try to stop the worsening tremors. The pain meds must be finally wearing off. Each breath hurt.

Her head was close to imploding. The truth was she probably did need help, though she wouldn't ask for it.

She should call the cops and get them out to that horrid place where she'd been accosted. They needed to fumigate that area, round up those bastards who had tortured her and send them off to where the sun never shone.

She needed a few more minutes on this computer to recheck her last bit of research—the reason she'd been near that wall on the far side of the park in the first place. She should input some details about the police officer she had followed out there, as soon as she asked the cops to chase the scourge from public places.

Yes, her brain was working now. She remembered why she had gone out. She had been tracking a female officer with an unnatural, unknown, mutated gene. A gene like nothing she had ever seen before.

She'd discovered it by accident, by stumbling across the cop's supposedly discarded blood sample for a rabies test, from her last hospital visit on record. Something in that sample had flagged Chloe's notice.

Thinking to do some unscheduled work—aka unpaid overtime—she'd tested for an anomaly in the officer's blood. A female officer named Delmonico.

The sample had tested positive for a gene that caused some interesting complications in her research. She had wanted more information about Delmonico.

Although spying wasn't actually in the fine print of her job description, she had followed the officer—God, was it only last night?—as Delmonico left the police station. Chloe had followed her on foot across that park, all the way to a set of wrought-iron gates leading to the big estate beyond. In hindsight, a stupid move. She shouldn't have been out there alone. Her boss at the university was not going to condone this highly irregular routine, since it had ended badly. But Chloe was good at her job, and took it seriously. An anomaly like the one she had found in Officer Delmonico's blood sample needed to be cataloged and explored. The officer herself needed to be studied. Possibly even quarantined.

Delmonico had met a man at the gate. Chloe had recognized Dylan Landau immediately. He was Miami's current deputy district attorney, and there was no mistaking him, with all that thick, shoulder-length blond hair she'd seen on TV on numerous occasions.

Delmonico and Landau had disappeared behind those towering walls. And five heathens had found her trying to scramble up one wall for a better look. After the first blow, she had been out of commission. As for the rest…

"No. Don't go there. Not yet."

There was so much to do. She needed to find out if those animals were watchdogs hired to protect that estate, and to sue them if they were. And if those scary, tattooed baboons weren't somehow related to the people on that estate, then what had they been doing there? Why had they come after her?

It would be impossible for her to go back out there now. She doubted if she could survive it. But the research was important, necessary. What if that cop harbored a contagious pathogen in her bloodstream and didn't know it? How many people did a police officer have contact with in a single day?

Chloe had been sidelined, big-time, by that gang. She had lost valuable time. But she was all right. Outside of a little pain, once she healed she would ask Delmonico to participate in further tests.

Chloe hit more keys, ignoring the insistent aches. Spying might not have turned out to be her forte, but knowing her way around a computer was.

D-y-l-a-n L-a-n-d-a-u, she typed. What would a D.A. think about the things tweaking his girlfriend's DNA?

Bingo! Dylan's father was Judge James Landau. She had not known that.

L-a-n-d-a-u. She cross-referenced the name to title companies. Some illegal hacking was involved, but she was fairly sure property ownership was public record. Bingo! Judge Landau owed that estate.

And for all her own efforts at becoming a one-person center for disease control, Chloe thought, she had almost died coming up with this information. Would have died, if it hadn't been for Parker Paul Madison, M.D., in all his tan, chiseled, werewolfian glory.

She stopped typing. Did it make sense that each and every time he came to mind, both the pain and pangs of longing mingled like drops of colored dye in a petri dish?

And wasn't it strange how the lines of information on the monitor had begun to swim in a wavy, greenish haze…? How her head's pounding had approached critical levels?

The aftereffects of someone who had been sliced open and left to die.

Chloe staggered to her feet. Each attempt to open her eyes brought sharp, piercing distress.

The tech closing up shop for the day grimaced and moved out of the way when she reached for the back of the chair with both hands, to steady herself.

"What? Do I look that bad?" she croaked, sensing his presence.

"Worse," he replied.

"Unable-to-escape-this-hospital-in-my-present-state kind of worse?"

"If you were a horse, I'd put you down."

"Damn."

"You're actually trying to get out? For real?" he asked, slinging on his backpack. "Without being noticed?"

"Yes, and the reason why is privileged information."

"Then check the drawers," he suggested. "I found Ray-Bans in that desk last week. Shades ought to do it, if you pull a blanket over your head and if no one looks too closely at the rest of you."

"You think?"

The tech shrugged. "Need I mention that your regulation hospital bathrobe has *conspicuous* embroidered all over it?"

"Thanks," she said, waving him away. Managing to hold on to the chair until he had left the room, she then reached for her head with shaky hands. Sickness roiled in her stomach. Her bare legs felt cold and weak.

If she did get away, where would she go? Back upstairs? Bad things were catching up with her. She was seeing glimpses of a man with very light hair in every shadowed corner, there and gone in a flash of incomplete memory each time she blinked. A big man. An evil man. The ghost of surgeries past, maybe? The result of all those medicines she had been fed? Why did she imagine she felt that bastard's breath on her face? Not Death's, his.

Unable to take a necessary breath, and hence supply oxygen to her brain—and with Parker Madison's name on her lips—Chloe felt the floor rush up to meet her.

Chapter 10

Parker heard the call for a cart to be sent to the research lab, and nerves churned in his gut.

The staff hadn't been able to find the girl. She had disappeared without a trace, and even his extraordinary senses hadn't picked up her trail in such an antiseptic environment. The hospital was too damned clean.

Now, though, with that call, a fresh sense of urgency curled up inside him. Moonrise was only minutes away, a fact he felt in the steadily rising thump of his pulse.

Working the rest of the afternoon had been difficult, with the woman out there somewhere. Normal daytime events in the E.R., such as kids falling from trees, had taken on a sinister cast. He scanned each body for potential teeth marks, bites. People were hurting all over the place, and he looked for *her* in the face of every patient he attended to. Would she show up again? Would he find her behind the next curtain?

His mouth tasted of burned coffee. The stale bagel he'd eaten was a distant memory. Was, in fact, hours ago. He'd worked right through his shift, staring at the door, the same door that Nikki Reese came walking through now, wearing a frown.

"Thought you might like to know about this first," she said, waving him over to a corner.

Parker knew what she was going to say before she said it. His body had already geared up to move.

"Some guy found our truant patient collapsed in the research lab, where she's been all day, apparently."

Parker thought he'd gotten past the phase of feeling responsible, but his heart resonated like thunder.

The doors to the E.R. opened again. Two attendants were wheeling in a cart. *Not her.* He glanced to Reese.

"She wouldn't come," the nurse said. "She got as far as the hallway down there, then vehemently refused treatment or assistance. She's asking for you."

Parker dashed from the room before Nikki had finished speaking, his heart virtually taking over his chest. This reaction was too much; he knew that. He didn't owe the young woman anything. He'd done his bit. The moon was calling to him through all six stories of the hospital, as if her light were seeping through the windows and walls. At the same time, his thoughts were scrambling. He wanted very much to see the wounded girl again. He would ask her about the marks on her arm before Wilson did. Parker had to find out about the other wolf he'd seen, and whether that creature had played a role in her injuries.

Dammit, Parker had to make sure she was all right.

He hit the stairwell running. The research floor was underground, beneath the hospital's main lobby. He reached the corridor before remembering to breathe, and halted when he saw two attendants on their knees flanking a length of bare leg that was shaking as if it had been Tasered.

Parker stifled the howl that would have threatened his current camouflage, and worked hard to control himself. His anonymous blonde sat propped against a wall, on the floor, with her head in her hands. She ignored the attendants' chatter, every few seconds gasping for air and swinging her head from side to side.

With whatever tenuous connection they had between them, she seemed to immediately feel his presence. Her body stilled as he approached.

She feels it, too.

Parker didn't speak to her. Not one word. Was he seeing something different now that he had added two and two together in a jumble of half-baked ideas?

He watched her green eyes open. As her gaze met his, Parker had no more doubt about their connection; he heard the damn thing snap into place. She also recognized it, Parker saw, in the widening of her haunting eyes—eyes that also revealed the extent of her pain. Dark bruises colored the skin beneath them. She had removed her bandages, leaving her facial wounds exposed. She had bitten her lower lip; tiny drops of blood pooled there.

And he noticed something beneath her pain, underlining it, hinting at a darker presence. He hadn't been wrong. This new presence had a scent that filled the space between them and left the air thinner.

It seemed to Parker as though she reached out to him, though her arms didn't move. The fine, undamaged skin beneath her left ear visibly pulsed, unbelievably fast, then slowing slightly to match the rhythm of his own racing beat. Using him as a model.

Parker held his breath. She held hers. He struggled to inhale, and she did the same. Although this woman might have looked to the casual observer like a patient desperately in need of help—damaged and petite, pretty and sick—the otherness in her slid behind her eyes like a splash of black liquid, there and gone in the dilating aperture of her irises.

Wolf.

The proof had been there, on her arm, all along. Whatever reaction that bite had caused was now transferring to other parts of her, while her body put up a fight.

This young woman was about say goodbye to her former life, the one she had clung so hard to. Soon she would confront the total, horrific rewiring of her system, if what had happened to Parker was routine. She would transition from human to woman-wolf hybrid soon now. Very soon. As if the pain gripping her at the moment wasn't bad enough.

Parker wanted to rip apart the walls, toss the attendants aside and freak out, because the legends were true, after all. And the timing couldn't possibly have been worse. Her eyes were pleading with him for help, and his own transition was on its way.

For whatever reason, he and this woman were tethered together by an invisible rope. She tugged on that rope while feeding off his every move. One beast looking for another.

Be careful what you wish for….

Not only had he found another werewolf, he had found two—if this girl managed to make it through the initial stage of her evolution. This lovely, damaged Jane Doe was no longer merely a patient, or merely human. And being close to her, after searching so long for another being like himself, felt like the final straw to Parker. The straw that might break him.

"I have her," he told the attendants, his vocal cords seizing as he waved them off. "I know her. I'll handle this. It's a mental case. Please leave us."

As soon as the men grudgingly rounded the corner, Parker

fell to his knees, driven there by lon-pent-up emotion. He brought his heated face close to her ruined one and sniffed. *Yes. Unmistakable. Damp hair. Musk. Animal.*

He growled and cleared his throat, so that he might make her understand he had only minutes, at most, to speak at all. Certainly not enough time for an explanation. The moon was calling.

"They can't help you here," he said, his knuckles aching for change, his shoulders rigid beneath his scrubs. "I can't help you here."

Tears of frustration were spilling from her glazed eyes. Her arms and legs twitched repeatedly. It was obvious she had lost control of her movements without being able to fathom why. Parker remembered this stage all too well—the fear, the pain, the uncertainty of a body testing its limits. It had nearly done him in, a man so much stronger than this small bundle of bones.

He winced when his spine cracked, the sound only slightly muffled by the length of empty corridor. He flinched, hearing the answering crack in hers.

In a few more minutes his molecules would rearrange. He would take the shape of the thing he harbored. He could not allow another slip, not inside the hospital. He had to get away from this building, fast.

The best way to help this woman would be to get away from her, too. But he couldn't leave her, not alone and hurting. How would she possibly have a chance of surviving this impending transformation if he didn't help? If she didn't know what her body was about to put her through?

Who else might get her through this night? A night from hell that had almost killed him when his turn had come?

That last thought hung in the air, suspended, almost solid, as Parker touched his cheek to hers. As he ran a fingertip, soon to sprout a long, pointed talon, under her chin. She knew something was dreadfully wrong; her lovely eyes told him so. They also told him that she trusted him fully. Him. Of all the people in the world, in Florida, in Miami, in this hospital—him.

She was struggling to draw air through passages narrowed by pain and panic. She was fighting with every last bit of energy she possessed to hang on to herself.

Careful of her injuries, Parker took her face in his hands and gazed deeply into her eyes, confronting the cause of her trauma. *You cannot have her yet, beast.*

A tear touched his fingers, warm, wet. He stared at that droplet, then brought his eyes back to hers. Angling his head, he covered her mouth with his, flattening her against the wall that supported her, needing not only to tend to her, but to conquer the thing that lay between them. This particular personal demon.

Two wolves in this hallway.

Her lips were soft, dry. She did not draw back into herself as his mouth shaped to hers. Nor did she cry out or try to move aside. Parker felt the exact second she let go.

Her trembling lips parted. She made a sound—not a groan of discomfort or rebellion, but a deep, low growl of relief.

The inside of her mouth began to heat. She clutched at Parker's shoulders with rigid fingers, attempting to pull him closer. On his knees, straddling hers, he exhaled a slow breath into her mouth, guessing at what she needed. This strange CPR would force air into her lungs and help her to breathe, even if it further entangled the two of them.

Yes, you can breathe, even if you think you can't. You will survive this, he silently told her. *I will see to it somehow.*

Parker blew air into her again, felt her chest expand. He squeezed his eyes shut to block out the thoughts begging for some kind of order.

Officer Delmonico had asked about a bite. Detective Wilson had been intrigued by the wound on this girl's arm. By all that was holy, both of them had to know about this. They had been looking for confirmation all along. Had they seen this sort of thing before? Did they *know?*

Hearing a second crack of bone on bone, Parker knew he was out of time. But his dilemma remained. How could he help this woman? Did he actually wish, now that he'd found her, for her transformation to be completed? Was he so selfish?

Maybe she had a chance to beat what swam through her veins. If it was caught early, would something as simple as a dose of penicillin help?

Maybe a wolf that had not yet shown itself fully could be stopped, its progress halted…despite every fiber of Parker's being wanting a mate.

There was, he knew, no time for more questions. The clock was ticking.

To hell with yourself! Fix this if you can! Save her the pain. You're a doctor, Parker. What must you do? What could possibly hinder a burgeoning beast?

Think!

Without the luxury of more time to investigate options, he knew one thing. The girl he wanted so badly had to be hidden from moonlight, removed from all reaches of the moon—and from him, since she was taking his cues.

She'd have to be tucked in a faraway place, kept from seeing him, hearing him, feeling him and his silver mistress. Hopefully, in return for the distance, the awful progression in her body might be stunted, halted, possibly even bested, at least until another day.

What he didn't know about this could fill a damned textbook. A hundred textbooks. Could a beast be stunted? Held back for a time? Hadn't he pondered those same questions in relation to himself for eight long months, only to have the answer be *no?*

"Not this hospital," Parker barked. "No help here," he repeated. He'd told the truth about that. The absolute truth. This woman needed a place used to dealing with anomalies, a safe haven, until he could think more clearly.

All right, then.

What he was about to do would amount to abuse, he knew. There was a chance she would never forgive him for this. There was a chance she wouldn't survive, no matter what he did or didn't do.

With claws pressing at his knuckles and his mouth still clinging to hers, he scooped the girl up, for the second time in the mere twenty-four hours he'd known her, and into his arms.

She clutched at his shoulders, trying to get closer still. Her mouth became hungry—as hungry as his. The frantic ebb of her emotion tore her apart, inciting her pain, pushing her own needs to the surface in full force, either because she had been moved or because she had been forced into such close proximity to one of her own kind. Either way, it was a hell of a thing.

Unable, unwilling to stop himself, Parker kissed her back. He caressed her mouth with his, licked at her warmth, nipped at her lips, sucked her moist tongue between his teeth...and the heat, so extreme, burned him up.

She was fire, her mouth an inferno. Her body strained toward his. Her arm wound tightly around his neck as if she wanted to climb inside him, melt into him, become one with him, have all of him. Every last bit. And those feelings were mutual. The moment was as frightening as it was powerful. Over-the-top bliss that came with a hefty price tag.

His beast's nearness flashed beneath his skin with the shock of an electrical flame, drawn by the rawness of their passion and the rightness of this wedding of their lips.

Whatever particles of beast she had incubating inside her—so tiny at this point, Parker thought, so minuscule—called to his, encouraging, demanding that this closeness be allowed.

It should have been foolish to resist such an invitation, yet the very thing they both wanted at that moment might kill her unless he did.

Her body's need was throbbing through him—pulse after pulse, in his neck, his chest, his groin. Their breath mingled like flames entwining.

Yes, he could have kissed her like this forever. He could have held her endlessly, taken this further, been consumed by the greed. But he would *not* hurt her.

Shocked by the strength his own conviction, Parker lifted his head. A blast of cool air slashed through the flames curling between himself and the woman in his arms. For seconds, minutes, hours, her green eyes bored into his. And then, as if separating from her had cut the strings of a puppet, her head fell back, her eyes fluttered closed, her mouth opened and she screamed.

Chloe heard the noises she was making and couldn't stop. There was no shutoff switch. She couldn't open her eyes or lift her head.

This time when the man who held her—the man who had kissed her, the man who had burned her with his reciprocal need for possession—closed his mouth over hers, it was to stifle the sounds. His lips made no further advances. His dexterous tongue did not dance. But somewhere within him, his soul cried out to hers. *Soul.* That ethereal part of people that made them what and who they were, distinguishable from all others. And because this touch felt so personal, so immediate, it manifested inside her as sexual longing.

Sick, breathless, Chloe wanted to be consumed. She

wanted more. Hotter. Parker Madison was in control of the flames, but even as he called them forth, he snuffed them out. A touch and not a touch. A call, yet not a call. An internal war she hadn't the ability to name, and was losing.

She'd been injured, then stretched too thin. Everything ached, from her toes to the roots of her hair. Raging hormones had shoved all that pain aside for a time, but it was only a postponement.

The blackness returned in the form of a wave. Chloe rode it like an inexperienced surfer, dipping in and out of that darkness, crashing, tumbling repeatedly. Parker's arms were corded with muscle that contracted against her back, her shoulders and her bare legs as she dangled in his grip. He was immensely strong, but she shouldn't have liked or admired that. She had always been independent to a fault, she remembered through a gap in her disconnecting consciousness, and didn't need to be carted anywhere in a man's arms. A man who was not just a man, but something extra.

Each time she opened her eyes, his face took on a darker aspect. A face unsure of what it wanted to become. What did he want from her? Would he take her upstairs and tuck her away? Wrap her up? Kiss her again? The longing for that kiss nearly overwhelmed everything else, except for the knowledge that her pain had moved in to stay.

The lights of the hospital hallway dimmed. The fraction of her brain still retrieving and processing data told her that the musty odor she inhaled was from the same hospital stairwell she took every time she worked in this facility.

The sinking sensations she was experiencing weren't entirely due to losing her grasp on consciousness, but because he, Dr. Madison, was taking her down the stairs. Not up to the lobby, the E.R., or back to a room in the ICU. Down, which meant the underground parking structure.

He was taking her out.
Away.

The moon's silver song played so loudly in his ears that Parker couldn't have ignored the call much longer.

Carrying his fragile cargo, and with her arms still wrapped around his shoulders, Parker strode briskly through the garage, keeping to the unlit spaces, dodging cars on his way up the long, winding ramp.

He wouldn't fully transition until he felt the moon's light on his body, and yet that invitation was powerful enough to vibrate through him from a distance—which caused the woman he held to vibrate in the same way, as if she, too, knew what would happen next.

Actually, she had no idea.

"Not long now," he whispered to her. A promise on so many levels. Any second now the creature inside her would feel the call of the wild, as he did.

Warm air found him as Parker exited from the garage. Night smells rushed at him. High in the sky, surrounded by thousands of stars, the moon blazed icy-white, her shine tickling his skin and quadrupling his energy output.

His beast acknowledged its freedom with a groan. His heart skipped a beat.

Her heart skipped a beat.

She was tuning in to him, mimicking, patterning herself after him, taking his lead as if he might know what he was doing. Realizing this, as well as that for the time being there wasn't much he could do about it, Parker spoke some of the last words he would probably be able to utter.

"You will hate it, at first," he said.

Chapter 11

Thoughts ripped through Parker's head. The moonlight beyond the overhang made his skin chill, then flash hot, as the familiar intoxication struck.

Moving fingers of silver hit his shoes, searching for a more direct route to the rest of him. Legs apart, body braced, Parker stood on the sidewalk, holding the girl. Streetlights glowed. After the quiet of the hospital, the city noises seemed deafening.

He couldn't linger. There would be no helping her once the change took place. There'd be no driving a car. If he had been right in his assessment of the girl's condition, her convulsions would return as soon as moonlight hit that part of her waiting for it. He had to keep her out of the light.

A sharp glance to his right brought into focus an EMT truck with its back doors open. Parker went over, hopped inside, grabbed a blanket, and from there examined the street.

The bus stop across the boulevard had a roof meant to keep day travelers out of the blistering sun. Watching for a break in traffic, Parker covered the girl with the blanket, then covered his own head and shoulders. Hooded, nearly blind, he ran to the bus stop and pressed the backs of his knees against the bench so that not one drop of moonlight would hit them.

"One down."

He punctuated those words with an oath. Calculating the distance to the next building's overhang, Parker took off again, praying he'd make it that far. He did.

But how many more stops to go?

Cold sweat beaded on his brow as he planned his next move. It would be hit or miss, finding shelter until he could make it to the safety of the park's trees. Would anyone see him and dial in for help? Hopefully not. In his favor, his blue scrubs might identify him as someone relatively trustworthy.

If they only knew.

Inside him the beast writhed, not at all happy about being restrained. Parker figured he had three more minutes, max, of this hide-and-seek game before the moon sent a punishment for holding back. If the moon loved monsters, what possible punishment might that be?

"Get a move on. Can't let the moonlight reach her."

He raced for the next overhang, and the next one after that, counting the popping sounds of his spine realigning. Four vertebrae had already separated in what amounted to a freakish structural miracle.

The scent drifting up from beneath the blanket was like an aphrodisiac, turning him on. His awareness of the weightless body nestling against him made things worse. He had to maintain a tight rein on his hunger, shun temptation. Heaven help him if his humanity were to slip any more.

It looked as if one more run would distance them from the hustle and bustle of the street. One final dash to tree cover, and then he could let go. He would need the beast's added strength to get the girl to the other side of the park grounds, and the couple of miles beyond it to the place he had in mind. He would ask the people there to keep her safe, if he could speak at all by then.

He'd take her to Fairview, a psychiatric facility and haven for anomalies, nervous breakdowns and dysfunction. He had no experience with it, but he'd never forgotten his meeting at a conference early on in his career with the striking female doctor who ran the hospital.

Dr. James was young, sharp, and known for her care and treatment of deviations of all sorts. He'd be willing to bet the fortune he didn't have, though, that she would have never seen anything like this, if moonlight touched his little Jane Doe. A woman becoming a wolf for the first time was sure to be a show-stopper.

"Maybe it will work. There's nowhere else," he whispered hoarsely to his precious cargo.

Stuffed away in one of Fairview's private rooms, this beauty who moved him in so many ways might contain what lay growing within her. Having never been exposed to the light, her beast might back down. Alternately, if the girl's beast recognized its time and got tripped by the moonlight between here and Fairview, she might go insane, just like he had, once upon a time.

The possibilities were endless. But she only had to make it through one night. Just one. Tomorrow, he would take her back. He'd get his hours covered at the hospital, drive out there, pick her up and take her someplace safer. He would watch over her, try everything.

Not an option. He understood this just as quickly. He

couldn't take responsibility for her when he wasn't sure how his own beast would react to another creature like itself, in the flesh. Look what had happened in that hospital hallway. No, he wasn't to be trusted with her, or near her. If she made it through this night, she'd need help getting through another. And another. For her first transition, she might need care for a week or longer. How many nights had it taken him to get through the indescribable ordeal?

Five, give or take.

Fairview had to agree. Parker would write a prescription for them to hold her. He'd...

"Ah. Shit." *The moon.*

And the girl in his arms had gone completely still.

Throwing off his own portion of the blanket, hugging his bundle tightly, Parker ran for all he was worth for those trees, willing himself to make it.

Madame Moon had other plans.

White light hit Parker square in the face as his hair streamed behind. The light caused his skin to glitter as if covered in sparkling confetti. His final fade began with the force of a soft but vehement slap on his back with a damp towel. Unavoidable moonlight did the rest.

On came the beast.

He skidded to a stop, roared, shook as his flesh tore apart and rearranged. But he hung on to the girl, careful not to let her fall. The sound of tearing cloth filled the quiet. His clothes. He kicked off his shoes.

Fully transformed, he opened his mouth and roared again as the girl stirred. But instead of twitching this time, she began a slow, provocative climb up the front of his body.

Like a vine.

Her arm squeezed tightly around his new shoulder musculature. Her bare, silky legs twined around his waist, so that her buttocks rested just inches—mere inches—from the engorged proof of his raging, ravenous need for her.

She tucked her face into the curve of his neck. His beast's neck. And the fight began. A beast's needs versus a man's powers of reason. If he moved, his beast would take her to the ground, stretch out on top of her and finally get his way. Mate. Rut. Find that hot, tight triangle of fur nestled between her sleek thighs. Maybe her molecules were urging her in that same direction. There was a possibility she ached for this as much as he did. If he didn't have her, both man and beast would explode.

But the nobler parts of Parker's mind kept repeating the same litany. She was too small to fight and too weak to protest. She was out of it, ill and oblivious to the perils of the night. Easy prey.

Back off, beast! We must help her. Do the right thing.

Shaking all over from the immensity of the struggle, Parker hauled himself back from the face-off and moved forward a step.

Yes. Do the right thing, he chanted.

Chapter 12

Chloe struggled to wake, gasping for air. The most important thing was to keep breathing. Everyone knew this. Her cells wouldn't die if they were processing oxygen.

She kept her eyes shut, afraid to open them, afraid she'd be unable to. Behind her closed lids she saw flashes of white light, yellow light, inky darkness, long gray shadows, and wasn't sure what those things were. She had an innate sense of having traveled, ending up somewhere she shouldn't be.

Her body pulsed irregularly with seismic internal hiccups. Pain was focused in one of her upper arms, sharp, insistent, though she didn't know which arm. One ache had become indistinguishable from another. Pain was everywhere, unyielding, unending, all-consuming.

"Are you awake?"

Sounds filled in around her. Chloe reeled with the sudden break in the quiet.

"Are you awake?"

More sound. Slightly familiar. Getting somewhere.

"Can you tell me who you are? Can you tell me who brought you here?"

Somebody was speaking. To her?

"Do you know why you're here?" the voice persisted.

No. She got that one. *Big fat no!*

"Can you open your eyes?"

No!

"Please try to open them now, if you can."

Don't want to. Don't ask me to.

"You're all right. You're safe."

They were the same words she'd heard before, only the voice wasn't the one she wanted to hear them from. This voice was female. Not her doctor. Not *him*.

She was no longer in his arms, feeling his heartbeat against the side of her face, able to hear that tremendous rhythm in her ears. She was no longer snug in his grasp, no longer experiencing the warmth radiating off him. She felt cold again, and hated the suddenness of its return.

"Go ahead. Open your eyes," the woman said softly. "See where you are. It's all right."

This voice was authoritative in a good way. Certainly it didn't belong to the dark?

"Let me help you," the woman said.

Yes. Need… "Help."

"Good," the voice acknowledged. "Good. You're here. You're with me. Will you try again to open your eyes and look at me?"

The voice was beguilingly persistent. Chloe found herself wanting to obey.

"I'm Dr. James."

Memories flooded Chloe's malfunctioning brain like the rerun of a movie. White hallway. Chilled floor. Inescapable shaking. His—Parker Madison's—confident approach. He had held her, taken her from the confinement of the hospital, allowed her room to breathe. How then had she gotten back inside?

"Can you look at me?" this doctor again asked.

Chloe opened her eyes, blinked at the brightness of the light and promptly closed them again. Light was torture.

"I'll turn the lights down. I'm sorry if they hurt you. Your eyes are sensitive, then."

The brightness dimmed. Chloe fluttered her eyes open, gasped in a breath of air that tasted of sterile environment, and felt a cool cloth brush across her forehead. The same forehead *he* had not long ago stroked with tender fingers. *Him. Parker Madison.*

Where was he? Who was she with now?

"I'm going to apply some bandages," the female told her. "Your scratches need attending to. Is that okay? Is it all right if I treat those areas?"

"Yes."

She remembered that now, too—tearing the gauze from her head, seeing the destruction in the mirror, looking at the face that was hers and yet not hers, one cheek marred by rows of sliced-up flesh, many blue nylon stitches in her forehead. This woman had said *scratches*. A gross understatement meant to appease her?

"You'll feel something cold. That's the ointment," the woman explained. "We've already given you something for the discomfort."

Another gross understatement: *discomfort.*

"What?" Chloe managed to rasp.

She actually felt the woman trying to understand what she was asking, but the thought of stringing together too many words at once for clarity's sake seemed daunting. She slid her jaw side to side, unclenched her chattering teeth, tried a second time.

"What, for pain?" she asked.

"I've given you a mild sedative. Are you in pain at present?" the voice reported.

"Yes." *Unending pain.*

"Where do you hurt?"

"All." Short for *everywhere.* Best she could do.

"You can have more medication in a while. Not one shot right on top of another."

Of course. A shot. More of her neural functions must be returning. That had been the pinch she'd felt. They had injected her with a painkiller in her left arm, the one with the broken wrist. But the other arm, her upper right arm, was now hurting like nothing she had ever encountered before, with pain that had taken on a life of its own.

How had this doctor known she was in distress, and if she might need meds? Was "shoot first and ask questions later" usual procedure? The doctor had no doubt found the trail of pinpricks from her escape stint from the ICU.

"Par-ker," Chloe said as the smell of fresh gauze filled her nostrils. She would loathe that smell from now on.

"Is that your name?" the doctor asked.

"His."

"Are you married?"

"No."

"Boyfriend?"

Chloe hesitated on that one. "No."

"Who is Parker?"

More smelly gauze. And sticky tape applied to her tender forehead.

"Doctor," she said, keeping the rest private, where those thoughts belonged. Keeping them close.

"There's no one here by that name. How did you get here? There's no car outside."

A fresh recollection of being carried out of the hospital and into the night made Chloe stutter, "W-where…am I?"

She clamped her teeth together again. The seismic pulses coming from her insides were getting stronger, not weaker. So much for the meds. She felt as though she had swallowed a small animal, still alive and kicking and wanting to get out. Perhaps, though, that feeling was just a metaphor for wanting out of wherever the hell she was. She was that small animal. *Trapped.*

Breathing seemed impossible. There were no tubes clogging her throat, yet nothing got past. Her arms and legs had started to twitch. Claustrophobia closed in, further dimming her surroundings. She had to get out of wherever she was, get outside. *Find him.*

"This is Fairview Hospital," the doctor said, and after a pause added, "It looks as if you've recently visited another medical facility. I don't think they would have released you without your clothes, so it would help if I knew how you got here. If you came here to get help for your injuries, this isn't the right place. On the other hand, if you came here seeking solace for other reasons, we'll do what we can for you tonight and call the proper authorities tomorrow."

Another pause, then, "Since your distress seems to be growing, I think you might need more medication, after all. Let's get you downstairs where you'll be more comfortable, shall we?"

"No!"

Did they listen to her protest? Had her cry even made it past her lips? For the second time that night, Chloe felt herself being lifted, this time by someone dowsed in aftershave.

She opened her eyes, focused on the face above hers.

Fleshy brown male face. Spiky brown hair. Brown expressionless eyes, not exactly unkind.

This was not the man she wanted to see. Where had Parker Madison gone? Why had he left her alone?

"Stop," Chloe said, forming the word distinctly.

"It's all right," the female soothed from behind. "You can decide what to do in the morning if you're feeling up to it. You'll be safe here until then."

Safe? She didn't feel safe. She felt sick. Her stomach was turning over. She couldn't get a handle on the shakes. The room spun around faster and faster…taking her with it.

Parker returned the next night, morphed and anxious. He'd barely made it through the day knowing he couldn't be near the girl, feeling guilty for having abandoned her. There was no way he could explain now. There had been two messages from Dr. James, which he'd had to ignore. He had dropped his she-wolf off on Fairview's doorstep, wrapped in a blanket, anonymously. He had rung the bell! How could he have stood there, naked, holding her? If he'd been arrested, how would that help?

How had Jenna James known his name, and where to place that call?

He paced like a caged wolf along the chain-link fence bordering the gate to Fairview's driveway, wondering which room his she-wolf might be in, and if he could climb up there. Moonlight followed him, highlighting the tracks he had already worn in the grass, adding to his agitation. What was happening to her inside Fairview? Had he been wrong to leave her there?

He hated himself for taking part in any of this. In his defense, the only one he had at the moment, if any staff from Fairview had laid eyes on him as he was now, in this mountainous form, they'd have checked themselves into their own damn mental facility.

He took a quick swipe at the air with his claws, listened hard, cocked his head and dropped to a low crouch. A growl bubbled up.

He wasn't alone.

Hunkering down, tightening his imposing shoulders, Parker sniffed the air, turned slowly and crept with the stealth of his four-legged relatives toward the open gate.

He sniffed again, searched the area, then abruptly stood.

Wolf. No mistaking the scent this time.

Apprehensive, and with an image of the pale wolf in his mind, Parker waited, leaning in the direction of the scent, every nerve fiber on alert. This was the kind of odor that had lured him to the Landau estate, which in turn had kicked off this whole series of events.

There! Movement! Along the fence on the opposite side of Fairview's front lawn something drew his attention. As whatever it was passed through a patch of unimpeded moonlight, Parker saw the outline of a beast. Not the pale-pelted version he might have expected, but a creature whose brown hide shone like bronze.

It was a huge male, moving like a predator.

The fur on the back of Parker's neck rose. Baring his teeth in an automatic reaction, he watched the dreadful beast's progress.

Friend or foe?

Just a minute more. I've waited this long.

God, how I've waited.

The big male moved in a graceful sweep of wolfish muscle and bone as it approached a second gate sitting open, on the far side of the circular driveway. As he walked, he stared intently up at the hospital's brick facade. At the gate he stopped to transfer his gaze to a car parked by the steps.

Four, Parker noted with trepidation. Four wolves now, counting the girl. Was that too many, or too few? This was the time to approach the brown wolf, reach out.

Parker slipped forward several paces, then halted when he saw his target head through that open gate. A security light immediately snapped on, flooding the section of driveway where the beast stood. He hauled himself up as if he'd been zapped by an invisible electric fence, and cocked his head, considering the light. The low, almost tormented growl he issued caused Parker to growl, as well.

Hearing Parker's retort, the werewolf spun around with his massive muscles rippling. Parker felt the instant his gaze found him standing there, black as the night, but highlighted by the shower of moonlight.

The brown wolf growled again menacingly as he advanced with a bound. After considering Parker for several seconds, he swiped a sharp claw across his chest, drawing a thin, dark line of blood. The scent of iron filled the air.

Rocking on his feet, and with that smell in his nostrils, Parker mirrored the other werewolf's gesture by tearing at his own chest. Was this some sort of species recognition, like male apes pounding on their chests to ward off competition?

Competition for what?

Daring to take his eyes off the brown werewolf, Parker glanced warily toward the hospital with a sudden buildup of bad thoughts. Had this other male ferreted out the girl he'd brought to Fairview, about to become a she-wolf? The girl he sincerely hoped was now safe and secure inside a werewolf-proof place?

Damnation! Unexpectedly, Miami had become crowded with genetic anomalies. Suddenly, Parker, his body rigid with tension, found himself wondering how many others there might be, and how many people he knew might be living with secrets.

Keeping his teeth bared in caution, Parker zeroed in on this new werewolf and waited for whatever might happen next. What did was yet another surprise. The gesture the brown man-wolf made with his great head and thickly muscled neck was universal for *follow me*. Then he turned, took a few purposeful strides and pivoted back to Parker, waiting for him to catch up.

The night had gone from dubiously dreamlike to surreal. Time seemed to slow as Parker watched the wolf. His surroundings narrowed until the hospital and its grounds faded into a hazy, colorless swirl, with not Fairview, but the impressively large brown beast as its epicenter.

Not just one wolf, were the words repeating in Parker's head. *Not just one, or even three, but four.*

With a boldness ingrained in his beast's tweaked DNA sequencing, Parker accepted the challenge by striding forward. The brown werewolf gave a nod, then headed for the trees. Parker followed, needing those answers now more than ever, not wanting to be the last wolf standing. Because this newest revelation changed everything. Again.

This moment was sure to be yet another turning point in his life. One of so very many.

The sucker was fast, but Parker wasn't about to lose him. Moonlight provided the impetus, the desire to push himself to the limits. His wolf body, like a well-oiled machine, allowed him to effortlessly cover ground in pursuit.

For a while, as he raced through the dark and the moonlight, Parker felt curiously freed from the mounting stresses of harboring secrets. With the balmy air in his lungs, the wind in his hair and the sacred light from above making this possible, he wanted to shed the last vestiges of normalcy and bay at the moon. He wanted to give in to the wildness of communing with the night. The feeling was new and wickedly exciting.

The big wolf eventually slowed, dropped onto his haunches and turned his head to await Parker's arrival. So there they were, inches apart, face-to-face at last.

The strangeness of this meeting was something Parker figured he'd never get over. This werewolf appeared to be startlingly similar to himself in every way, but still, there were noticeable differences, just as in the simple allotment of two eyes, a nose and a mouth, there were differences in people.

It might have been irrational to feel a kinship with another monster, but he did. This guy shared his plight. A man resided somewhere inside that huge body. Who was it? What did he do for a living when not running wild in the night? Were there others?

The wolf beside him was silent, yet so intent that Parker almost expected him to speak through those elongated jaws. Intelligent eyes outlined in gold fixed him with a serious expression. The spell was broken when an echoing noise interrupted their little bonding session. Gunfire, it sounded like. Two rounds in succession, and fairly close. A contemporary, modern-day call of the wild.

The brown Were leaped to his feet, snarling as he acknowledged the noise. Parker caught the fever and snarled back. As insane as it might have been, he and this wolf had connected through those vicious vocalizations. They were on the same wavelength.

Trouble lay ahead, and they were going that way.

Chapter 13

"I've given her two sedatives and she's still shaking," the female voice remarked, sounding faint and faraway. Chloe's head continued to spin, and her heart beat way too fast, like an accelerator pedal stuck to the floorboard of a car in neutral.

"She can't handle any more. I won't chance it," the woman continued. "I'd like to change those bandages she's pulled loose before she hurts herself. Can you hold her?"

A male baritone replied, "Sure thing, Dr. James. Will we need a jacket?"

They were speaking as if Chloe wasn't there. As if she were unconscious. She forced her eyes open and saw the grim expression of the doctor above her.

The woman had a lovely face, surrounded by auburn hair, pulled back in a clip. Her big eyes were framed by dark lashes, and her skin was perfectly smooth, an unblemished, unwrinkled ivory. The lips that parted to formulate her next words were full and unglossed. Not pretty, was Chloe's immediate assessment. She was too beautiful, too perfect, to be considered merely pretty. Had to be smart, too, to be a doctor.

"Hello," Dr. James said. "Can you hear me?"

Chloe blinked once. That's what people did in the movies to signify a yes. She didn't trust herself to speak, afraid of screaming.

"Do you understand what I'm saying?" The doctor's penetrating eyes seemed to bore into her.

Chloe blinked again, slowly. The pain seemed to trace the edges of her body now, as if she'd been outlined in black ink.

"You're at Fairview Hospital," Dr. James explained, starting over. "You've been having seizures, so we've sedated you. The seizures might be related to your head wound. Do you remember getting that wound?"

"Yes." Chloe hadn't screamed, after all, though the urge to do so made it dangerously possible.

"Were you attacked?"

"Yes."

"You've been treated. I see the stitches. Did whoever sewed you up let you go? Did you find your own way here?"

Chloe tried to shake her head, and a bolt of fire sliced through her, inciting reactionary movement from every muscle. Her arms, head and legs moved independently of her brain. She tightened as many pieces of herself as she could, and shrieked with the effort.

The doctor's voice registered deep concern. "You're about to seize again. Can you tell me your name? At least that much?"

Chloe wanted to comply. She tried to say her name, but her chattering teeth and side-to-side head movements seemed to be addling her thought processes. She felt nauseous.

"Stay with me," the doctor said. "Try to focus. Stay with me."

That request was impossible. Chloe's body was thrashing so violently that she had to close her eyes for fear they'd fall out of their sockets. She didn't want to close them. Doing so meant slipping back into darkness.

"Keep her in the ward?" the baritone asked, applying pressure to Chloe's shoulders with his big hands.

"For now. We might need restraints, but God, I hope not. That last sedative should kick in soon."

"Do you know what this is, Doctor?"

Yes, Chloe seconded. *Tell me what's happening!*

"She's in shock. She's had some sort of trauma that's being kept inside. It's in there festering, physically and mentally. Problem is, we have to placate the body before we can deal with the mind. We have to try to keep her comfortable until she can speak."

"Maybe restraints would help to keep her hands away from her face?"

"No. Not unless it's absolutely necessary. We'll wait to see if that sedative works. I don't want to cause her any more discomfort than she's already experiencing. I don't want her to think we're part of the problem. I think she… I'm afraid she might be…"

"Yeah, Dr. James?"

"Well, I'll stay with her awhile. Can you can start the rounds, Jim?"

"Whatever you say," the baritone agreed.

Chloe swore—aside from all of what was happening to her, and with her eyes closed—that she felt Jim leave the room.

"Can you hear me?"

Chloe came to again slowly, with no idea where she was. Her first realization was that her pain seemed to have diminished. That in itself seemed a miracle.

She was able to lie still and to breathe through her nose. She also knew she was being stared at by someone waiting for a question to be answered.

"Yes," she said, wading back to the question itself. "I hear you."

"How do you feel?"

"Ill." She hadn't wanted to admit that, but did anyway.

"We've reached a limit on the medication," the voice explained. "I'm using hypnosis to get you to relax, and to provide a brief respite from the pain, which seems to be getting worse. Do you know where you are?"

"Hospital."

"Can you tell me your name?"

"Chloe."

"Chloe what? What's your last name?"

"Tyler." She heard a ticking noise in the periphery, as if they were sitting next to a clock. It had a calming effect. This woman's questions didn't.

"Where do you live, Chloe Tyler?"

"Used to be the desert. Phoenix. Now, by the water."

"Here in Miami?"

"Yes."

"Do you live alone?"

"Yes."

"Did you bring yourself here? It's an important question, Chloe, so please answer."

"Parker brought me."

"He is the doctor you mentioned earlier."

"Did I mention him earlier?"

"Chloe, listen to my voice, please, and answer this question. Where is he? Where's the man who brought you here?"

Was the ticking somewhere in the room or inside her head? Hard to tell.

"He's not at the other hospital, so where might I find him?" the doctor asked.

An answer formulated that Chloe would not say. She would never do so. If everything he had told her was the truth, in any way, shape, form or parallel universe, her delectable doctor would probably be running through the dark out there, playing werewolf. But then everybody had a flaw or two, right? Chloe's was a massive stubborn streak, plus moments of outright rebellion. Hadn't her parents always warned her about those traits? Did her behavior even matter now that her folks were gone?

"Why did he bring you here without speaking to me?" the doctor asked.

"He couldn't speak."

"Why not?"

"Moon," Chloe said, wondering why she had, again feeling compelled by the nature of the questions and the tone of the doctor's voice to answer correctly. Then there was that darn ticking. She felt her heart adapt to the tempo.

"Moon?" the doctor repeated, her voice changing slightly, enough for Chloe to gain a foothold on that old rebelliousness. She would not say another word. Would not.

"What about the moon?" The doctor had returned to her former tone in such a way as to absolutely require Chloe to answer the question.

She felt her mouth opening, heard herself say, "Werewolf," her resoluteness slipping as quickly as that. "He is a werewolf."

Although a silence fell, the room wasn't completely quiet. Chloe's uneven breathing sounded to her like a chugging freight train.

The doctor said, "Did he make that wound on your arm?"

"No." Chloe squirmed, wanting to run away from that particular answer. *No going that deep.*

"Who did? Who did this to you?"

She clammed up tight, didn't want to think about her arm, but seemed unable to resist the images flashing in front of her, sketched in paint and ink by the doctor's voice. The nasty men were there, near Landau's wall. They had caught her, thrown her to the ground, kicked her in the ribs, punched her in the face. But they hadn't finished the damage. They had merely warmed her up for someone else, a monster who had appeared so quickly, she hadn't registered his approach. Like a shadow, he'd come on. A nightmare. A man with no face, just…just all that pale hair shielding his features. An evil presence that brought overwhelming pain and suffering.

"Was this doctor, Parker, trying to help you by bringing you here?" the doctor asked.

"Yes." As though a dark cloud had lifted, her avenging angel's beautiful face filled her memory, replacing the other, darker thing, bringing back a longing for him that was so strong, it produced a noticeable moistness between her legs. With Parker Madison's scent in her lungs, she awaited the doctor's next question.

"All right, Chloe. We can try this again later. You're tired."

Yet another pause from the doctor. More ticking sounds.

"I'm going to count from three to one," Dr. James eventually said. "When I get to the number one you will wake up. Are you ready, Chloe?"

"Yes."

"Three…"

The ticking started to fade, as if it were attached to a dimmer switch.

"Two…"

Chloe felt herself sinking downward, and feared she was going in the wrong direction.

"One."

The betraying body parts began their polka of twitching and shaking all over again before the word *one* had stopped resonating inside Chloe's head. Her shout of defiance, loud and pathetically shrill, escaped from between her teeth without any conscious help from thought processes.

"He will be back! He promised!"

They ran side by side, Parker and the brown werewolf, their strides equal, covering ground as if they had been created to be running machines.

Parker didn't stop to consider why he had followed this beast. The echo of the gun's retort drew them forward, the sound hanging in the air like a loud shout, easy for his inner navigation system to lock on to.

East. Trouble to the east.

His blood pumped through his veins. He felt excited, wild, wary, different in an altogether new way. He decided that looking too closely at the creature running alongside him probably wouldn't be a good thing. Parker's own beast had taken over this chase, instinct fueling the fires that drove him on. Obviously, somebody else's beast had done the same thing.

Bodies in sync, he and the other wolf passed through the shadows of overarching trees, scarcely sucking air. Quickly, they covered acres of grass, until they neared the stone wall that now seemed to Parker like a magnet for adversity. Sure enough, the trouble was there.

He felt so stunned when he saw what had transpired in this place that he stopped, backpedaled and howled with his head thrown back. The brown wolf rammed him hard to direct his focus. He circled Parker, growling, then repeated Parker's hollow cry.

Two bodies lay on the ground beside the wall. Human bodies. Buck naked. Faceup. Each of them shot once through the heart. Bull's-eye.

Parker gaped. What kind of monster would do a thing like this?

The brown wolf yowled again, this time with a baying sound that tore right through Parker like a sonic boom. He'd heard that before, near a wounded body. The last time, he had been approaching a wounded female, and the howl had come from the mouth of a pale, half-morphed Were.

Even more disturbing to Parker, the brown werewolf's baying was echoed by a replacement, originating on the other side of the stone wall beside them.

Parker felt otherness coming on—that sensation he was unable to pinpoint, and dreaded as much as he wanted it. Chills arrived, cooling his overheated skin to lukewarm. He turned his head warily, watched as another beast appeared atop that cursed wall. A beast who leaped nimbly to the ground not three feet away.

It was another large brute—larger that himself and the brown, very obviously male, with a rust-colored, furred back.

The world turned upside down. Parker felt himself tilt, and shuffled back a pace as a second new werewolf jumped down off that wall on the heels of the first. This one was even more impressive, frighteningly so. Thick silver streaks, glistening like sterling in the moonlight, ran through a black pelt as fine as ermine. This huge creature beat out the rust-colored wolf in size, and was older; Parker knew it intuitively. The Were radiated grace and attitude, and his very presence reeked of danger.

Parker fell to a crouch, teeth again bared, not quite sure how to handle this situation, refusing to believe his eyes. He spun around, more chills raising the hair on his neck as a third wolf landed next to him, with a pelt almost as dark as the last one, minus the streaks. Though smaller, this wolf was wiry, lithe and not one iota less impressive than the rest.

Whipping his head to take them all in, Parker caught a whiff of fragrance rising above the other smells vying for his attention in a this-can't-be-happening sort of way. The smell emanated from the closest werewolf, the smaller one. Musk, damp fur, and…gardenias. An all-too-familiar concoction.

Where had he smelled those things before?

Apprehension gripped him tightly. Parker let loose a baying shout that severed the night as completely as lightning when the answer to his own query came. A ridiculous answer. Totally unfeasible. Yet he was suddenly sure he was right.

The small beast next to him was one of Miami's finest. None other than the dark-haired female cop he had spoken with over coffee at the hospital. Detective Wilson's ally in the department. The bite-savvy cop who had asked probing questions about Jane Doe's wound.

His mouth gaping, Parker fixed his eyes on her in disbelief. This was Officer Delmonico. *Dana* Delmonico.

Was he mad to think so?

Showing very sharp white teeth that real wolves used for tearing flesh and God knew what else, and aware of his scrutiny, the she-wolf growled back, as if to warn him to stick to the situation at hand. The others, four not counting himself, were nosing around the dead bodies, their great shapes livid with anger. Not one could say anything or voice his distress, because none of them could speak. Yet they were formidable, drenched in moonlight as they were. Their eyes all flashed with the same glint of gold, as if that color somehow connected them.

Tonight, the moon directed the game. The game that wasn't a game anymore—a fact that had become all too clear.

Parker didn't have to worry about being an anomaly. What he did have to worry about were those two bodies on the ground, and not ending up like them. Violence had been done near this wall twice. It occurred to Parker that someone else knew about this barrier and about the genetically altered people behind it, and didn't take to the idea. The girl might have been a mistake, but two dead souls in the same area made this look a little like target practice.

Sharpshooting target practice, by the look of those perfect holes in the victims' chests. Holes in skin tinted by the blue cast of death. With a shot to the heart, these guys would have died instantly.

The wolves were offering up a series of whines. They probably knew these people, these two men who'd just happened to be out here, naked, near the Landau property. Two werewolves, reverted to their human shape in death?

Had the killers used silver bullets, like in the horror novels, to keep them down?

Was the Landau estate a vortex for the supernatural?

The others seemed to be waiting for the silver Were to act. Leader of the pack, then? Easy guess. The call the silver creature made next hit Parker square in the forehead with the force of a slap, instantaneously translating into a single word: *hunt.*

A chorus of howls went up from the gathered group. All the creatures surrounding Parker sprang into action at once, of one mind, moving as a pack of predators away from the scene of the crime and into the moonlit night. A dangerous, churning sea of muscle and madness that swept Parker along.

Chapter 14

The odor of their prey floated in the heavy humid air like summer heat shimmering off asphalt. At least two humans ran ahead, Parker knew, and they would have the guns that had brought the two werewolves down. Still, whether they were armed or not, it would take more than human legs to keep those killers distanced from an angry pack on the move.

Parker clung hard to his humanity as he ran, needing to maintain the subtle hints of himself peeking out from inside his altered outline. Losing himself completely seemed only a breath away. Madness felt closer than that.

He had to drag his attention back to his she-wolf to keep everything from blurring into the beast's excitement—the woman he'd kissed, then dropped off. If he let go of himself completely here, tonight, what would happen to her?

Wildness filled his lungs. Humidity dampened his fur. The moon hung like a flare above the trees, and the park had grown quiet beyond the unique murmurings of the many morphed, fur-covered limbs doing what they were designed to do—a sound comparable to the rustle of wind in the treetops.

The effects on Parker of running with this pack were substantial. The farther he went, the more feral he felt, the more the night suited him, the more he wanted to leave the old Parker and his reasoning behind. This group had not questioned his being among them. The brown wolf had led him to the wall, invited him along, and now ran at the black-and-silver-pelted wolf's side.

Did all werewolves stick together? Find each other eventually? Maintain their own secret cult? These wolves had all come from behind Judge Landau's secluded gates. Certainly a piece of the puzzle of Parker's own existence had been found.

She wouldn't have to worry now, he told himself. These other Weres were sure to know more about their species and would fill in the blanks. A cop ran with them, just as fierce as the rest. A female cop. Perhaps her presence made these Weres good guys by association. His she-wolf wouldn't be the only one of her sex, that was for sure. His Jane Doe wouldn't have to grope for enlightenment if Delmonico knew the ropes.

The trees thinned on the eastern side of the park's acreage. Buildings appeared in the distance, rising above streets teeming with civilization. If the killer reached those streets, this hairy group would be out of luck.

It was a conclusion they obviously had all come to simultaneously, since their speed kicked up.

Parker's vision sharpened. Navigating through the dark at a full run was easy. Believing this to be real was the hard part.

And then Parker saw them. Two men, ahead.

What would happen now that his pack was closing in?

What would his fellow wolves do in retaliation for the slaying of their kind, possibly their friends?

The thought fled Parker's mind when the silver-streaked wolf in the lead gave a sudden, bone-chilling command.

"Chloe?"

Again voices came from far off. From another planet, maybe. Chloe's body was thrashing too hard, too violently, for her to pay attention. Trauma vibrated through her as one of her arms hit the wall, followed by her shoulder. She cried out in surprise over the return of a dagger-sharp pain.

Her broken wrist burned. The room was so white, and seamless. If this was a hospital, where were the people who had been hired to help?

"Chloe, we'd like to restrain you," the voice announced calmly, sounding closer now than Mars. "I'd like your permission because it won't feel very nice. It might even seem scary."

Yes. Do it. Do it, for God's sake, before I kill myself!

"Can you look at me, Chloe? I need to see that you understand."

A face swam into view. Recognition hit as Chloe waded through round fifty of the shakes. This was the female doctor. Dr. James.

"Yes, that's it," she said with audible relief when Chloe faced her. "I'm sorry, Chloe. The sedation works for only fifteen minutes at most on you. You've had three injections already. I hesitate to give you more."

Chloe found herself standing on trembling legs. Well, almost standing. She leaned on the wall, with her head against it. The surface was padded and smelled like Lysol-coated vinyl. The white room was tiny, and the lights had been dimmed, probably in deference to her sensitive eyes.

Across the space stood the auburn-haired doctor, alone now. Dragging her gaze over the woman's face, Chloe saw worry etched there. Patients never wanted to see expressions like that cross their doctor's face, she thought numbly.

Why was she looking at Chloe in that way?

In a low tone, Dr. James said, "I think the wound on your arm is infected."

"Great. That's what's wrong with me?" Talking was hard. Thinking was harder. Chloe didn't know how she had gotten that much out past her chattering teeth.

"You'll need other medical help," the doctor added soberly. "Antibiotics. Possibly more stitches. I can help with some of that if you can stay still. I'm not sure whether your head injury is causing the seizures, along with the possible hallucinations you're experiencing, or if it's something else altogether. I have to be sure before treating you further, and before calling someone else in."

The doctor's voice lowered again. "Do you have family here, Chloe? Someone I can call? Would you like to be transferred to a facility better suited to help?"

"No." *To all of those.* The only person she had trusted had deposited her at this place, wherever the hell it was. Had it been for her own good? Her dark angel must have had a reason.

"What is this place?" she asked, afraid of the answer, her body tipping toward the wall as her knees weakened drastically.

"Fairview is a psychiatric hospital," Dr. James replied.

"What?" The question reverberated in Chloe's throat.

"And your story is that another doctor brought you here."

"Yes. I—" Chloe gave up what she had been about to say. She was trusting a man who thought himself a werewolf.

"A doctor who didn't check you in or leave a prescription.

No paperwork. You do see why I'm puzzled?" Dr. James said. "We found you on the porch, under a blanket."

"He said…" What had he said? That they couldn't allow a drop of moonlight to touch her. That she would hate what was happening to her at first. Did this make sense? Would Dr. James lock the door and toss away the key if she were to repeat those things?

"I can't legally keep you here longer than twenty-four hours, and then only on your own reconnaissance," the doctor explained. "I'm taping this conversation to make sure we have that approval on record."

Chloe had to work harder than ever to keep from throwing herself across the room. The terrible energy gathering inside her made her want to ping off the padded walls, race through the hallways and get outside, into the open air. The only explanation for this behavior had to be that her head injury caused an affliction similar to Tourette's syndrome.

Maybe Parker had known she would have this reaction. Maybe that's why he'd left her here. Didn't his hospital now induce artificial comas to protect patients from suffering through hardships like hers?

The pain in her head got sharper each time she thought of Parker Madison and his sickness-free bio. A perfect record of perfect health for a perfect doctor. Perfect. But what gave doctors a get-out-of-jail-free card against illness, when hospital personnel were exposed to every known virus in the city on a daily basis?

Only a handful of people in the public domain could actually brag about their clean health records and immunity to bugs. These few were termed Super People in her research.

Her research. Yes, she remembered that now, too. She'd been studying the Super People phenomenon at the cellular level, looking for reasons why some people got sick while others didn't. Her job at the university was to seek answers for this phenomenon in test tubes, blood and DNA samples. She'd had to dig real deep, crack open at least a hundred computer systems, to come up with the handful of extraordinary subjects she'd found.

That's how the whole ordeal had started. She had been looking through police files for the possibility of coming up with a supercop, she remembered as she bounced off the wall for the tenth time before falling to her knees in front of Dr. James. But she was excited to remember those things.

Instead of a supercop, what she had found was something stranger. A malfunctioning set of cells unlike anything she'd ever seen before. Those cells belonged to a female cop. Officer Dana Delmonico.

Curious about Delmonico, she had followed the cop to a meeting with Dylan Landau. She had watched them both disappear behind the gates in the stone walls, beyond the park— the ones she now knew to be owned by a Landau. She'd been positive there had to be more than a romantic link between Officer Delmonico and Dylan Landau. Links were how research worked, one thing leading to another. If Landau turned out to have a similar cell pattern to Delmonico's, the next logical step would have been to check out his father and mother, her parents, and so on.

And in tracking down those links, Chloe had ended up beaten there, by Landau's wall. Her last thought before being struck down had been to wonder what might happen if whatever swam in Delmonico's bloodstream were to contaminate those miraculous Landau genes—the ones determining the high cheekbones, chiseled physiques, intelligence and all that thick blond hair.

If she could find a pattern, determine what it meant, and if it turned out to be a contagion…and if she could work up an antidote to reverse those effects...she'd have bagged a Nobel Prize.

Trembling out of control, she clung to Dr. James's white coat as the woman knelt beside her. Maybe, Chloe thought as the doctor took a firm grip on her shoulders, Parker had brought her here because he had once been a resident at Fairview himself—to get treatment for those werewolf hallucinations.

"Sorry, Doc."

Assuming the apology was meant for her, Dr. James nodded.

And just maybe, Chloe thought, her mind as tormented by thoughts as her body was with the tremors, she could look that up. Parker and Fairview. If she could manage to get to a computer and check Fairview's files, that was.

If she could stand up.

"I will stay here," she said, for the benefit of those tapes the doctor had told her about. "For...for the record. Of my own free will."

With a worried expression furrowing her otherwise smooth brow, James helped Chloe to her feet. But the doctor's grip made her cry out in agony, after which Dr. James's expression changed yet again, to one of surprise.

Chloe didn't have time to ask about it. Her shaking got rapidly worse until she was sure her insides would explode like a bottle of aggressively mishandled champagne.

God, she had liked champagne once. The golden color, the bubbles, the sweetness of those bubbles going down. She had liked birthday cake, starry nights and drooling over unaffordable designer shoes. In that order. All fleeting thoughts, like parts of her life flashing before her eyes.

The fresh batch of tremors nearly took Dr. James to the floor with her. The doctor rallied gamely, yanking Chloe to her feet with astonishing strength, turning, pressing her backward onto a cot riveted to the wall.

"You told me you were attacked. Your wounds are fresh. The attack was last night?" she asked, releasing Chloe slowly.

Chloe nodded.

"How did you come by the wound on your arm?"

No. Don't want to think about evil. Don't want to go back there, into the dark. Please don't ask me to.

"Chloe, listen to me. Your answer may make a difference in what you need. I'm trying to understand."

Since she was unable to pry her teeth open, the only way to communicate was through charades. She ignored the doctor's question, instead asking one of her own. With difficulty, Chloe faked typing with her fingers on an invisible, imaginary keyboard. Her hands shook.

"Computer? You work on a computer?" the doctor asked.

Ramming herself against the wall behind the cot, this time dislodging the splint on her broken wrist, Chloe cried out, and nodded. Hot tears gathered in her eyes.

"I'm sorry," Dr. James said sincerely. "I'll call for another sedative. I'll have to restrain you somehow, for your own protection, while I splint that wrist. I'll wrap your hands to keep them from your face."

Chloe typed again in the air, and pointed to the door of the room, which was open.

"You're asking to use a computer? You want to write something down?"

She nodded, knowing her eyes were wild with pain, yet implicit in her need to get this point across.

Parker. Fairview. She kept focused on that.

"There's one at the end of the hallway," the doctor said. "I don't know if you can make it, or use it when you get there."

Chloe nodded her head vigorously. She damn well would use that computer. She'd type in Parker's name. If there turned out to be no connection to him and this place, she'd have a message waiting when he returned to the hospital after indulging in his nighttime games.

Remember me? she'd write. And maybe something a bit more cryptic, such as What the f—?

"All right." Dr. James helped her stand, then called for assistance. With Big Jim's help, bless him, Chloe made it through the door without breaking anything else.

Parker found himself surrounded by a dark cloud of apprehension much the consistency of mud. He ran at a slower pace now, each movement an effort, each breath an insufficient oxygen draw.

The group of wolves around him matched his pace, but it also may have been the other way around. Their concentration was centered on the two men they were closing in on. Men who would be no match for such tweaked, wolfish beings.

Again Parker wondered what would happen when they caught those guys. A terrible, yet necessary consideration. Would Delmonico's presence mean that justice would be served in the usual way? She didn't appear to be in possession of handcuffs at the moment. Who here, in their wolfish nakedness, had a cell phone?

Having seen two of their kind murdered, what were the chances these wolves might actually hand the yokels off to the authorities?

And what might these two killers tell the cops if they were handed over? That a pack of wild animals had chased them into custody? That the two men they had killed weren't men at all, really? Such a disclosure might get them sent off to the loony bin for a while, until someone like Detective Wilson came snooping around. They might even be sent to…*Fairview*.

Parker's pace faltered at the same time that another cry went up. The wolves were close enough now that he saw the stiff muscles of the men's backsides and smelled the anger pouring from their sweat glands. They smelled also of the metal of the guns they had used. Parker could make out the outline of the handles of those guns tucked into the waist-bands of their jeans. One each.

It was a matter of another minute at most before the bad guys and the good guys—the latter meaning himself and his companions, at least in this situation—would end the chase.

A cry came from Delmonico. Her wolfish jaws open, her lethal teeth exposed, she was a blur of movement in the night beside him. Parker felt the heat radiating off her from two feet away.

And then the silver-streaked wolf lunged at the closest runner, knocking him to the ground. The brown wolf Parker had followed took the second guy down in the same manner. Easy as pie. Humans, even murdering criminals like these two, who had just killed two people in cold blood, were no match for werewolves, after all.

Parker and the other two wolves skidded to a stop, quickly forming a circle around those on the ground—just as the gangbangers who had accosted his girl and then tried to accost him had done. That similarity struck a nerve.

Like the others, he stared at the silver wolf, waiting for whatever would come next.

The night went as quiet as if they had all fallen into a black hole. As unbelievable as it was, the killers didn't utter a word—an odd thing for Parker to digest. Surrounded by a bunch of big bad monsters in full werewolf form, which ought to have caused cardiac arrest, the two shaved-headed murderers lay facedown on the grass with their mouths shut.

An eerie premonition washed over Parker, one he saw

echoed in the sudden tilt of Delmonico's head. Why weren't these creeps making noise? At the very least, screaming?

When Delmonico snarled, Parker cast a glance over his shoulder, then whirled to face a new terror.

Chapter 15

The computer was on, Chloe saw with relief. That would save her some time.

A wooden chair sat beside the small table holding the PC. Probably this was where Jim, the doctor's assistant, wiled away his time when he wasn't tranquilizing patients or standing guard by their doors. She had to hand it to him, though, and award him gold stars for his gentle treatment. He helped her to get seated, then pushed the tiny button to activate the monitor for her.

There was no time to offer him an appreciative smile. She had to concentrate hard to type, with her body refusing to calm down. She actually felt her synapses frying with each effort, and experienced short spurts of mental blankness following them. Grunting, trying really hard to stop shaking long enough to do this, she pecked at the keyboard with her index fingers.

I can do this.

Seconds longer than usual, though in a short enough span of time, she had logged in to Fairview's mainframe. No Parker Madison. As Dr. James moved to stand behind her, Chloe quickly logged on to Metro Hospital's mainframe, and accessed her chart. Dr. James read it silently. "Okay," she said simply, signaling for Jim to help Chloe back to the padded room.

"Wait!" Frustrated, Chloe held up a hand, pleading for a minute more, and was about to knock out that message to Parker Madison when she stumbled upon a connection to Dr. James's computer. She pulled up what the doctor had last typed in, hoping it might provide some clue as to what was happening to her.

A word flashed on the screen. Just one word.

Werewolf.

They had visitors. Looking at the three new, fully morphed werewolves that had appeared on the opposite side of the expanse of lawn felt like gazing into a mirror.

Parker's entire world rearranged in that instant.

The rust-furred werewolf next to him, the only male besides Parker himself who wasn't busy attending to a murdering son of a bitch on the ground, snapped his teeth—which in turn drew the attention of the silver and the big brown wolf, each kneeling on the back of their prey.

Parker tried to glean whether or not these visitors were friendly. Appeared pretty much *not*.

The silver wolf howled a menacing warning that no one would have misunderstood, and sprang to his feet, one of which was still pressed firmly in the center of his prey's T-shirt-covered back. The guns the murderers had used to fell the beasts at the wall swung from the brown wolf's claws like a woman's heavy dangling earrings.

The largest of the three Weres across from them issued a reply, without advancing. What the hell was this? A stand-off? Over what?

Parker's attention slipped to the guy trapped beneath Silver Wolf's heel. Although his movement had been slight, his head had turned toward the newcomers. There was a smile of triumph on his face.

Mother of God. These murderers knew the other Weres, Parker realized. The guys on the ground were waiting for those beasts to rescue them.

His thoughts split into new directions. Had these two men been sent to kill members of a rival group?

Were these two humans decoys sent to lure a few more wolves away from the Landau lair?

Could it be a planned attack? A kind of werewolf turf war? Wolf against wolf?

No time to think on it. Delmonico, the smallest of them all, moved. She grabbed one of the guns from the brown wolf's hand and backpedaled for tree cover. As soon as she had ducked beneath the shadows, the unmistakable sounds of her reverse transition filled the air. Really quickly. Five seconds, at most, and then a naked Delmonico appeared, crouched on one knee, with the gun aimed at the Weres in the distance. She fired off a warning shot, yelled, "Back off!"

The largest werewolf opposite them pounded his chest once with a fisted paw, in the same way Parker had seen the brown wolf now standing on the prone guy do, back at Fairview. Silver Wolf mocked the gesture.

Dana Delmonico shouted, "You know what's in these chambers, right? And what it can do?"

The Weres opposite were clearly agitated. The three kept changing positions, like a shuffled deck of cards, without moving any closer. Their teeth were bared, their ears back.

Sharp claws swiped at their own fleshy hides, producing stripe after stripe of maroon-colored blood nearly as dark as the night itself.

Perhaps they hadn't they been fleet enough to help their friends. Maybe they hadn't planned on encountering someone with Delmonico's lightning-swift reaction time. Whatever the case, two things about this situation became relevant to Parker.

One: the wolves next to him, including Delmonico, knew these others, in a bad way.

Two: it sure seemed possible, after Delmonico's brief discourse, that there truly could be silver bullets in those guns.

More truth to those legends, after all? An important detail for a werewolf to know.

Parker became aware of the fact that he was snarling under his breath, and that he was shifting his weight continually from foot to foot as if he might cut loose at any minute and run over there to confront those foreign Weres. The sheer intensity of the whiplash energy swirling through him made him acknowledge that he had chosen sides.

As if reading his mind, the rust-colored wolf next to him stepped closer with his teeth snapping together and his lips curled back. Was anyone here expecting those wolves to make a play? The intruders might fight with other Weres, but against the same guns already used that night to fell a couple of beasts? Was anybody that stupid?

A spasm of distaste pulled at Parker's mind. It took another few seconds to hear what Delmonico was saying.

"Toss a phone here!"

He glanced at her. They were all naked except for the guys on the ground. His own cell phone had been left behind in his locker, inside his jeans.

"The phone!" Delmonico again yelled. And this time

Parker got it. He stepped back, still eyeing the distant Weres, and crouched down. With one claw, he ripped the back pocket of the closest criminal, and out popped a cell. Giving the phone a good kick, he sent it sliding across the grass and right into Delmonico's free hand. He heard the trill of numbers connecting, and wondered if it was even possible to dial 911...given what they were.

"Park. East side. Two down, two g-b's underfoot, and a bunch of growling," Delmonico said into the phone. As if that sort of cryptic description would make sense.

Guess it did. Parker heard the sirens. Multiple sirens, closing in fast, as if they'd been on standby.

The Weres across from him heard them, too, and yowled in displeasure. In unison they broke from their huddle, running straight for Parker and the rest of his group with intention to do damage.

Parker and the rust wolf sprang forward to meet them, reacting on autopilot. The three Weres, in a wave, struck, smashing their big bodies into him and the rust wolf as if they had gone berserk.

Parker fought them off, fury making him mean. The rust wolf was a pro at fighting, and had to have seen this kind of action before, he noted peripherally, just before a claw belonging to the wolf who'd done the chest pounding raked a set of deep grooves into his right forearm.

Hissing through his teeth, Parker sent those teeth toward the wolf's swiveling neck and found a hold. With a sharp turn of his head, he tore a decent chunk out of the Were, who made an awful keening sound, half anger and half something akin to demonic possession.

Delmonico shouted, "I have these two," shifting her aim to the guys on the ground, releasing Silver Wolf and Big Brown from their duties. Silver Wolf came on like a fifty-ton truck, pushing in on Parker's action. The brown wolf did likewise. The attacking Weres didn't seem particularly happy to see reinforcements, and turned away.

Another howl split the night. A harrowing, haunted cry. Parker spat out the chunk of flesh in his mouth with disgust. His body rippled when he saw who had made the sound.

A ghostly pale werewolf stood in the distance, across the grass. There was no mistaking this guy. Parker's heart lurched.

The pale wolf was fully shifted this time, and menacing in his stillness. A nightmare come to life. But it wasn't his size that seemed so threatening; in fact, he didn't appear to be any larger than Parker or the rest of the silver wolf's pack. What made him stand out was the gathering of darkness around him. That darkness licked at his body in the same way that a man lapped the private place between his lover's thighs. Waves of hatred shot out from him, thickening the air.

Parker blinked, taken aback. When he opened his eyes, the ghostly apparition was gone.

A closer sound snapped Parker out of his stupor. He glanced sideways to see that the three invading wolves were running off, chased by Parker's pack mates.

Only then, when the silver wolf came back to stare down his long muzzle at them, and the sirens were loud enough to burst eardrums, did the two werewolf slayers on the ground start to whine.

Parker's hackles rose as the sound of doors opening in the distance reached him. Cops! He fired a glance to Delmonico, saw her nod her head. She would stay to see that the wolf slayers got what they deserved. She stood at the edge of the shadows with her legs splayed, naked as the day she was born.

His instinct was to run, and in doing so, keep his secrets and his medical degree. Then again, he really needed the answers he'd been seeking, now more than ever. If he left the pack now, would he be allowed back in?

The silver wolf barked at Delmonico, and after that to the others. Strangely enough, Parker understood that bark to mean "Go."

Swiftly, Silver Wolf stepped into the safety of the shadows. A single crack, as brief and innocuous as the sound of somebody cracking a knuckle, was the only hint that the mighty Were had changed back to his human guise. Nevertheless, there he stood, next to Delmonico—a tall, well-built man in his sixties, with angular European features punctuated by bright blue eyes, short-cropped silver hair and the regal bearing of a Viking.

Parker recognized him at once. Anyone in Miami would have. The silver wolf was none other than the Honorable Judge James Landau himself. The man who owned the secluded property behind those stone walls. The man that Miami law enforcement trusted to dish out justice, and good citizens trusted to uphold their rights, was a genetic mutant.

Unable to help himself, Parker looked toward the distant boulevard, wondering if the entire Miami justice system might draw its strength from the goddamn moon.

At least he was in good company.

He laughed at the unlikelihood of it all. Well, howled actually.

"Go," Judge Landau repeated. "Gather the rest. We'll take it from here."

With that, the judge hauled the two pathetic, murdering gangsters to their feet and ordered them to strip. They did, no questions asked. Landau was beyond formidable. So, Parker guessed, was the gun pointed at them.

Landau threw a T-shirt and a pair of jeans to Delmonico,

and each of them hastily dressed. They looked ridiculous, probably smelled even worse, but who was going to question such things, to their faces?

The brown wolf Parker had chased bumped him. *Time to go.* Leaving the scene, as they had been directed to do, Parker ran beside the two Weres he had fought beside this night, quiet now as they headed back the way they had come.

Back toward that genteel Southern house and its damned stone wall.

The room was a blur of white and red and black. A swirling, moving mass that kept Chloe sick to her stomach and barfing up bile that tasted of meds.

She felt trapped, isolated, angry. She'd lost the use of her fingers. Her hands were swaddled in tight white bandages that gave them the appearance of Q-tips.

Now and then a face appeared at the door. Sometimes Dr. James would bring in a needle. Chloe lost all sense of time, as well as the ability to speak, protest and even think clearly. In between the random moments of mental firepower resided a white fluffy haze of pain and blinking lights. Like being in Vegas on a bender.

There also was an image of a black fur coat. It covered her arms for a while, as inky as Parker Madison's hair, and caused Chloe to sweat. After each drenching, a fresh blue gown would arrive, and she'd be helped into it. She'd given up count at nine.

More blurring. More sickness. And then she saw a new face at the door. A man. *Not Parker. Not Jim.*

The man pressed his face against the window glass, closed his eyes, then entered her little white space. No features registered. He could have been anyone, but he held up a hand to show he would not harm her, and spoke to her in a tone reserved for calming feisty children. She went to him, felt another sharp pinch of a needle, which brought instant oblivion.

As if her life were attached to a fast-forward button, Chloe came to in what had to be a car, spread out on her back, on a leather seat. She smelled the hide, car wax and the faintly musty interior of the space. She smelled herself. She smelled emptiness on the seat beside her. No doctor sat there. Chloe was alone in the vehicle except for the man in the front seat, driving. He smelled like trouble.

All was dark outside the car. Through the window, from her position on her back, Chloe watched stars go quickly by. For that to happen, the driver had to have a heavy foot on the gas pedal.

More blurring. Those stars whipped by.

"Just a few more miles to go. We can make it," the man said over his shoulder, as if aware that she had woken. "Two more miles, max." He added in afterthought, "Timing is everything."

Chloe had no way of knowing what was going on, except to note, oddly enough, that the pain that had been jerking her around had lessened slightly. Somebody had removed her from the padded cell and from the hospital. The darkness inside and outside the car was a sudden blessing.

Until the vehicle changed direction and the moonlight reached her face.

Cold burn. Icy fire. Sudden numbness…and then her shaking started all over again, quickly reaching an intensity that rocked the seat.

They skidded to a stop. The driver tapped the horn twice, and was out of the car like a rocket. The door beside her opened. A sea of hands took hold of her, lifted her.

White light appeared, bright, focused, replaced by more

dimness. She'd been carried into a house smelling of lemon oil, old wood, aged carpets, cotton, pie crust and people.

No, not people, exactly.

Where had she been taken? What did they want from her? Had she gone insane in that hospital?

Her last thought this round, before the comforting smells faded and her synapses gave up, was to pray that whatever they wanted from her, there wouldn't be a cage involved.

Chapter 16

As a werewolf hitting his stride at a full run, Parker found that taking the stone wall was a breeze. All three of them were up and over it, and heading for the house. The stately mansion Parker had staked out was, at the moment, so much less of an enigma. A werewolf lived here. A werewolf with werewolf friends.

This was a place where nightmares, secret longings and plenty of wishful thinking came to a head, all rolled together in Parker's sigh of relief.

They ran right onto that wraparound porch. The door to the house opened and a tall, stately, gray-haired woman came out, one hand gripping the glossy string of pearls at her neck, the other waving them inside.

Parker nearly laughed again out of sheer disbelief. The image of a woman facing three big wolves with what amounted to open arms seemed so strange.

He followed the other wolves toward the door. About to cross the threshold, he jerked to a stop. This was like going to Grandma's house, where little Red Riding Hood might be waiting. These people expected him to follow. It had been years since he'd lost his family, and a long time since he'd allowed himself to get close to anyone.

Except *her*.

And now that his Jane Doe had reentered his mind, she filled it. He could almost feel her presence. He smelled citrus and flower petals in the air. These…people could help her, he reminded himself. He was in no shape to go and get her, not like this, but he'd get her as soon as he could manage.

The others were inside, already out of sight. Parker continued to hang back without knowing why, breathing heavily, as if he had run too fast and stopped too quickly. He rested his hand against the door frame, aware of the warm, welcoming glow just steps away. But who would the beasts in there turn out to be? Did he want to see their real faces?

He caressed the doorjamb, lost in thought, afraid to become Parker the man again. He tasted blood in his mouth— another werewolf's blood from his own savage bite. He wasn't sure if it was possible to tear at a throat one minute, then simply return to being a human the next, with no gray area in between to act as a buffer. He was cold, though the wooden door frame felt warm against his fingers. He was anxious, uneasy, and wiped his mouth on his arm.

Hell, he did smell flowers.

The gray-haired woman came back to stand in front of him, unafraid. Having no further urge to fight, Parker merely waited where he was while she looked him in the eyes, smiled and nodded her head. "Only vampires have to be asked in," she said in a light, lilting voice with no evidence of age in it.

Thrown off balance by her personal invitation and her tone,

Parker advanced a step, reluctant to check his worries at the door. She moved aside so that he could enter, and he did, but a wafting scent stopped him again in the foyer. He stood for a minute more with his eyes locked to a wide wooden staircase.

His gaze rose up those steps to settle on the man standing halfway up. He cradled a woman in his arms—a slight wildcat of a woman who twitched, kicked out and babbled nonsensical syllables.

She was blonde.

Parker felt shock; he felt rage. With the roof over his head blocking the moonlight, his body began its transition back to human.

He stood his ground. Stood tall. No doubling over, no panting as his body sucked itself inward. He didn't take his eyes from the woman in that other man's arms.

Reverse ordeal over, his bare, overheated flesh continued to ripple from the quickness of this change as he took the stairs two at a time, defied the man there with a steady gaze and reached for the girl curled up in his arms. "Mine," he said fiercely.

He met with no resistance when he took his she-wolf for himself. He groaned with relief when her softness settled against him.

He had found her. Here, of all places. Among the wolves.

Little Red Riding Hood was Jane Doe.

Her body went slack as he closed his arms around her. She'd been shivering with a major convulsion, but stilled completely when he whispered, "I'm here."

She opened her eyes—those green, heavy-lidded eyes that had bewitched him before. As they focused, and briefly cleared, she smiled. She reached for him, wrapped her arms around his neck, hid her damaged face against his chest.

God...

A light hand on his arm made Parker spin. He might have

unconsciously struck out at anyone else who dared disturb such a moment, but the gray-haired woman who had invited him inside stood there, wearing an expression of earnest concern.

"You know this woman?" she asked.

"Yes. No." The truth was so very complicated. "How did she get here?"

"A friend brought her a short time ago. He found her at a nearby hospital."

"Fairview," Parker said. "I…I left her there."

The woman scanned the foyer below, probably searching for the others who had arrived with him. Parker didn't care to look. He didn't want to move, savored the feel of the woman in his arms, shook off the urge to pound on his chest the way the other wolves had, to prove his ownership of what he held. Although he didn't know where he was or where to go from here, finding the little wolf was all that mattered.

"She needs help," the woman said to him in a gentle, unassuming tone.

"I'm not in any shape to do that," he confessed, heartened by the sympathy on the woman's face. "I hoped Fairview might protect her until I—"

The woman's pressure on his arm assured him that he needn't explain. "We can help her. That's why she was brought to us. Will you let us do that?"

"What will you do? Who are you?"

"I'm Sylvia Landau," she said quietly. "This is my home, and you are welcome in it. We call this estate The Sanctuary, because we protect our own here, including those falsely initiated."

"Falsely initiated? What does that mean?"

"Please," she said. "We need to take her now. The others are waiting for you. They can tell you what you need to know."

Parker's arms tightened around his she-wolf protectively. Her shaking was fainter now. But her breath rattled in her chest.

"If you want her to live," Sylvia Landau said, "you must let her go."

"Will she live?"

"There are no guarantees for the recipient of a bite. Nevertheless, we will do all we can, I assure you. We've seen this before."

"Your husband is the judge?" Parker's voice wasn't steady.

"Yes."

"Are you a—?"

"No."

Silver Wolf had a human wife, then.

"The gene runs in my husband's family," she explained, "and transfers from father to son."

Parker nodded his head gravely over that. It was a gene. A damned gene that caused the body such havoc. A gene or a bite. And since he hadn't been bitten, it seemed he was a genetic mutant, after all.

"I'll take her where she needs to go," he said. "If you'll lead the way."

Sylvia moved past him on the stairs, signaling with one hand for the man who had been carrying the girl to follow— a large man, wide-shouldered, immensely strong, shirtless, with rusty hair curtaining a face too mature for its age. The face of a soldier who had seen battle and been too close to the fray. This was the rust wolf, Parker instinctively knew. The fighter.

He nodded when Parker knowingly glanced his way.

"How many—" Parker began, cutting himself off in order to absorb his she-wolf's shudder. Loosening his taut chest muscles, he recalled what had passed between them the last time he'd held her.

"How many wolfmen are there?" he finally said.

"In the world?" Sylvia Landau asked. "Or just Miami?"

"Jesus," Parker whispered. "As many as that?"

If he had expected a medieval-dungeon type of environment in the room he entered, Parker couldn't have been more wrong. No shackles or iron bands furnished this place. It was merely a bedroom, high up in the house, painted a light green and containing a bed, a chair and not much else.

The room had two windows. Heavy blinds on them erased all hints of moonlight from the other side of the glass. There were, Parker noted with dread, finely wrought metal bars behind the shades.

Following Sylvia Landau's direction, he laid his she-wolf on sheets that were feminine floral pinks and yellows, and smelled of fresh air.

Werewolves on the floor below, and springtime upstairs— as if to negate that monsters could exist on an upper floor, so close to the moon.

Sylvia Landau waved him back from the bed once he had released the young woman. He didn't want to do what she asked, and he sent her a look of stern reproval.

"It would be best for her if you left her," Sylvia said. "Being near a wolf in her state will prolong the pain and slow the process."

"Being near me?" Parker queried, already knowing that what she said was the truth. His Jane Doe had mimicked him, trying to follow his lead.

"She will react to any wolf, but especially a male. Mating instincts are strong among you. Your presence would draw her out before she's ready."

Yes. Hadn't she clung to him, opened for him, with her own brand of desperation?

"It's obvious the two of you have imprinted," Sylvia Landau said. "Which makes your presence doubly difficult for her."

"Imprinted? What the hell is that?"

"A physical phenomenon that links you together. An unbreakable bond."

Parker closed his eyes briefly. How had that happened, when he barely knew her?

"*When* a bite occurs is extremely important to someone without the Lycan gene," she said. "If bitten after the moon's full phase, the recipient has a month to begin to adapt. If the bite occurs close to a night when the moon is full, or on the night of a full moon, those changes begin too soon, too quickly, too strongly."

"Then she was bitten," Parker said.

"Oh, yes."

"I wasn't."

"No. You are different. I can see it in your face, and in your eyes. Yet your Blackout wasn't much fun, was it?"

"Blackout?" For Parker, the very word had a bad taste.

"Blackout is what we call the start of a body's rewiring process. The time when the wolf blood kicks in and all hell breaks loose at a cellular level. You do remember that?"

"Yes. God, yes." He had thought he would die. Parker looked at the girl on the bed, the memory of the experience like a jolt to his mind. "Will she make it?" he asked, sorry for what she'd be put through. Needing her to live.

Was that all part of the *imprinting* business?

"Maybe," Sylvia Landau answered truthfully, and although Parker wanted to protest, he knew this outcome lay beyond his medical skills. "She might."

"Blood transfusion?" he suggested, groping.

"Too late. Seconds after a savage bite, it's already too late."

Parker ran a hand through his hair helplessly. The phrase "savage bite" echoed hollowly in his ears. If he had gotten to her earlier, she might have been spared.

"She's stronger than she looks," he said. "She's a fighter."

"That's good news."

"What will you do?"

"Keep watch. Keep her comfortable. Give her herbs for the pain."

"Medicine?"

"Secret remedies handed down from family to family."

"You have done this before," Parker said.

Her unflinching smile was her reply.

"What about that thing out there?" He waved toward the window.

"We open the blinds a little at a time once she's well into the Blackout. It's the best way to get new wolves acclimated."

Acclimated.

His she-wolf was still a woman. And alluring. She no longer wore the hospital's bathrobe. The folks at Fairview had dressed her in a fresh hospital gown, blue, and put soft slippers on her feet. She rolled from side to side on the floral spread now that he'd been separated from her, slamming her splinted wrist against the mattress. Her hair was damp with perspiration and stuck to the bandaged side of her face. Fresh bandages. Fairview had done a few things right. And yet— he wished he could take some of the pain from her and give her a rest. He wished he could spare her this terrible trial by fire.

An unbreakable bond. Unless she didn't make it.

"She must go through this, and on her own," Sylvia Landau explained. "No one can take this from her. Even you. What we can do is watch over her, see that she comes to no further harm."

It all made a certain crazy kind of sense to Parker now.

Remaining here by her side, refusing to leave her, would be a selfish act.

The big man, still in the room, eased up beside him with body language that spoke volumes. Whether or not Parker knew her, and whatever their relationship was, he had to leave her now.

The rust wolf also tossed him a pair of pants and a white shirt he had taken from the closet near the chair, only then reminding Parker of his nakedness.

He slipped his arms into the sleeves, certain that if Sylvia Landau housed a pack of Weres, she had probably seen it all many times before, but glad of the distraction. The shirt was snug, soft, and it covered his private parts well enough. Without taking time to fool with the buttons, Parker leaned over the bed, over his sick little wolf. He kissed her wounded forehead, then kissed her mouth without lingering, a feather-light touch, waiting for her to open her eyes, hoping she would, hoping she wouldn't, and realizing again that any kind of prolonged closeness could hurt her.

Speaking to her gently, he repeated words from their first meeting that he prayed she would somehow recognize as the truth.

"Hang on. I'll be back," he said. "I promise."

Attentive to Sylvia Landau's tap on his shoulder, Parker reluctantly went to the door. Pausing with his hand on the knob, he said to the silver wolf's wife, "Keep her alive. For me. Please."

Chapter 17

Four men waited in the room off the foyer. Fortunately, they didn't speak until Parker had climbed into his pants—another pair of well-worn jeans that didn't fit too badly.

Settled a bit on the outside, though he felt numb beneath, Parker faced these werewolves in their everyday shapes, reconciling where he was and wondering what would happen next.

"What did you do with the two dead men?" he asked. It wasn't quite the requisite icebreaker, but it was the best he could manage.

"Who are you?" The question came from the man nearest the shuttered windows, whose lined, sober face placed his age in the forties. His hair was a mild chestnut-brown and shorn to a buzz cut. Exceptionally broad shoulders stretched at the seams of his striped cotton shirt.

Not the brown wolf, Parker's intuition told him. But all of

these wolfmen were in incredible shape, and they looked fairly normal with their clothes on.

"Name's Parker," he said. "Are we going to have to get all the pleasantries out of the way before you answer my question?"

"They've been taken away," a voice close to him said. "Their families have already been notified."

Families. Parker hadn't thought that far ahead. He didn't want to think about it now.

The man who had given him that piece of information was young, strapping, with an energy that made the room hum. He wore his dark blond, shaggy hair long, to his shoulders. Sorrow surrounded his eyes like dark circles.

"They were friends of yours?" Parker queried.

"Close friends," the man by the shutters replied.

"I'm sorry," Parker murmured.

"So are we," the older man remarked, staring out of the window.

Parker had waited for this—communing with creatures similar to himself. For eight long months the possibility of doing just this had headed his list. Now that he had found a houseful of them, he dreaded asking for help. They were mourning the loss of their friends. Two were down, and two more of their pack were still missing—Delmonico and the judge. Asking these men to shed light on the whole werewolf phenomenon, how it worked, how it had come to be in the first place, would have been a grave imposition.

"What will the authorities say when the murdering bastards talk?" Parker asked instead.

"Talk about what?" the young wolf countered.

A stroke of uneasiness jabbed at Parker, which the man by the window must have noticed.

"The murderers will say nothing," he clarified. "It isn't in their best interest to talk. They won't fear prison half as much as what would be waiting for them on the outside if they did."

Parker spoke up. "Are you vigilantes, then?"

"No," a third man replied—medium height, long red hair, cleft in his chin. "Nothing like that. We'd like to be left alone, as a matter of fact. But things have gotten out of control lately, and ignoring what's going on around here is no longer an option."

"Meaning the escalating violence in the park?" Parker recalled Detective Wilson's all too brief explanation about that, and Delmonico's fill-in about the recent deaths out there. "Does that streak of violence tie in with these gunslingers and the wolves who attacked us tonight?"

"All caused by the same pack," the man by the window replied, his disgust audible. "The police cleaned them out recently, but a few of the worst offenders got away, including that crazy son of a bitch alpha."

"That alpha has already gathered new troops, mostly street gangs always up for a turf war if there's money to be made," the young man added.

"Why?" Parker felt ignorant. "Why would they go after the men by the wall? Didn't they know what they—*we*—are?"

"It was a hit," the young wolf replied. "A warning for the judge and the rest of us to stay out of their business."

"What business would that be?" Parker wasn't catching up fast enough. He felt as if time had slowed to a standstill. He wanted to head back up those stairs and stretch out on the bed, beside *her,* keep her safe. He'd been on the right track in thinking the Landaus drew darkness to them. If he'd been lured to the wall around this place, why not somebody else with his or her own agenda?

"They dealt in drugs at first," the young wolf explained, pacing the room like a caged animal. "But the bastard has added kidnapping, torture and murder to his short list. He doesn't take kindly to people trying to disrupt his illegal operations. He has enough money to bribe half of Miami in order to keep himself out of prison."

"But why," Parker asked, "would one wolf want to kill another?"

The man by the window took that one, sounding surprised it had even come up. "Wolves don't kill each other, as a rule. We have a healthy respect for territory. We try to lead normal lives within those parameters, and keep a low profile. But in came one insane son of a bitch to change the rules."

"There was more than one wolf out there," Parker pointed out.

"That filthy alpha has created them all, made them into what they are—Frankenstein versions of Lycans. He creates them and then tortures them in unspeakable ways until they fall all over themselves to please him and stay alive."

"He creates them?" Parker noticed his drop in tone. "How?"

"He bites," the young wolf said. Parker wanted to grab him by the shirt and sit him down in a chair. The kid's agitation was making it hard for Parker to think.

"And when they are ready to turn," the young wolf continued, "and in the middle of their rebirth phase, he tosses them into a ring. It's no fight ring that bastard runs, it's a *bite* club. His own wicked version. Wolf pitted against wolf, drugged up against the pain of their first transition, crazed, and expected to fight to the death. The winner lives to serve his master."

"And sometimes," the red-haired wolf added, with an echo of madness in his own tone, "he throws a man into the ring with them. For fun."

Parker bit back his horror over the idea of such an atrocity. A man wouldn't stand a chance against one crazed, tortured werewolf, let alone two, or a warehouse full. It would be murder in its most abysmal sense.

Nothing Parker might say would do justice to the information he'd just garnered. Hearing about those things had brought the darkness closer. He had an urge to button his shirt to keep that darkness away from his skin.

"I thought I might be the only one," he confessed, running his hand through his hair. "The only man-wolf hybrid."

"How wrong you were," a voice remarked from the doorway.

Sick to death of surprises, Parker spun around with his hand still raised. His eyes widened. He felt his brow crease as Detective Wilson strode into the room.

But Wilson's face belied his benign exterior. His formerly passive cop expression was tight. He wore a black T-shirt that showed off his honed physique. "I just found out," he said to the men gathered. Addressing Parker directly, he asked, "You were there?"

"Yes." Wilson hadn't asked what *form* he'd been in at the time.

"Who else?" Wilson said to the others.

Those men looked at Parker.

"I guess," Wilson said, "they'll want to know who you are before disclosing anything more dealing with their privacy."

"Understandable," he agreed, his surprise over seeing the detective wearing off. Wilson was a homicide detective and Landau a judge, so maybe the two had frequent run-ins.

"I can leave the room so you can talk freely, but I won't leave this house," Parker said.

Wilson's expression registered puzzlement.

"She's here," Parker explained. "I won't leave her again."

The detective's brow furrowed. Seconds later, the truth dawned on him. "*She's* your Jane Doe, Madison? Bless her, I thought she looked familiar, but had no real way to gauge who she was."

How the hell did Wilson have any idea what he was talking

about? Parker wondered. How had the detective possibly
made that leap from the patient at Metro to a patient in Sylvia
Landau's care? The girl had been half-covered with bandages,
her features hidden. In order to match that bandaged form to
the one upstairs, Wilson would have had to have seen her
arrive here. But how had she gotten here?

"Jenna," Wilson said seriously over his shoulder, just as
Parker was about to ask that very question. "You're good at
math. What are the odds?"

Jenna? Parker's eyes traveled down Wilson's body to his
right hand, which was, he saw now, interlaced with a set of
paler fingers. With his hopes of making sense out of any of the
evening's events dashed, Parker waited for the woman whose
hand Wilson held so possessively to emerge from behind him.
And when she did, Parker glanced from the woman to Wilson
to the group of gathered werewolves and back to the
woman…and felt like laughing. Because the world and everything in it had turned upside down. Or maybe inside out.

The woman by Wilson's side was, of course, familiar—a
stunning, stately beauty with ivory skin and a flurry of tousled
auburn hair, Jenna James.

Parker's mind went into overdrive. He recounted events
leading up to this moment, his mind jumping from one thing
to another as if he were seeing his life flash before his eyes.

Officer Delmonico was a dark-pelted wolf with an experienced trigger finger. Judge Landau, an alpha in every sense
of the word as Parker understood it, owned a wolf sanctuary. Detective Wilson was in the loop with all of this, and
known to all of the wolves in this room. His presence here
suggested he might be helping Landau and these wolves in
some way. There was a distinct possibility that Wilson had
been on the other end of the phone call Delmonico had made
from the park.

So, if Wilson knew about werewolves, it was likely he also knew about the drug-running, the bite clubs and the rogue Weres who bit people, not only in order to populate a pack, but for a maniac's entertainment.

Wilson might in fact be a major player in the hunt for this criminal alpha freak.

"Jenna," Wilson said, his face back to immovable steel, "meet Daniel, Max, Marcus, Brian...and Parker."

Jenna's eyes glowed in the foyer light—bright eyes flecked with amber and cloudy with the aftereffects of sex. If nothing else in the world made sense at the moment, how about the fact that Jenna and Wilson were a couple? And Wilson, Parker realized in that instant, couldn't have taken Delmonico's call for backup, because while some of this assembled group had been chasing killers, Wilson and Jenna had engaged in a tryst.

Lucky Wilson.

Whether he liked it or not, Parker's own repressed libido responded to the thought of sex with a stiff rise that would have been plenty embarrassing had he not been given the jeans. He tore his gaze from the velvety-smooth planes of Jenna's face, and jerked his attention back to the stairs, able to feel *her* up there. Able to feel the wolf in her by way of the strange connection they had. *Imprinting*.

He would have torn the place apart to get to her if the woman with her hadn't been the soft-spoken, entirely human Sylvia Landau. He considered doing so anyway.

"You're *her* Parker," Jenna said, her voice deep, sexy and serious. "Parker Madison."

His heart was hammering for no apparent reason at all that he knew of, outside of the conglomeration of really irregular events. But his instincts, bombarded as they were by all this new information, told him suddenly to get up those stairs. His instinct shouted *protect her.*

He looked back at the gathered faces. Nobody had moved. No one was after the little she-wolf up there. Probably nobody cared, unless Jenna James blamed him for leaving her at Fairview in the first place.

Another hand rested on his arm with an empathetic touch, but he jumped just the same.

"Matt brought her here," Jenna told him, as if either she knew what he was thinking or could read his face. "I wondered about the signs, but didn't know for sure until I saw him with her, and how he handled her. I'd never come across a she-wolf. My fear was of being unable to manage what she was going through at Fairview, if that's what she was to become."

A sudden disturbance caught his attention and he whirled toward the door. Everyone else in the room had done the same thing. The hair at the nape of his neck bristled. He growled low in his chest, a sound echoed by every one of the present members of Judge Landau's pack.

The scent of blood drifting through the open doorway was heavy, strong, close. Before Parker knew it, he found himself one of four heading for the yard.

The young man he'd spoken with inside was the first to shift shape, tugging his T-shirt over his head and tossing it to the lawn. The man who had stood by the windows followed, not bothering to remove any clothes. The red-haired fellow stopped just short of the steps, his weight a solid barrier keeping Parker from reaching moonlight. Wilson brought up the rear.

The moon was huge and full, hovering in the sky like an alien spaceship too close to the earth and blotting out most of the stars. Her light cut a wide swath across lawn and flagstone driveway, turning the shiny hoods of two parked cars into mirrors.

Not a sound could bc heard.

The Weres on the lawn were as motionless as statues. It was an odd sensation for Parker to be standing on the porch, among the others, wondering about that damned scent of blood.

"Human," the man blocking Parker announced, his muscles visibly dancing.

"Male," Parker added, having no idea what made him think so, but knowing this for a fact.

"It's unacceptable," the red-haired man stated. "And it's a trap."

"No," Wilson corrected, his voice low, his eyes thoughtful. "It's a challenge."

Parker searched the dark, muttered, "Fill me in."

"Chavez." When Wilson whispered the name, his mouth twisted with such disgust that Parker felt another chill slip down his back. He had heard that name only once, yet hadn't forgotten the tightness that had appeared in Dana Delmonico's shoulders when she'd mouthed it at the hospital. Chavez, the man who had gotten away in the raid on his warehouse. The criminal wanted for an undercover detective's murder, among other atrocities.

"Rogue wolves *and* a crazy criminal mastermind, all at once?" Parker said. "Isn't that a bit much, even for a judge to have to handle?"

Wilson faced him with anger in his eyes. "Not *and,* Doctor. One and the same."

Parker examined the two motionless Weres on the lawn, then transferred his attention to the wall beyond the driveway. "What does Chavez want?"

"Miami," Wilson answered.

"What is he willing to do to get it?" Jenna James asked, stepping out from doorway.

"Anything," the rust wolf replied.

"And that includes killing every other Were in the city so there will be no one left with the strength to stop him," Wilson said. "Starting at the top."

"Every *other* Were?" Parker got hung up on that particular word. "Oh," he almost shouted, as enlightenment finally arrived. "Oh, shit." He again glanced to the wall, thinking that *dark* didn't begin to describe the vibe it had taken on in the last two minutes. "Chavez is the crazy werewolf," he said. *One and the same.* "And Judge Landau is…"

"The top of the food chain," Wilson finished.

"And in Chavez's way," the red-haired wolf added.

The sound of the red-haired wolf shifting shape next to Parker was like bottled danger suddenly uncorked, and happened so quickly he did a double take.

"How recently was that warehouse where the fights took place cleaned out?" Jenna asked.

"A month ago," Wilson said.

"If a lot of those Weres were destroyed, how could Chavez repopulate his pack in that amount of time? Is this the first full moon since the raid?" Jenna queried.

"The raid happened during a full phase, so yes, this would be the first full," Wilson stated.

"Then the wolves he has are the ones who escaped with him," Jenna reasoned. "Plus the shooters he seems to have acquired, like the two guys caught tonight."

"Along those lines," Parker said, "just how many cops and detectives know about…us? The call Delmonico sent out was fairly cryptic. I believe she mentioned the word *growling*."

Wilson nodded. "She called Scott."

"Who the hell is Scott?" Parker snapped, tired of playing catch-up.

"Adam Scott," he elaborated, "is an officer of the law and

recent inductee to the clan. Scott has a personal interest in Chavez and has been searching that park for signs of him for the last two weeks."

"How personal?" Parker had to ask.

Wilson sighed in obvious frustration over the answer he was about to give. "Scott," he said, dragging out a beat of time before continuing, "has had the pleasure of being a participant in Chavez's bite club."

"You said 'inductee,'" Parker pointed out, shaking off the image that arrived with this last piece of news.

"Adam Scott was torn to shreds in that underground torturefest, and would have died, but for that raid and the woman who provided the whereabouts on how to get there. She saved him by—"

"Offering just one more bite?" Jenna said, filling in that sentence as much for Parker as for herself. "The woman who pointed the way to Chavez was a wolf?"

Wilson nodded.

"So that makes two Were cops on the force," Parker said. "Delmonico and Adam Scott. Right?"

Gazing out at the night, Wilson said softly, "More or less."

Chapter 18

Enough was enough.

Chloe opened her eyes, checked out her surroundings, took a moment to try to recall where she was, and couldn't.

A face swam in her memory, and it wasn't the face of the woman sitting in a chair beside the bed that Chloe found herself stretched out on. She remembered something about a car, stars flying by and seeing the man with the serious face again. She saw glimpses of a white room and a padded cot, heard the echo of a ticking clock and felt ghostlike pricks of needles.

"Am I possessed?" she demanded.

The question surprised the woman, who immediately turned her way.

"Why can't I stop shaking? What's happening to me?"

"I might ask the same question," the woman answered in a mild, pleasant voice. "Do you know where you are?"

"Hell?"

"You're in my home. You were brought here so that we could help you."

"Those doctors couldn't help?"

"What's wrong with you wasn't in their realm of expertise, I'm afraid."

"So I am possessed?"

"Yes, in a way. But not how you're imagining."

"Then why do you look so stunned?"

"I'm surprised because you're talking, and coherently, when by all rights you shouldn't be." The woman leaned closer. "You've been ill. We didn't expect you to be better for a long time yet. How do you feel?"

"I don't know." Chloe waited to estimate the level of the pain she'd been fighting, but didn't feel anything. She moved her fingers, her head, and felt a dull, lingering soreness in her neck. "You took away the pain?"

"The herbs helped with that. But not enough, surely, to—" Instead of finishing that statement, the woman said, "I'd like to open the window shade."

"Is it still night?" Chloe asked.

"Close to midnight."

"How long have I been here? A week? A month?"

"You've been here an hour."

An hour? Chloe put a shaky hand to her forehead, felt the outlines of the bandage. "My face doesn't hurt. Neither does my head or ribs. I can breathe."

"You remember about all that?"

"I doubt if I'll ever forget it."

"Then you remember how you got the wound on your arm?"

Chloe didn't want to see the monster that had caused that wound, but his face came hurtling back, called to mind by the woman's question. Dark face. Milky-white hair. The dreadful black, bottomless eyes. She heard an echo of the sound of her wrist breaking in his grasp, felt his breath on her bare skin as he slid his wet mouth down from her shoulder to the softer part of her upper arm.

The memory forced Chloe upright. The room spun around just once as she heard the shade being drawn, and then light—fierce and cool—streamed in through the window.

She gasped as the light hit her bare legs, her arms, her face. She opened her mouth to unleash the sound choking her. Her skin turned black, then white again, then black as her body seemed to stretch beyond itself. Awful noises accompanied the changes. Wet sounds. Grinding sounds. Ready to scream, she looked desperately to the woman beside her, who promptly closed the shade.

As the light receded, Chloe fell back to the mattress, felt herself suck inward with a quickness that left her reeling. After several moments, her breathing evened out. Her nausea disappeared, leaving her feeling lighter, almost shockingly euphoric.

"It's going to be all right now," the woman told her in a hushed voice that seemed very loud in the confines of the room. "Can you tell me your name?"

"Chloe." She barely got that out, sure that the air carried a foreign scent she couldn't place. Sensing a distant vibration, she looked to the window, certain that a voice out there was calling to her.

"Chloe, can you tell me if you have ever been bitten before?" the woman asked, whispering now.

Bitten? Yes, that's what had happened to her in the park. That was the horrendous part of her beating she had chosen to block out. The monster had chomped on her arm, taken a bite. He'd pulled away her flesh and some of the muscle, leaving his mouth a bloody mess. She'd been so scared, fearful she wouldn't make it if she retained that image. Her brain had complied by providing a blackness, a void where that event could be hidden, at least for a while.

"Think back further," the woman suggested, "to anything significantly like a bite?"

"Rattlesnake," Chloe said. "I was bitten by a rattler when I was thirteen."

The woman nodded her head, as if something had just made sense to her. "And you survived that bite, too. Maybe that's it, the key to your body's quick adaptation. Venom, and the effects it produced."

She'd come close to dying that time, too, Chloe recalled. Two bites, two near fatalities. Two too many, for sure. But she wasn't at all clear about what the woman was suggesting.

"The desert makes you strong." Chloe repeated her mantra. "What's the voice out there?"

"The moon."

"The moon has a voice?"

"Oh, yes. For those who can hear it."

Chloe glanced at her wrist, no longer in its bandage. "This should still be hurting."

"From now on you'll heal very fast," the woman said. "Supernaturally fast. The creature who hurt you in the park carried an ancient virus in his saliva, and infected you."

And there it was. The answer. The reason for the tremors, the sickness, the hallucinations and the rolling blackouts. Not just superficial wounds and stitched-up holes had caused her reactions, but a damned, freaking virus.

"This virus's effects are ruled by the moon," the woman explained. "By a full moon in particular."

Chloe felt light-headed as those words sunk in. Behind them appeared a face she wanted to see, curtained by straight black hair, the color of midnight. She could smell this man's scent, feel the taut contours of his muscles, remember the words Parker Madison had whispered to her.

Can't let one drop of moonlight reach her.

She delved further back, groping, her head starting to spin.

I don't know about the werewolf part. I don't understand how the wolf thing came about. That's why I'm out here tonight, looking for answers.... Problem is, I've started to like the changes. At the same time, I have to wonder how much longer I'll be able to keep the old me together.

And—

The night the changes began I was sure I was dying of some lethal disease. Excruciating, debilitating, draining.

Oh. No. Hell, no. God, no.

"Are you telling me that I'm a...werewolf?"

"Welcome to The Sanctuary," the woman replied.

The three Weres on the lawn issued a series of snarls just loud enough for Parker to hear. Warning sounds. Threatening. Everyone on the porch froze.

"They're here," Parker said. The scent of wolves out there beyond the wall was strong enough to make the smell of blood seem subdued by comparison. There were several wolves, he figured.

"Let's hope so," Wilson replied.

Parker faced the detective. "What did you say?"

"Let's hope *all* of them are here, in full force. Every single one."

"Dammit, Wilson," Parker muttered. "Were you expecting this?"

"Sooner or later. What else could Chavez do when we've been closing in, narrowing his territory night after night, making sure not too many of his guys get out or back in? His warehouse was destroyed, as was most of his pack. His kingpin days are over. He is wanted by every law enforcement agency in this city, and by us. He can't go to prison because even Chavez fears what might happen to him there when those folks find out he's a freak." Wilson shook his head. "He was a fool to stay in the area. And his lapse is our gain."

"What? You'll call the cops out here to help fight them off? How can cops handle fully morphed werewolves? How do they even know about that?"

"Only a few cops and officials are going to lead the parade," Wilson explained. "These rogue bastards killed one of our own, among scores of others. We don't take losing one of our guys lightly, or anyone else for that matter."

"So why didn't Chavez leave the city, if he realized it might come to this?"

"Only two reasons that I can think of," Wilson replied.

"The term *criminally insane* comes to mind," the rust-haired fighter interjected.

"And those two reasons might be?" Parker pressed.

"Revenge," Jenna James answered, as if she had been asked that question. "Revenge often drives the unbalanced mind when reason fails. That or…"

Everyone on the porch waited eagerly for her to finish her statement, Parker included.

"Love," she finally said.

Now she had his full attention.

"The sick bastard might be doing all of this for love?" the rust wolf said disbelievingly.

"No," Jenna clarified. "Revenge would be the larger goal, since he is here and pressing his presence. I'm just saying that men, and not only those we've categorized as insane, have been known to do a lot of strange things in the name of love."

As if Parker didn't already know that.

But he hadn't done those things out of love for the little she-wolf. He had wanted to help her, felt protective of her after seeing the damage she'd sustained. She was to become a wolf, in a time when he hadn't known there were many others.

Was that so? his mind nagged at him. And what about the feelings of possessiveness? The attraction that had him spending the night in her hospital room? What about the stabbing feelings of loss he had experienced when she'd disappeared? The bliss of finding her again? The erotic kiss? The hunger for what lay between her legs? What about the feel of her soul pulling against his? How about when she had climbed up the front side of his body, virtually nailing him to the spot?

The word *love* loomed large in his mind now. So much so that he whipped around to face the open door. With rogue wolves licking at their heels on the other side of that wall, and the real reasons for their presence eluding him, Parker wanted nothing more in that moment than to get to *her*. His Jane Doe.

He took a step toward the doorway, paused when the young morphed Were on the lawn snarled again. Parker sensed the density of the wolves now, near the wall, waiting. Everyone else here sensed them, too. How many rogue Weres were out there? How nasty had their master made them? Would the elusive Chavez lead his pack against Landau's home when Landau wasn't here to protect it?

Had those two shooters tonight been decoys, after all, to get Landau away? Had this all been a trap, as had been suggested? A wolf trap?

There were three Weres on Landau's lawn, fighting ready. Their pelted bodies were picking up scents and clues with each and every fiber that made them what they were.

Parker went over his count. With himself, the tally of

wolves this side of the wall equaled five. On top of that, there was a detective who probably had a gun stashed somewhere, and a shrink who could fell a man with her smile. But these rogues weren't men at the moment. And Jenna wasn't smiling.

Inhaling the night, Parker centered himself and cast his senses outward. *Ten.* His inner radar perceived ten Weres in the area. Maybe a few humans with weapons, too. All in all, a lethal enough dose of anger to exact some serious revenge.

While here at The Sanctuary there were women to protect.

Cracking his thick neck with a sudden twist, the rust wolf hit the second step, shedding his shirt. By time he had reached the fifth, he looked about as lethal as anything the rogues could have thrown at them.

Sensing something in the wind again, feeling that draw on his soul, Parker threw a quick glance to the open doorway. *She* was calling him, and he couldn't desert his post. *She* was moving, and he feared it would be toward him. Was she hurting? Crying out for help? Needing to be calmed?

No! He sent the message to her with as much force as he could muster, hoping the connection they shared would make her heed his warning. *Wait!*

But she wouldn't wait, he knew. Not this woman. Not for anybody. The feistiness with which she had clung to life and to him were examples of the tenacity of her will.

How he wanted her, lusted for her. Did that mean he loved her?

The purr of a sports car's engine spun him around. The car was coming fast, had to have clocked eighty miles per hour on the long stretch of driveway, but it eased to a stop in front of them. The driver-side door of a red Porsche flew open, and a man jumped out. Without bothering to close the door, he lunged for the stairs, making it in two strides.

This guy looked like another damned Viking—tall, built, angular-featured and fair-skinned. His clothes reeked of a bulging bank account, and his long, light blond hair was gathered in a band at the base of his neck. He was handsome, but able to pull off a ruggedness suggesting he might be more than he seemed. The set of his features hinted that this was a man to be reckoned with, and a Landau, no doubt about it whatsoever.

This guy had to have been werewolf for a very long time. Perhaps the longer a man spent sharing his body with a beast, the more virulent his presence became.

"Are we ready?" he asked simply.

So, he was here for the inevitable fight? Parker leaned against the door frame, awaiting the answer to that question.

"Dylan," Wilson acknowledged. "Glad you made it. Yep, we're in place. What about the judge?"

"Got the two assholes booked."

Dylan Landau, Parker acknowledged. Judge Landau's son. Miami's deputy D.A.

"What about Dana?" Wilson asked Landau.

"She's with my father. Where's Scott?"

"He's out there. And Tory?"

"In the car."

Somebody named Tory was in the car. Parker checked out the Porsche, unable to see past the tinted windows.

"Any minute now, he'll come knocking," Wilson stated.

"I'm sure he thinks his ruse did the trick," Landau agreed.

"But we lost two good friends," Wilson said.

Landau nodded. "Too many fine people have fallen to this creep. Time to take him out." He caught sight of Parker in the doorway. "And you?" he said, with the voice of a damn good D.A. cross-examining a witness on the stand.

"Parker," Wilson answered for him. "Friend of mine."

Landau nodded his acceptance, cocked his head, sniffed the air. "New female?"

Jeez, these guys were like homing devices. Parker spread his legs to fill the doorway and stood his ground. Then he felt a pull on him so strong, so complete, that he forgot Landau and the others, knowing on some sublevel of consciousness what it had to be, damn her little werewolf hide.

Slowly, he turned. And there she was. Incredibly, unimaginably, his towheaded patient stood on a step halfway down the Landaus' grand staircase. She wore a man's baggy shirt that partially covered her bare, lean, shapely thighs. Her blond hair was slicked back from her face, where her wounds, unbandaged now, stood out lividly against her porcelain skin like slashes of red lipstick. She wasn't shaking. Her green eyes were blazing.

In spite of everything going on, and what the night would bring, Parker wanted to run up those stairs to meet her. He wanted to do all those things to her, with her, that he'd been dreaming of.

But timing truly was everything.

Chapter 19

Chloe gripped the railing as if her hold on the wood might be the only thing keeping her tethered to the earth.

A tingling sensation floated along the surface of her skin, nourished by the heat she felt from Parker's nearness. As her eyes met with his, past feelings of hopelessness over the parts of her life she had lost were quickly replaced by something bigger, better, brilliant, and as hard as steel.

Her sickness had gone. She was relatively pain-free. "Transition" was the term for this state that Sylvia Landau had described in detail. First came the trauma, the bite, the virus exchange. Then the sickness and resistance of a body trying to adjust to the invading pathogen. Chloe had been lucky, and had made it through this illness. Sylvia had told her that only a small percentage of the people who entered the transitional phase ever made it out. Blackout, the process was called. A sort of werewolf test to ensure the survival of the fittest. And her own transition had been unusual. Highly irregular.

Unlike Parker, she wasn't a genetic Were, those whose blood was ancient and whose powers were tenfold what hers would ever be. But she was close enough. The fact foremost in her mind now was that Parker had been telling her the truth all along.

Her pulse beat against her skin, now ravenously hot. She was almost completely healed, and pretty damned invincible.

Scared, and invincible.

She couldn't publish the results of her research on that female cop's anomaly when she was now just such an anomaly herself. Maybe more so. She was a blonde with a jet-black pelt. Another irregularity.

Color change, Sylvia Landau had explained, was sometimes due to the force and extent of the trauma one experienced in becoming a wolf. And sometimes pelt color just had to do with feelings. *Feelings.* Like the ones she had for the black-haired man in the doorway. *Hunger.* For him—the man gazing at her with a hint of danger darkening his stunned face.

"Chloe," she said to him, knowing he would hear and understand. Just that.

Only this one particular sound that split the night could have torn Parker's attention from the woman on the stairs. He'd heard it before. Now, as then, it brought a chill.

"It's the pale wolf," he said, spinning back to the others on the porch with his heart racing. Her name was Chloe, and the rogue wolves were at the doorstep. Landau's Sanctuary had to be protected at all costs. *She* had to be protected.

"Yes," Dylan Landau whispered. "Chavez sets his trap."

"You know this wolf?" Parker asked.

"He," Landau replied, with the tone of an unspoken oath, "bit Dana."

"Good God," Parker muttered. The pale-pelted bastard had bitten two women—Delmonico and Chloe. Parker had been out there in the park with Delmonico, had seen her run, roll and expertly position the gun in her hand. If she had been bitten by this bastard, what chance had Chloe had against him?

A second harrowing howl came right after the first. But this one didn't originate on the far side of the wall. It came from inside the house.

Parker felt a rush of energy course through him, leaving live trails of flickering fire. His body stiffened in reaction, getting hard in all the right places, at the wrong time.

Jenna James pushed past him while he stood there straddling the line between fantasy and reality, movement and stillness. Jenna headed for the stairs. But so quickly he didn't have time to blink, a fevered, half-naked body tore past him and Jenna, heading out into the night.

Chloe.

She hit the porch steps like a woman possessed, before anyone had time to even consider stopping her. Hands fisted, hair flying, she leaped to the driveway, landed in a crouch, then sprang back up, legs splayed.

The muscles of her torso rippled dramatically beneath the oversize shirt. She flung her head back as if to confront the moon straight on, parted the swollen lips that Parker had greedily tasted and howled. The anger in her call was red-hot.

Parker shuddered with the first notice of an imminent shift. As if the call had been meant for him, he leaped down after her, tearing at his clothes, feeling his outer shell slip into a more accommodating shape. Chloe was confronting not only the moon, but her tormentor. That howl had been intended for the pale wolf who had sampled her flesh.

After that, events happened fast. Chloe swayed and caught herself. She held up hands from which claws visibly sprang. Her shoulders were next to go, broadening, straining against the compactness of her slight frame. The rest of her body more or less flowed into its new shape, cracking, groaning for a few seconds only. Fur sprouted from her pores, covering those parts of her still visible. Black fur as dark as Parker's own. When her body had finished rearranging, she swayed again and drew her lips away from her teeth.

The passenger-side door of Dylan Landau's red Porsche opened with a snap. The person Landau had identified in passing as Tory jumped out. For a few seconds it was hard to discern who this was, dressed all in black from head to foot. But when the light made contact with her face, female features filled in. A riot of curly hair tumbled over slim shoulders, hair that matched its color to the scent of blood in the air, Landau's Porsche and Chloe's anger. *Red.*

That person's change happened in less time than it took for Parker to blink his eyes, and so smoothly it would have been evident to anyone watching that she was a master at transitions. She was also graceful, beautiful, regal and, Parker sensed, as dangerous as any of the males here.

The two she-wolves on Landau's lawn faced each other. Then the sound of more bodily manipulations came from behind them. Dylan had morphed into an imposing light-pelted werewolf. Caught up in the moment, Parker almost missed the next shift happening beside him.

Christ, it was Wilson. Wilson was one of them. Big, dark brown, naked now and without his badge or gun.

The last noise came from the porch steps. Lighter footfalls padded to join the circle. Parker glanced into the eyes of a third she-wolf. Putting two and two together in this instance equaled—the stunning Jenna James.

All of them were werewolves. It was insane. Unbelievable. All of these people had gathered at The Sanctuary for a reason, tethered together by a mutated gene pool. These were the others that Parker had waited to find as he had perched atop Landau's wall. People from all walks of life were here, sharing this one secret. Why? To protect the missing judge? To keep safe and secure the place where werewolves roamed freely and could find refuge?

Parker flicked his attention to the red she-wolf, Tory. Who was she? The question scarcely had time to settle before a silent message passed between Wilson, Landau and Tory. Then Tory, like a flaming arrow, sprinted for the wall.

The others followed, racing after her, spreading out to cover more ground. Except for Parker, who held Chloe back by corralling her with his body.

She pressed up against him, bumped him back, growled in agitation, snapped her teeth. Parker knew he would be needed out there, over the wall, if there was to be a showdown, and that he couldn't remain here, no matter how badly he wanted to protect Chloe. There was the matter of his own revenge against the wolf who had done this to her and so many other innocent people.

He wasn't alone. No longer did he have to fear the future. He would find the answers he sought, and was in good company. The future looked more promising, almost shiny…if all these wolves would come back alive.

In a moment of indecision, feeling Chloe's angst ride his skin like the threat of an imminent cyclone, Parker let her go.

Chapter 20

He ran beside her, with the breeze in his face and her scent in his lungs. His blood pumped furiously through him, part exertion and part fear. He would keep close, watch her, protect her with his life. Theirs was a connection not to be broken by something as dreadful as a werewolf named Chavez.

The scent of his pack was like a visible directive. They had not traveled far from the wall, had in fact stopped just short of the trees. The only wolf missing was the red one. Tory. And Parker got it then, realized what the plan had been. Part of it, anyway. The red wolf was going to be the bait—to catch a killer. Why?

Jenna's words came back to him as he herded Chloe off toward the closest tree cover. *I'm just saying that men, and not only those we've categorized as insane, have been known to do a lot of strange things in the name of love.*

The red wolf was the bait. She would set this wolf trap.

The red wolf, out of everyone here, was the bait because… Chavez wanted her? Because Chavez *loved* her?

Would Chavez, a master criminal and murderer, be waylaid from his plan to go after the judge by his longing for a flame-pelted wolf, even if he did want her? Or had he gone over the edge of sanity once and for all?

A series of calls went up, but Parker's mind was stuck in a loop. *Trick* was the word that Chloe had said to him when he'd found her. Possibly she'd been right. A master criminal of Chavez's caliber had to be as intelligent as he was insane. There was a chance that Chavez had indeed been smart enough, lucid enough, to set this very night in motion through a series of events. He'd been squeezed into a narrower vision that included the red she-wolf as a prize. Maybe that's why Chavez hadn't left town. He had one more thing to do. Maybe two. Take the red she-wolf for himself, and do some damage to the pack she preferred.

There were wolves everywhere. Parker smelled them, felt them. Chloe did, too. Growls emerged from her throat as she pressed herself tightly to his back. She wanted to be a part of whatever was happening.

Whose trick would succeed tonight? Whose plan? For surely that silent message passed between Wilson, Landau and Tory had confirmed there was a plan. It could not be as simple as luring Chavez out and then letting the fight begin, winner take all. It had to be way more than that on principle alone. Good guys versus bad guys?

Anxiously, Parker waited, holding Chloe back, feeling her breath ruffle his hair, and fighting his beast's instinct to say the hell with the rest of them, and to take her somewhere safe, someplace where he could have her for himself.

Selfish bastard.

She was shaking with anxiety, and smelled like unmasked

desire, raw nerves and feminine seduction. Being near her was a wild intoxication. All he had to do was turn, and he'd be ready to show her how much he wanted her. Yet…God, yes, with all of that, he knew also that Chloe wouldn't be able to rest or accept any of this until she had settled a score.

The call they had been waiting for came—vicious, threatening. *Chavez.* Had to be. Parker tensed, and felt Chloe tense behind him.

An answering howl, equally as strong and no less menacing, went up. *Tory?* And— No! Shit! Chloe followed that call, darting out from behind him, running for all she was worth.

Parker went after her, sprinting as fast as his legs would take him, and he still had a hard time keeping up. They weren't alone, he knew for a fact. Several werewolves hid among the trees. It was a game of hide-and-seek, with a myriad of scents clogging up the mix and not one wolf appearing in the open.

Then, all of a sudden, there were two wolves ahead of him, the females, stopping side by side on the grass, caught in a beam of moonlight so bright, it highlighted every feature on their faces.

Parker drew up short and threw his weight sideways. He had no idea who Tory, the red wolf, was, but she truly was magnificent. By her side, Chloe, brand-new to her current shape, and with her black pelt shining like polished ebony, was every bit as magnificent, and evocative as hell.

Parker's nerves flared again. His loins ached with a growing, insistent throb. The way Chloe stood there, independent, head lifted, weight on her toes, made him want her all the more. But he knew better than to ruin whatever game plan was in play.

He had to wait this out. From beneath the trees, he sent his senses outward, fishing for clues as to where everybody was, thinking they had better be really close and prepared to move. The two wolves were alone up there and exposed, seemingly. Anything could happen, at any minute.

Another howl went up. Parker's hackles lifted. He dropped to his haunches, ready to spring. This wasn't a call he recognized.

Another noise spun him around. A wolf joined him, leaping silently in from the shadows. It was the young wolf from the judge's Sanctuary, greeting Parker with a snarl and a hand to his chest, signifying *same*.

Same what? Side? Species?

The pale wolf he now knew to be Chavez had done the same thing, but there had been nothing similar between them if pain and torture were that wolf's idea of a good life.

A third howl went up, this one from the red she-wolf standing defiantly in the moonlight. Her vocalization was loud, harrowing, and caused every single hair on Parker's body to stand on end. He made a second sideways jump, rocked on his toes and got a bump from behind. The young wolf had his back, that bump told Parker, but what would happen next?

Chloe had to feel his attention, but she kept mute as a large male stepped out from beneath the trees. Parker snapped his teeth, inched ahead, then rocked back again. This was no pale monster. It was the missing brown wolf who had led Parker from Fairview to the wall, and eventually to the judge's house—taking Parker right to the source of his dreams.

The brown Were planted himself four feet away from the females with an attitude that had *bodyguard* written all over it. A message clearly stated, and an answer to the challenge Wilson had mentioned? If so, Parker thought, swear to God, it smacked of the shootout at the OK Corral.

Chloe's ebony pelt visibly ruffled. Watching her carefully for signs of fear that would have had him by her side in seconds, he moved toward the light. The wolf beside Parker broke his forward momentum by applying a stiff swipe with very sharp claws to his shoulder blade. *Wait.*

Waiting proved to be nearly impossible. The males might have been mimicking the shootout, but Chloe stood there like one of the damned virgins in fantasy novels who were tethered to a spot and designated as dragon fodder. Would Chavez be so bold as to take this bait, stride right in here, when Wilson and Dylan Landau were close by?

Parker's attention was riveted on Chloe, the woman who had been half-naked in his arms not an hour before. The woman who had shown courage in this same place, and was showing it again now by taking a stand. He would not, could not lose her, he realized. He could lose the rest, even the answers to the puzzle of his existence, if she were by his side. With that startling thought in mind, he willingly joined the party.

Positioning himself shoulder to shoulder with the brown wolf, Parker found his breathing settled into a rhythm. The tension of the moment was like nothing he'd ever known, not even remotely similar to the fight in the park. This tension was denser, weightier, aggressive. It was also exhilarating.

A low murmur went up, disturbing the trees, the grass, the air. Parker scented *him* among those bits of nature gone awry. Chavez. The scent quickly melted into a taste that Parker had missed with the distance of their prior meeting. Chavez was like the bitter taste of burned coffee, perhaps hinting of the black, burned-up soul he possessed.

And Chavez, the elusive pale wolf, appeared now like an apparition on the edge of the shadows, seemingly alone, although that, too, was an illusion. The area virtually pulsed with otherness, as if too many anomalies had been crammed into a space too small to hold them.

Chavez was a sight, fully morphed. All Weres, Parker had

found, were larger than their human selves, but Chavez was one of the largest Weres he had seen so far. The eeriness of Chavez's white pelt was further intensified by the directness of the monster's gaze. Intelligence shone there, yes, and also that creepy gleam of someone who had obviously left reason behind.

The wolf at Parker's side snarled. Chloe's responding snarl caused Parker's jaws to clench. This was the monster who had hurt Chloe, bitten her, infected her, changed her life forever.

Tory, the red wolf, remained silent. What was her story? Parker wondered. How had she garnered the attention of this criminal in the first place?

There was no time left for pondering anything else. Chavez's wolves started to close in from the periphery, one step at a time. Parker recognized the ones he'd faced when the gunmen had been taken down. The surprise was that there were only four beasts in Chavez's entourage. Behind them, still hidden but smelling like the metal of the firepower they wielded, were two humans. Replacements for the two taken away earlier.

But Parker had sensed more Weres than this. At least ten at last count. He did a quick recalculation of the surroundings, inhaled, and let the number of remaining Weres roll across his tongue. Yes, more were there, and now that he'd sampled some of them up close, he could pick out the rust wolf and the young wolf. He knew that Dylan Landau was here, and Wilson. He smelled the sweetness of gardenias that came along with Dana Delmonico. With himself and the big brown wolf, that made seven Sanctuary Weres to Chavez and his four. Easy pickings if it weren't for those humans and their damned silver bullets. And if he knew about the count, so did Chavez, who had so obviously been a werewolf longer than Parker.

Uttering a feral, deep, rolling growl that instantly stopped all movement from Chavez's pack, the red she-wolf twitched. Her fur vibrated as if she'd met with a stray breeze.

The pale wolf only had eyes for her. That much was clear. If a wolf's muzzle could smile cynically, Chavez's did. And in the manner of not giving a fig about whomever else was there, he moved toward Tory with intent to do what? Hurt her? Kill her? Jump her? Ignoring the rest of the Sanctuary pack present?

Maybe he really had jumped off the sanity bridge.

Tory snapped her teeth when the big brown wolf made to move closer. She snapped at Parker when he stepped in front of Chloe. He seemed to hear what she was thinking. *Mine.* But that was just silly. Or was it?

Again, Tory moved faster than the eye could follow. She halved the distance between herself and Chavez, and then she was on him. And not in the way Chavez might have anticipated. Certainly his wolf face seemed startled.

Her teeth were on his neck in a flash of red. She twisted her body, sank her canines into Chavez with the fury of a wolf who had been wronged. But Chavez hadn't bitten the red she-wolf, Parker knew. She was something altogether different, as were the Landaus. She was fast, terrible in her fury, and unearthly strong. Realizing this too late, Chavez began to fight back.

All hell broke loose. Bullets flew. Parker jumped aside, taking Chloe with him. The brown wolf went after Chavez's nasty pack, and after making sure Chloe was safe, Parker did the same.

Claws were slashing all over. Teeth grazed Parker's skin, beading up lines of blood. More wolves arrived. Bodies were so tangled that the bullets stopped coming, the humans perhaps fearing they'd hit one of their own.

There were shouts and human cries, then silence from the gunmen. Into the space beside Parker, Chloe landed, her own teeth bared, her arms and legs a blur of motion. She leaped onto Chavez's broad back as Tory clung to his front. Her teeth sank into his neck where Tory's had left off. Although Chloe didn't appear to be strong enough to do any major damage, she succeeded in distracting her target.

Chavez screamed, whether in anger, frustration or pain, Parker couldn't guess. The young wolf and the rust wolf were there now, their added strength turning the tide. Blood flew in the fighting. Howl after angry howl filled the humid night. And then, miraculously almost, certainly way too quickly, the fight was over.

Silence fell.

Chavez was on the ground, with four wolves on top of him. Four more bodies lay scattered around, back to human form in death. Tory stood aside, her face covered in Chavez's blood. But the criminal wasn't dead. Chavez, mighty in his own right, and well used to the pitfalls of the fights he had sponsored in the name of torture and entertainment, lay there motionless, as if he had simply given up.

Parker could not believe he would do that, or that he had been a fool for love. Complete insanity seemed more likely. But there was no time to think further on that, or about what would happen to him now. The brown wolf hauled Chavez to his feet. Delmonico and Wilson, still morphed, stood on either side. They dragged him toward the wall, herding him like a dog caught in a moving cage of muscle.

Done deal. Miami's monster, without the rest of his pack, which had been killed in the raid, had been taken down. And every one of the Sanctuary's pack had been left standing.

Parker heard Chloe's labored breathing and turned to find her crouched on her haunches. Bloodstains tipped her sharp teeth. She had a strange look in her eyes.

He was with her in a second, pulling her to her feet. With a roar. She stared back. Then Parker ran, with his she-wolf in tow.

He headed for the wall, for the Landau's house, for The Sanctuary, which would allow them to get back to their human forms. He needed to see her, speak to her, comfort her, hold her. Needed so much more from her that his heart nearly burst in his chest at the distance they still had to go.

And it felt good, running beside her—more exciting than the fight, or freeing Miami from a monster—and equally as important somehow.

It felt right.

Chloe's body undulated as soon as she reached the porch. She staggered as they raced through the open door, and nearly fell as Parker, changing shape while he took the stairs two at a time, refused to slow.

She ventured a glance at herself as she followed. Her hand once again resembled her hand. No claws, no black fur, only a fine-boned arm and wrist, naked, with all bones intact.

Parker pulled her through the doorway to the bedroom where she had made her first full transition, and fell back against the door as she tumbled onto the bed. It could very well have been an awkward moment, for so many reasons, with both of them completely naked. Yet Chloe felt as if she knew Parker at the soul level, and as though she had been waiting for him for a very long time. He was a noble, honorable man who sacrificed himself for others on a regular basis. Case in point, herself, and what he'd done for her. Second case in point, his being here tonight, helping the others.

Plus he was absolutely spectacular naked.

Chloe gasped as she eyed his male perfection, her hungry gaze traveling over the soft dark hair on his well-muscled chest, to his narrow hips. Was she quivering for him, or was her body shaking off leftover remnants of werewolf?

Parker moved away from the door, eyeing her right back.

It didn't take a rocket scientist for her to realize the cause of her quivers. It was the anticipation of finding out everything about him, starting with the very male, very large, rock-hard and completely visible erection for which he wasn't the least bit embarrassed.

As a matter of fact, neither was she.

Getting to her feet slowly, Chloe looked up at his devastatingly handsome face. With everything that had happened, she simply said, "Hello, Parker."

"Chloe." His voice was hoarse and filled with longing.

"Thank you." Her own tone was breathy. She could scarcely take in air. He was close up against her now, and smelling of wolf. She couldn't think of a better scent for a man, wouldn't like any other scent after this.

His attention throbbed against her belly, and she wanted to be nearer to him still. Breathe him in. Take him in. Give back. All the sensations flowing through her were new, thrilling and not quite human.

"I didn't get there in time to keep this from you," he told her, his blue eyes luminous, his voice as compelling as the rest of him.

"You saved my life," she said, thinking that she now had a family of sorts, if this pack would let her stay. If Parker's soul was anything like she assumed it was, she would be a part of something special.

"Are you always so…"

"Pragmatic?" she finished for him. "Accepting? Flexible? Yes. Always. Well, almost always. I'm a rebel, too. You should know that."

"Oh, I know it." His grin made her tingle all over. His eyes shone with a gleam that wasn't remotely civilized.

"I'll help in any way I can," he said. "What do you need?"

What the heck. Showing him what she wanted would be

so much better than any attempt she might make to answer that one. Reaching up, she took his face in her hands, met his eyes, said, "You kissed me in a dream."

"Funny. I dreamed the same thing," he whispered.

"I'd like you to do it again."

"You're…"

"A werewolf. Yeah, I get that. And one who should be wanting answers. But we'll have a long time to talk those things over, right? Go through the details?"

Did she look as hopeful as that sounded? She no longer had control over her expressions. Her heart pounded as she waited for his reply.

"A *very* long time," he said.

And those words made Chloe rise onto her tiptoes. She brought her mouth close to his while his hands, so warm and so talented, stroked down her spine slowly, going over every vertebra as if it was a new adventure to savor, leaving a trail of fire that scorched her flesh.

As his fingers slid to her waist, his lips parted. As his hands dipped farther, tracing the shape of her buttocks evocatively, erotically, Chloe sighed and closed her eyes.

He cupped her with both hands at the exact same time that his mouth met with hers. A wave of heat soared through Chloe, shooting sensations right through, bringing on an ache that wouldn't be appeased by a kiss, no matter how perfect it was. Tonight, she was both Chloe Tyler and someone else. Some*thing* else. And whatever that was added to her need for this man.

"Now!" she said, her demand spoken into his mouth, her tongue and breath dancing with his, her heart matching the rapid tempo of his own.

She was on the bed a split second later. On her back, with Parker stretched over her, balanced on his fists. She felt the sheets beneath her, felt the heat of her own sighs. She felt Parker enter her body, and heard herself cry out.

She heard the voice beyond the window shade quite clearly, and knew she would always hear it. But the moon wasn't warm, or able to do the things Parker was doing to her. Wonderful things.

She tasted passion, lust, longing and salt, as she lapped her tongue over his shoulder and bit down lightly, needing to hang on to something, anything, as Parker eased back, then pressed himself into her again and again—the tempo of his thrusts building as her legs opened wider, as she tugged at him, closed herself around him, encouraged him deeper, wanting it all.

And when he struck the spot she had needed him to reach, sending her over that damned moon and into the realm of the clouds, she screamed. No, not a scream, a howl. A sound that Parker Madison matched as he shuddered along with her, his body locked to hers, his essence emptied into her, a part of her.

But a strange longing remained, even after that, nestled down inside her. Disturbed, Chloe opened her eyes.

"Yes, little one," Parker said, with his mouth hovering above hers, as if he had been waiting for this to happen. "It's the beast rising. Time to get out and explore, let it out. Let it have its way."

Chloe smiled then. "Can we control it?"

"Not for long."

"Long enough?"

The sound of Parker's laughter filled the room. As his legs pressed hers open and he came back for a deep, drowning kiss, the kind that would make any woman's inhibitions take a hike, Chloe was almost completely sure that the moon could wait a little longer. Just this once.

* * * * *

*Harlequin offers a romance for every mood!
See below for a sneak peek
from our paranormal romance line,
Silhouette® Nocturne™.
Enjoy a preview of REUNION by USA TODAY
bestselling author Lindsay McKenna.*

Aella closed her eyes and sensed a distinct shift, like movement from the world around her to the unseen world.

She opened her eyes. And had a slight shock at the man standing ten feet away. He wasn't just any man. Her heart leaped and pounded. He reminded her of a fierce warrior from an ancient civilization. Incan? She wasn't sure but she felt his deep power and masculinity.

I'm Aella. Are you the guardian of this sacred site? she asked, hoping her telepathy was strong.

Fox's entire body soared with joy. Fox struggled to put his personal pleasure aside.

Greetings, Aella. I'm the assistant guardian to this sacred area. You may call me Fox. How can I be of service to you, Aella? he asked.

I'm searching for a green sphere. A legend says that the Emperor Pachacuti had seven emerald spheres created for the Emerald Key necklace. He had seven of his priestesses and priests travel the world to hide these spheres from evil forces. It is said that when all seven spheres are found, restrung and worn, that Light will return to the Earth. The fourth sphere is here, at your sacred site. Are you aware of it? Aella held her breath. She loved looking at him, especially his sensual mouth. The desire to kiss him came out of nowhere.

Fox was stunned by the request. *I know of the Emerald Key*

necklace because I served the emperor at the time it was created. However, I did not realize that one of the spheres is here.

Aella felt sad. Why? Every time she looked at Fox, her heart felt as if it would tear out of her chest. *May I stay in touch with you as I work with this site?* she asked.

Of course. Fox wanted nothing more than to be here with her. To absorb her ephemeral beauty and hear her speak once more.

Aella's spirit lifted. What *was* this strange connection between them? Her curiosity was strong, but she had more pressing matters. In the next few days, Aella knew her life would change forever. How, she had no idea....

Look for REUNION
by USA TODAY *bestselling author Lindsay McKenna,*
available April 2010, only from
Silhouette® Nocturne™.

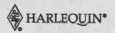 **HARLEQUIN®**

INTRIGUE

WILL THIS REUNITED FAMILY
BE STRONG ENOUGH TO EXPOSE
A LURKING KILLER?

FIND OUT IN THIS ALL-NEW
THRILLING TRILOGY FROM TOP
HARLEQUIN INTRIGUE AUTHOR

B.J. DANIELS

WHITEHORSE
MONTANA

Winchester Ranch

GUN-SHY BRIDE—*April 2010*

HITCHED—*May 2010*

TWELVE-GAUGE GUARDIAN—
June 2010

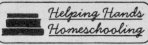

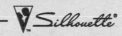

SPECIAL EDITION

**INTRODUCING A BRAND-NEW MINISERIES
FROM *USA TODAY* BESTSELLING AUTHOR**

KASEY MICHAELS

SECOND-CHANCE BRIDAL

At twenty-eight, widowed single mother
Elizabeth Carstairs thinks she's left love behind
forever....until she meets Will Hollingsbrook.
Her sons' new baseball coach is the handsomest
man she's ever seen—and the more time they
spend together, the more undeniable the
connection between them. But can Elizabeth
leave the past behind and open her heart to
a second chance at love?

FIND OUT IN

SUDDENLY A BRIDE

*Available in April
wherever books are sold.*

HER MEDITERRANEAN PLAYBOY

Sexy and dangerous—he wants you in his bed!

The sky is blue, the azure sea is crashing
against the golden sand and the sun is hot.

The conditions are perfect for
a scorching Mediterranean seduction
from two irresistible untamed playboys!

Indulge your senses with these two delicious stories

A MISTRESS AT THE ITALIAN'S COMMAND
by Melanie Milburne

ITALIAN BOSS, HOUSEKEEPER MISTRESS
by Kate Hewitt

Available April 2010 from Harlequin Presents!

www.eHarlequin.com

HP12910

HARLEQUIN® Romance®

ROMANCE, RIVALRY
AND A FAMILY REUNITED

THE BRIDES of BELLA ROSA

William Valentine and his beloved wife, Lucia, live
a beautiful life together, but when his former love Rosa
and the secret family they had together resurface,
an instant rivalry is formed. Can these families
get through the past and come together as one?

Step into the world of Bella Rosa
beginning this April with

Beauty and the Reclusive Prince
by
RAYE MORGAN

Eight volumes to collect and treasure!

www.eHarlequin.com

HRI7650